MOUSE

A novel by D. M. Mitchell

The Agamemnon Digital Press

ISBN – 13: 978-1483995908
ISBN – 10: 14839° ̄°°°

D0970166

Other novels by D. M. Mitchell:

THE DOMINO BOYS
THE SOUL FIXER
SILENT
THE KING OF TERRORS
MAX
THE HOUSE OF THE WICKED
PRESSURE COOKER
THE FIRST D.M. MITCHELL THRILLER OMNIBUS
THE SECOND D.M. MITCHELL THRILLER OMNIBUS

But long it could not be
Till her garments, heavy with their drink,
Pull'd the poor wretch from her melodious lay
To muddy death

Hamlet
William Shakespeare

1

Laura Leach

Some things never seem to change, she thought. It was exactly the same view framed by the arched window; the same view she used to look out onto as a child, as a young woman, all those long years ago. Why is that, she thought bleakly? How can it be that the view can stay exactly the same but people change so, so much?

Her breath fogged up a circular patch on the rippled glass, which shrank and grew again with every exhalation. I never loved this view, she thought. I never loved this place, but I am here all the same and I am destined to stay till the day I die and I am laid to rest in the very earth I find hateful, never able to escape its embrace even in death.

The land she stared at was flat. Not a hill of note for miles. A vein-like network of rhynes scored through the earth, centuries-old drainage systems sitting alongside more modern affairs, taking away the water that troubled this low-lying landscape, taming it, bringing it under man's industrious hands. It was an ancient landscape, the customs and practices of its people little altered by time. The many fields were largely given over to grassland, to teasel and willow grown commercially as it had been for many generations, a small amount of peat extraction in some areas, and the remainder set aside for arable. But when the rains came down hard – and it was a place where rain was plentiful – and the ditches struggled to cope with the rapid influx of water, the area could easily resemble acres of sodden paddy fields.

There were trees in abundance, but spread out thinly and not enough to stem the wind that raced unfettered across the land, causing the shivering grasses to grow low and sturdy, the hawthorns to arc painfully, and the restless, rustling reeds that lined the dark waters to rock delicately back and forth before the blasts, as if they took the wind in their embrace and danced with it.

In the heat of summer there was little shade out here on the Somerset Levels. The ground baked hard, the grass scorched yellow, and the few cows lay as best they could beneath the cooling shade of the odd-oak tree, left to grow for just such a purpose. Skylarks dribbled song down from a pristine blue sky; bees droned like distant conversations; fish teased the surface of myriad streams, and anyone could be forgiven for thinking this was some ancient idyll unsullied by the modern world. Especially so as the summer heat wave of 1976 continued, and day after day the blistering Sun refused to back down, in fact seemed to grow ever stronger with each passing hour.

Nothing appeared to complete the illusion of being transported to an altogether more bucolic and halcyon time than Devereux Towers. It stood alone in the middle of a field accessed only by a single dirt-track road; a squat, four-storey-high hamstone building studded with windows on all four sides, the majority of the golden stone surface draped in a shimmering cloak of ivy.

The name Devereux Towers was misleading; there was only one tower protruding from a corner of the building, rising bold and high and topped-off with a conical roof of red slate, atop this a badly rusted weather vane bearing the coat of arms of one Lord Devereux who had commissioned the building's erection around the year 1750.

At the time, such a folly, for that's what it began life as, was not unusual. Some say it was intended to be a representation of a Scottish castle, but Lord Devereux either ran out of money or ran out of enthusiasm, or perhaps both, and only a single tower out of the planned four ever got built. It even boasted a moat at one time, local legend had it, but this had long since been filled in.

Over time the building fell into disrepair, the elaborate geometrical gardens Lord Devereux had constructed to encircle it became overgrown and were eventually ploughed up, leaving the folly standing alone and incongruous in the middle of its bland field, so encased in ivy it almost appeared to have grown out of the ground. Eventually its roof all but collapsed and all that remained were four sturdy walls and the single chateau-like tower.

It looked destined to disintegrate entirely and become absorbed by the land, had it not been for Doctor Alex Leach in 1948. A successful London surgeon he made good on a number of wise investments and decided at the age of forty-one to retire early and become a man of leisure, choosing Somerset for no other reason than it was even then cheaper to buy a house and live here than it was to settle in one of its richer relations of Dorset, Devon and Cornwall. He was never one to waste money unnecessarily. So it came as something of a shock when he declared to his wife and three young daughters that he'd seen a most interesting house and that he had made up his mind to buy it and restore it to its former glory.

When he drove them down the track and pointed out what remained of Devereux Towers his wife declared him mad. The children – then aged ten, six and two respectively – thought it the most wonderful adventure and ran excitedly around the sorry building, leaving their mother and father to argue about the viability of turning this heap of neglected stone into a house and home. This would be the perfect place for them, he said. The ideal place to bring up their children away from the crime and filth of the city. Moreover, think how delightful their collection of antiques would look set against its restored grandeur. He took his wife through imaginary rooms, pointed out where his study would be and where he would display his prized collection of tribal artefacts, his wooden masks, statues and clubs from Hawaii, Fiji, Africa and South America, testament to their many exotic trips abroad. She was not immediately impressed. She disliked his primitive collection anyway, so in her eyes it was hardly an argument for taking the place on.

Laura Leach was aged just two at the time. She had only the vaguest recollection of that first visit, more, she reckoned, someone else's memory implanted in her through the many well-worn stories recounted of the day by her sisters. What she did vividly remember was her mother's warnings about the instability of the crumbling walls and that they might at any moment come crashing down on her young head and crush it like a red grape. She remembered being faintly annoyed that her mother called her back and hung tightly onto her little hand, preventing her from fully exploring the folly with her sisters, being told she was far too young and might fall down a well or some other disguised danger waiting in the sea of weeds for careless little girls.

In the end, Laura Leach's father got his way. Men invariably did. They found a perfectly nice cottage to rent in the small market town of Langbridge a few miles away – a town that had grown on the site of an ancient crossing-place over the crawling, lethargic, sinuous Lang – and restoration of Devereux Towers began in earnest. Her father refused to let any of the girls go to the local school, deciding that it was a little too rustic, a little too provincial, full of the common sort and not for people of means. So he engaged the services of private tutors. They were kept very much apart from the local children; indeed the entire family existed in a self-imposed bubble which only select people of the desired class and standing were allowed to burst. Laura Leach became very aware at a young age that whilst all around her there were many miles of open countryside they were allowed to see extremely little of it, and even then only under close supervision. Laura grew a little afraid of it. There were many unseen dangers for the unwary, she was told by both mother and father, and in her imagination the flat, ominous countryside became not something to enjoy but to fear.

Her childhood, she recalled, was very claustrophobic, and yet all was done in the name of love, for she was adored by her father, being the youngest, and he was berated repeatedly by her mother for failing to treat all the girls as equals, an accusation he vehemently refuted. Yet he named the tower Laura's Tower, and told tales of princes coming to the place almost every week and rescuing princesses from it, because there was always some unfortunate beauty being locked up in it back in those faraway times when princes and princesses were ten-a-penny.

It took a full two years before they could move into Devereux Towers and it was truly magical. She remembered – this time they really were her memories – smelling the fresh paint and varnish, the beeswax polish on the wooden panelling, of new carpets and a hundred other such things that assailed her reeling senses. And finally into Laura's Tower, where her father proudly opened a door onto a wide, circular room that he'd made into her bedroom, a tremendous arched window looking out onto the land that stretched out beneath her like a rumpled green blanket.

Their visits into Langbridge were infrequent, being mainly on a Saturday morning to collect the groceries from the various small shops in the cramped high street. A regular pattern, hopping from butcher to fishmonger, greengrocer to baker, and finally to the post office to buy stamps and envelopes and writing paper, to buy postal orders and to post letters back to friends and relatives living faraway in London.

Then one day they passed the cinema. The Empire, they called it. It had a date in stone above the main door: 1926. It occurred to her that she could not recall the last time she went to the pictures and she pestered her mother relentlessly to take her to see a film. Her mother resisted at first. It was probably infested with fleas, she said; they get passed on from sheep and cows, she'd heard. But her father pooh-poohed the idea and said that it looked perfectly charming, all things considered. It reminded him also that it had been an age since he went to the cinema, something they used to do regularly when back in London, he said, winking at his wife and mentioning something about the back row, which elicited a scowl in return.

So going to the cinema was the only real time she spent amongst the local people, sitting in the dark in the Empire, not being able to make them out properly yet hearing their strange but comforting country accents, hearing them laugh and joke amongst themselves in a manner her mother said just wasn't proper for their family to emulate. So they sat in silence and ate their popcorn. But to compensate there was always the film. It did not matter what she saw – musical, comedy, adventure – she lapped up the sumptuous excitement and escapism they offered her, for a few hours transported to a Technicolor-bright world where women were beautiful and men were handsome and the land about was safe and warm and loving. Where good prevailed and evil was defeated, and cowboys wore either black hats or white hats to help you differentiate between the two. Ironically, in this multi-coloured world everything was black and white, with no grey areas to trouble you, everything being either one thing or another.

When the time came the girls were sent away, one by one, to boarding school, Devereux Towers falling quieter and lonelier with every departure till finally Laura was the sole remaining child, having the place almost entirely to herself. But with her sisters gone her father grew ever more protective of his last little girl. He told her once that she was like a tiny bird he'd hatched from an egg; rearing it, feeding it, showering it with his love, knowing eventually that it must fly away and leave him and dreading the moment it did. She remembered how sad he looked as he told her. How odd, she thought, that love can cause such hurt.

Then one day it was her turn to be sent away to boarding school. She was both excited and nervous at the prospect, but her father could not bear to accompany her so it was left to her mother to drive her to the station, to take the train with her. Laura had never been so far away from home before; had never been without the company of her mother and father.

St Catherine's School for girls in Kent had been solidly recommended to her father for anyone wanting their daughter to be brought up in a manner befitting a man of standing and property. Her mother complained it cost far more than they were spending on the other girls, but her father got his way. Men invariably did.

Laura was taken to see the headmaster, Mr Donahue, a stern-faced, red-cheeked, pale-eyed man who squinted at her as if she were a specimen laid out on some table or other and he was undecided what he should do with it. He introduced her to Miss Franklin, the deputy head, who seemed to Laura to be a version of Mr Donahue in a tweed skirt. Laura cried every night for a week and was teased mercilessly by the other girls. She found she did not know how to make friends, but she was very skilled at making enemies. And so began many years of lonely torture as she strove to become a daughter befitting a man of standing and property, enduring a daily routine of punches, nips and kicks, and whatever other means of physical punishment young girls are capable of dreaming up, accompanied by their verbal and psychological equivalents. She hated St Catherine's. She hated the loneliness. She felt that she wanted to die so that her spirit could fly back at once to wander the empty corridors of Devereux Towers.

Except that she didn't die. In the ensuing years everyone else had died. First, her eldest sister, who drowned whilst on holiday in France. Then the middle sister was knocked down and killed by a car. Her mother was inconsolable and died soon after, some say of a broken heart. Then finally it was the turn of her father who had died of a heart attack two years ago, back in 1974. She came to Somerset to bury him. Devereux Towers was bequeathed to her, along with a small fortune in investments, in shares and dividends and money sitting in the bank. She needn't ever work again, the solicitor told her, perhaps sounding a little too envious.

Envy? She would gladly trade her lot for his. If only he knew what she had been through. No amount of money could repair the damage done in the name of love. So she scuttled back to Devereux Towers and crept around the many rooms like a lonely little mouse, staring out of its windows at the never-changing view outside; afraid of it, afraid of its people, yet desiring to be part of it, part of them, and yet too fearful to move far from the confines of Devereux Towers.

But she did go to the cinema. To the old Empire. There she felt she could be safe, sitting at the back inconsequential and unrecognised, amongst the people but not of them. Here she could transport herself away from this wretched world for a couple of hours. Be taken somewhere wonderful, somewhere truly magical. A place where good prevailed and evil was defeated and the land about was safe and warm and loving.

* * * *

2

Vince Moody

Just now, the Empire was a dead place. Cold, dark and lifeless.

Early in the morning, regular as clockwork, the cleaners descended on the old cinema like a flock of raucous crows settling on a newly planted field. They rattled around the place with their galvanised buckets, vacuum cleaners, mops, brushes and dirty jokes, congregated in the tiny staff room for a quick cup of tea and a fag or two, then threw on their coats and tramped noisily out again.

From there on in he was left pretty much on his own till mid-afternoon, cocooned in a welcome sepulchral hush. Those few hours, that narrow window of quiet when the building was largely deserted, was when he felt it belonged to him. At those times he liked to think of the place as his little Empire.

Vince Moody avoided the cleaners if he could. There were four of them, all women, and to a woman they didn't have anything nice to say about men, not a single thing. Their own men belonged to some universal class of men they all appeared to recognise and share; useless good-for-nothings and lazy cider-swillers who frittered away their wives' hard-won earnings on the horses or down at the local pub. The cleaners swigged their tea or sucked on their fags bemoaning their sorry lot in life and on the lookout for some handsome, rich foreigner who'd come along and whisk them away to better times.

Vince hated having to go into the canteen when they were all together. He'd even avoid them individually if he could, ducking smartly out of their way if it looked likely their paths would cross. But all in one room? It was like being fed to the lions.

Monica was only thirty years old but looked ten years older than that. Her middle name, he discovered, was Dorothy, named after Judy Garland's character in *The Wizard of Oz*. Vince thought she looked more like the scarecrow. She was the group's unofficial leader. Loud-mouthed, chain-smoking, tending towards the fat, greasy hair. It would have been a desperately sorry rich foreigner who felt impelled to invite Monica along to his chateau. As a kid she must have been the type who pulled the legs off spiders, or who put unwanted kittens into sacks and threw them into rivers. She certainly treated him like he was a legless spider or a helpless kitten. As soon as he appeared within her sights she'd turn her full attention on him.

'Here he is,' she'd say. 'Had a woman yet, Vince? Know what one is, Vince? Bet you wouldn't know what to do with one if you had one, eh, Vince?'

Always the same little jibe intended to make him blush. To make him squirm in discomfort. And he couldn't help but feel his cheeks get all stoked up before her nasty button eyes and vindictive yellow-toothed smile.

'Come on, Vince; show us what you've got,' she'd carry on, if she was in the mood to really get stuck into him, if her daily gripe hadn't been sufficiently offloaded onto her cronies and she needed a straw dummy to beat till she felt she'd gotten the crap out of her system. 'How big is it, Vince? A little worm, I'll bet,' she'd say, holding up a crooked little finger, causing him to lower his gaze in embarrassment. 'I'd get more satisfaction from this here broom handle!' she'd titter, and the other three cleaners would laugh in unison. Invariably one of them would tell her to let him be, and say it in such a pitiful way that it would make him feel even more like a legless spider or bagged-up kitten. Their feigned pity stung as readily as if they flung felt-covered rocks at him.

So unless it was absolutely necessary, Vince would avoid the cleaners. Even Martin Caldwell, the Empire's manager, steered well clear of them if he could. Mind you, he tended to steer clear of everyone. Vince wasn't sure exactly what he did as manager. Caldwell had the tiniest of offices located in one of the many back corridors and spent a good deal of his time shut away in there doing whatever he was paid to do and leaving Vince to get on with what they paid him to do. It wasn't much of an office for a manager, thought Vince – a desk, phone, filing cabinets, and a badly-made reproduction of an Oscar that Caldwell had brought along with him, a film-related gift from his wife to help him settle into his new job. Oscar was kept on his desk as a paperweight that never had any paper under it. Caldwell didn't like it but as it was a gift it had to stay there, staring at him and constantly reminding him he didn't know much about the world of film.

Vince Moody was Chief Projectionist. That sounded rather grand, as he was effectively a chief without any Indians, so to speak. Once upon a time, when Vince first started work at the Empire, there had been three of them sharing the projection booth shifts: the Chief Projectionist, an elderly man called Alan who sported a badly-cut mop of unruly grey hair, thin of frame and slightly stooped, with a habit of looking at you from under his large, furry eyebrows in a most sinister way; there was Michael, the Assistant Chief Projectionist, who was fat, bald, religiously ate a bag of sugared almonds every day, rode a motorbike and lived at home with his parents; then there was Vince, the new kid, the trainee projectionist, who landed the job mainly because he shared a passion for Fritz Lang's film *Metropolis* with the Chief Projectionist and it just happened to come up in the interview.

Those days were long gone. The Chief retired and died the same year; Michael was promoted, stayed a while and then followed the lure of better money with the Rank chain of cinemas, ominously declaring to Vince that the Empire was dead and finished and that he ought to get out whilst he could. That left Vince, and a local part-timer they wheeled in when Vince was on holiday or they had an extra shift, to pick up the reins in what was proving to be tough economic climes for cinemas. It was tough for everyone these days, he thought.

Everyone was blaming TV. Why pay to sit in an old, draughty cinema when you can sit at home in comfort and watch films – and in colour too? The aged manager of the Empire decided he too had had enough, cashed in his premium bonds and went off to live in Spain. So the company brought in a relative youngster, in cinema manager terms, to turn things around. A new broom, they said, and gave him a broom cupboard of an office to work from.

Martin Caldwell was everything Vince wasn't; nicely spoken, well educated, wore a suit, handsome like David Essex, had plenty of money, drove an MGB GT and married to a very pretty woman like the kind of models who appeared in him mum's Littlewoods catalogues. Not long after he'd started, Caldwell sat down with Vince in his broom cupboard of an office one day.

'The future's big for cinemas,' he enthused. 'How old are you, Vince?'

Vince didn't see the connection but humoured him anyway. 'Twenty-six, Mr Caldwell.'

'And how long have you been here at the Empire?'

'Ten years, Mr Caldwell.'

He looked surprised. 'As long as that?'

'Started straight from school, near enough,' explained Vince. 'I like film,' he added, because Caldwell had made it sound like ten years in the Empire was decidedly unnatural.

'Well, never mind,' he said. 'The future is going to be big! We've got plans for the Empire,' he said. 'Think about it; lots of small screens instead of just the big one. More films, more bums on seats, more X-rated films of an evening, securing your future and mine. What do you think about that, Vince?'

Vince didn't think much about it if he had to be honest. He liked the Empire with its large auditorium, the massive pleated curtains that hid a tremendously huge white screen, the Art Deco detailing on the ceilings and walls. He knew *2001: a Space Odyssey* would have looked naff on a small screen instead of it being projected in stunning 70mm as it had been when it was first screened at the Empire. That was an event. But it wasn't his place to say anything so he didn't. What he did notice was that Martin Caldwell appeared to be trying to convince himself more than anything and was using Vince as a sounding board.

Anyhow, that was two years ago now and recently Mr Caldwell had taken to shutting himself away from the world, every now and again popping out to see Mrs Kimble in her small office. She was an elderly bookkeeper who did bookkeeper things like typing, doing the banking and sorting out the weekly wages. Then he'd duck back inside his own office and close the door on everyone. Whenever Vince saw Mr Caldwell, and that wasn't often, he looked paler, thinner, increasingly stressed with each passing week, having all the appearance of a man shipped out to the colonies, lost in the far reaches of the Empire, so to speak.

Apart from one other man who was contracted to maintain the ancient electrical and plumbing systems, and the two women who came in to man the ticket and refreshment booth in the foyer, that was everyone at the Empire. And for a lot of the time it belonged exclusively to Vince Moody.

When he'd first started at the Empire he thought all he'd do was project films. That's what projectionists did. But, as assistant, whilst the Chief and sugared-almond-Michael swapped stories he was never a part of, Vince had to go around emptying bins, changing light bulbs, cleaning up what the cleaners didn't clean, then polish the tiled floor with an electric floor polisher, take out and wash air filters, fetch and carry cans of films from the lockup outside in the yard, make tea, get the fish and chips for lunch, answer all calls at the back door and a multitude of other tasks which the Chief had put on a long list of weekly chores that only Vince appeared to be in charge of, and all of which had little to do with projecting films.

Finally he was let loose on the twin projectors. They looked faintly frightening, like two prehistoric beasts in a dull lead colour, relics from the 1940s, he guessed, lit not by bulbs but two arc-light copper rods, one positive the other negative, which when brought almost to touching point erupted into a sun-like flame. He found it difficult to keep the rods in the correct position as they burned down, adjusting knurled knobs on the side of the projector to keep them aligned. He soon brought the beasts under his control. So too he mastered the lacing of the projectors with film, in and out of sprockets, under levers and through gates in a complicated order that, if gotten wrong, tore up the film which raced through the projector at twenty-five frames a second.

He learned how to do the changeover from one projector to another, waiting for the black changeover dots to appear on the film, the change from one reel to another, from one projector to another, never even noticed by the cinema audience. And the orchestrating of the many lights around the auditorium, all done from a bank of around thirty switches that controlled ceiling lights, sidelights, lights in front of the curtain, lights on the floor. And when it was all done in conjunction with the moving of the black masks over the screen, the fading of the auditorium music, the dimming of the lights, each bank at its allotted time, the slow peeling open of the curtains and the final appearance of the film on the screen as the last of the lights faded into dark – now that was masterful! That was when he felt like he was conducting a huge orchestra, all the different parts coming together like sweet music. And no one knew of the skill and artistry it required.

This had become his Empire. His refuge from the world. A place where people came to forget the power cuts, the endless news reports of industrial unrest and strikes and the bombs in Ireland. The Empire was a place of dreams. And before the people filed in, and after they had all left in the evening, the Empire returned briefly to him. No one knew it like he did. He was the cinema's longest-serving employee now. He'd tour the old building whilst it was wreathed in quiet, wandering up and down the many rows of empty seats, onto the stage, behind the screen, up into the lofty dark roof space, down into the basement where dusty old things had been stored and long forgotten, down the many corridors that laced through the building like mould in Stilton.

It suited him, this job. He was on his own most of the time. He was never comfortable in the company of others, often painfully shy and uncommunicative, except when he talked about film. He knew tons about film and didn't have anyone to share it with. Mr Caldwell only cared about figures, profits and losses, and especially the losses. Vince adored the Empire. It was a sort of second home. In fact he felt more at home here than he did in his real home. The Empire was more of a mother, he thought, than his real mother.

And when the film was running and the rods were set, the light and sound were good, he'd often creep out of the projection booth and stand in the dark behind the last row of seats. He'd simply watch the film for ten minutes or so, listening to the sound, looking over the focus, feel the heat in the auditorium – not too hot, not too cold – but sometimes he'd people-watch. Check out the backs of heads, guess who they were and where they'd come from; the singles, the couples, the groups. Here he was in charge. People looked to him, to the man with the faceless head sometimes glimpsed at the tiny rectangle of glass in the projector room wall, though they did not know this. They didn't know him, he didn't know them, but they were united by their love of film and for a few hours they were in his capable hands.

He secretly envied the couples, though he was too embarrassed to stare too long at the courting couples in the back row. But you never miss what you never had, his mother often said and he'd try to convince himself that this was so. He'd never had a girlfriend, never even kissed a girl, and something inside him missed that no matter how he'd try to tell himself otherwise.

He wasn't exactly handsome, but he wasn't ugly either. He was so plain as to be invisible, he guessed, and his crippling shyness didn't help matters either, didn't endear him to the opposite sex who appeared to like their men straight from a Marlborough advert. The only female attention he'd ever got was from the cleaners and he began to believe that this was all he deserved; it was all that fate had in store for him in that particular area.

Nobody knew he was here. No one cared he was here. In some ways that suited him just fine. It was a place to hide from disappointment before disappointment struck. Ten years had passed him by in a blink, and he supposed the next ten, and the ten after that, would come and go just as fast. It never occurred to him that things could change, either carving up the Empire into smaller pieces of itself, or that he might one day fall in love.

But fall in love he did. It had been on one of those trips down to the auditorium during the feature. He happened to glance over the back row and saw her, her face lit up by the light reflected from the screen. A woman sitting all by herself. Small, neat hair, maybe a little on the plump side. But he was inexplicably smitten with her.

He wasn't rightly sure what was happening to him, because the emotions were so alien. Couldn't understand why he couldn't take his eyes off her. Why his heart leapt on seeing her, why his stomach went all empty and fluttery. Or why he had to keep coming down to try to look at her, to see if she came back to the cinema. And he was delighted to discover that she did. When that happened it was always the same seat she occupied, though it might be weeks between visits. Yet the effect on Vince Moody was always the same; sheer elation on seeing her.

Once, he lingered just a little too long and then noticed that the picture was growing darker. He ran back up to the booth in a panic, managing to adjust the rods so that the light burnt bright again, before it went out altogether and triggered the alarm bell and accompanying boos and shouts of displeasure from the audience.

But that would have been a small price to pay. He loved her, this unknown woman, even though he didn't know what love was. He'd seen enough of it on the big screen, however, to convince himself that's what it must be. So she wasn't pretty in a Marylyn Monroe or Jane Russell way, but neither was he Steve McQueen or Robert Redford, and that fact alone told him they were made for each other.

But when the picture finished and the lights went up, when the people all went home, the dream was over. His life, though, had changed subtly. No longer was the Empire the refuge of before. Without her it was cold, dark and lifeless. Without her he felt cold, dark and lifeless. He felt dead. A corpse. She became his life. A reason to live.

* * * *

3

The Witch of Devereux Towers

Vince Moody owned a tiny terraced house in the most rundown part of Langbridge. He liked to think he owned it but in reality he had borrowed the sizable deposit, and more besides, from his parents, who didn't have much in the way of money and constantly reminded him of the fact, but in truth he knew they had been desperate to get the last of their four children off their hard worked hands. There was no way Vince would have been able to afford to buy a home otherwise, rundown area or not, so he was grateful, up to a point. Having to be forever beholden to his parents and shouldering the guilt he felt at being a major contributor to their supposed poverty being exactly that point.

He was anxious to pay them back, but the wages at the Empire had never been brilliant, even for the position of Chief Projectionist, and had in reality been standing perfectly still for a number of years whilst inflation had decided to take off like a Saturn Five rocket. So the little spare cash he had he squirreled away to pay back the loan, which meant he led a pretty Spartan life. He rarely bought new clothes, left it ages between haircuts – though the fashion was for long hair, which helped disguise belated trips to the barbers somewhat – he ate frugally, could not afford to smoke or drink even if he had the inclination, which he didn't, and instead of owning a car he owned and rode a bicycle. He would have loved to have taken driving lessons, shoot around the lanes in an MGB GT like his boss, but that wasn't going to happen in a hurry.

He was also partially trapped by his lack of ambition; or more to the point his crippling shyness, which in turn hobbled his ambition before it ever got going. It had been one of the driving factors behind his parents' scraping out the dregs of their savings to pay for a deposit on a house for him; anything to get him out into the real world, to give him that little bit of oomph, as his father used to say. They were almost embarrassed of him. He wasn't so much the black sheep of the family as the bald one. They liked to brag off about the other siblings, who had all gone on to really good, steady jobs, even married and provided grandchildren. But Vince? Well, Vince was always considered not very bright, not quite with it, even before he went to school. He was the baby that took the longest to walk, the longest to talk, the longest to potty train. It suited his parents to have him out of the house and out of sight, a distant, almost invisible slur on their genes.

Still, the things he could indulge in that didn't cost anything gave him some pleasure. He loved film, and his job gave him some access to that. In theory he had free passes to the cinema that he could use to come in and sit down and watch one properly, but given that he was the only real projectionist and had to work every day except Sunday, when the cinema wasn't even open anyhow, he never got to use the passes for himself. And when he was on holiday – a brief two weeks in summer, one week in winter – he wasn't in the mood for going back to his place of work. So he gave the passes away to his mother and father, who never went out because they had no money, they said, putting the passes into an old wooden biscuit barrel they used to hoard unpaid bills.

Another love was the detective novel. The library was free and they had a good stock of all his favourites, Agatha Christie in particular, though he had read every James Herbert books ever since *The Rats* scared him half to death, and he couldn't go into the dark storerooms in the Empire for ages without taking a shovel with him. Both occupations added cheap thrills to an altogether un-thrilling life. But Vince wasn't complaining. Vince rarely complained. To do that you had to have an opinion and his opinions counted for nothing. You also had to have the guts to voice them and he didn't have those either.

What he had been able to afford was his bicycle. A brand new Carlton Criterium in polychromatic bronze with lightweight five-speed derailleur. He could be at the Empire in under ten minutes, and in the absence of any other transport – no car and the buses were so infrequent they were a local joke – it meant his small world could at least be extended a little wider, limited only by the strength in his legs and the hours in a day.

It was this shining bicycle that he rode through the streets of Langbridge. Today was Saturday, market day in the town. The June sunshine was beating down on the sweltering shoppers, eager to grab their groceries and cheap tat from the market stalls before magically disappearing around one o'clock, when the town centre would fall almost empty again.

Vince breathed deep the warm summer air, the tang of oranges and lemons and the earthy smell of potatoes still caked in dirt wafting over from the fruit and veg stall. He loved this time of year; people swanning around in T-shirts, girls in light summer dresses, transistor radios playing in the streets. Made him feel like he'd like to stay on his Carlton and keep on riding, just take the road that led out of town and see where he ended up.

He leapt off his bike before the twin gates that led into the Empire's rear yard. It was his job to unfasten them and pin them back every morning, and to close them again at night after everyone had left. He was fastening his bicycle with a chain underneath a ramshackle corrugated shelter as Mr Caldwell drove into the yard in his MGB GT. He let the engine growl a second or two and then the yard fell silent, the fumes coming over to Vince thick and strong.

Martin Caldwell was a little younger than Vince, if only by a year or so, he thought. But he appeared far more worldly wise. He was tall and lean, almost too tall for his MG; his hair was long but expensively cut, feathered in beautifully and held in place by vast amounts of Falcon hairspray for men; he wore a wide-lapelled chocolate-brown suit, even though he didn't need to wear a suit, with a matching brown kipper tie; his shirt was cream with tiny daisies on it. Though fashions had changed and it was now OK for men to wear flowers – and even the colour pink – Vince could never see himself being brave enough to don daisies, ever. Caldwell's platform Chelsea boots click-clicked over to where Vince was just finishing off fastening the padlock on his bike lock.

'Morning, Vince,' he said. He smiled briefly, only to be polite. 'How are you?'

Though Vince replied that he was fine he could tell his manager wasn't interested whether he was fine or not. He'd already walked off in front to the back door, fumbling with a hefty bunch of keys. Vince could smell Aramis aftershave, lots of it. He went through a number of keys before shrugging and letting Vince open the door for him.

'Thanks, Vince. Why are there so many damn keys?' he said, thumping open the door.

'I don't know, Mr Caldwell,' he said.

'We need to rationalise,' he said. 'Get them down to three or four. There must be twenty keys here, all told. Is there really any need for that many different locks?'

Manager and Chief Projectionist didn't share another word, Vince leaving Caldwell to nip into his office and close the door, whilst he went up to the projection booth. The twin projectors stood like two massive hounds waiting silently and obediently for their master's return. Furniture was sparse. The long wooden table that took up most of the centre of the room had on it a device for rewinding film and a splicer, and little else except for a bottle of black blooping ink for putting changeover dots onto the film, and a small reel of tape beside the splicer. There was a hard wooden chair and a coat stand. That was it.

The room was always cold and dark, even in summer. There were no windows except for two small viewing panes, one beside each projector, and the glass panels through which the projector beams entered the auditorium. There used to be a selection of old film posters on the walls to help lighten things up, make it feel less like a mausoleum, but Caldwell had ordered him to take them down. All that was pinned on there now were a sign banning smoking and a yellow health and safety poster filled with a veritable desert of dry text that no one ever read.

Vince went through the morning ritual of working through the jobs on his list, wandering through the building, keeping the old girl ticking over as he liked to call it. Then he prepared for the Saturday matinee. A couple of shorts and a feature for the kids. Today it was an episode of Buck Rogers and another called Rocket Man – ancient black and white things – followed by an old black and white cowboy film. The kids loved it, though. Martin Caldwell didn't. He had to go out on stage before the films started and pretend to be the kids' uncle, make jokes, which he positively loathed.

'Fucking kids!' he'd say. 'I'm not a fucking clown so why do they make me behave like a fucking clown?' And he'd stomp away to his office as soon as he could.

Vince liked it though. The kids called him Uncle Vince and waved up to his window and he'd wave back. Then he'd have to go down to the auditorium afterwards with a plastic bag to clear up any crap left over because the cleaners didn't have to work on a Saturday.

But Vince was particularly excited today because there was a new evening feature being screened and he was hoping that the woman would come in to watch it. It was her type – a bit of romance, a bit of adventure. So he couldn't wait until the afternoon and the time of the first screening. He was disconsolate when he scampered down from his booth to the auditorium only to find her seat on the back row empty.

'Hello, I've not seen you before,' said a shrill voice behind him.

He turned to see a young slip of a girl with a square tray of ice cream and lollies strapped around her neck, ready for the interval. She was a pale-faced thing, her skin peppered lightly with acne.

'Are you new?' said Vince, avoiding eye contact. 'Not seen you either.'

'I finished school this summer. This is my first job,' she said in a whisper. Acne aside, the dark made her look quite pretty, thought Vince. 'It's so exciting, isn't it? Are you Vince, the projectionist? My name's Edith,' she said.

'Yes, I'm Vince,' he said.

'Aren't you supposed to be projecting?'

She unnerved him so he said that yes, he was, and dashed away to his booth. He peered down and saw the young woman. She looked up and waved energetically at him and he stepped back, out of view.

Vince's luck changed at the third and final screening of the day. She was there, sitting in the back row. He stood some distance away, lost in the dark near the exit, studying her, finding her more attractive every time he saw her, he thought. In his mind he was going over a variety of ways he might approach her, but they were all pretty frightening and each filled with disappointment and disaster. At least he could stand here in the dark safe in the knowledge he hadn't been disappointed, the bubble of his dreams remaining intact and un-pricked. Better to be here with hope than talk to her and have that hope dashed. He couldn't bear to live with the thought of rejection.

Just before interval little Edith came up to him. 'Hi again. It's so exciting, isn't it?' Vince couldn't quite make out what she found so exciting but she was definitely a live wire flushed through with it. 'It's a good film, isn't it?' she whispered.

'It's OK,' he said, annoyed that his attention had been diverted. These opportunities wouldn't crop up that often and she was ruining it for him. He had to be back in his box soon.

'Oh, look!' she said, pointing a finger at the back row. 'She's here!'

'Who's here?' Vince said.

'Her – can't you see? The woman over there, sitting all by herself on the back row. You know, fuddy-duddy hairstyle.'

He realised she was pointing at the object of his desires. 'You know her?' he asked.

'Oh yes, don't you? She's the Witch of Devereux Towers.'

'The witch?' he repeated, frowning. 'What do you mean?'

'Well, not exactly a witch, I suppose,' she said with a giggle. 'That's what all the kids at school used to call her. She lives all alone in Devereux Towers, you know, that creepy old place in the middle of that field a few miles away.'

'I know the place,' he said. 'I thought it was empty.'

'It used to be. She's been living there a couple of years now. Lives all alone, like I said. My mum says she's a very strange one. Keeps herself to herself, doesn't get involved with things, doesn't like to talk to people. A regular little mouse, my mum says, hiding quietly away in the dark. The kids call her a witch because that's what kids do. I'm not saying she's got a cauldron or anything. Do you suppose she could be a witch?'

He scowled. 'Don't be silly!' he said. 'Do you know her name?'

'Laura Leach. All her family is dead. Some say she killed them and has them buried in the grounds of Devereux Towers, or walled them up or something.

Cooked their hearts and ate them for breakfast. That's what the kids say.'

'Well that's just stuff and nonsense,' Vince defended. 'She looks a very nice lady.'

'Just saying, that's all.' She fell silent and then nudged him with her sharp point of an elbow. 'Do you fancy her?' she asked, a bright mischievous light in her eyes. 'You do, don't you? You fancy her like crazy!'

'No I do not!' he returned, a little too loudly because someone turned around and hissed at him to be quiet. 'Stick to selling your ice creams, you silly girl!' He stormed away up to the projection booth, his cheeks afire.

He could hardly concentrate the rest of the evening.

* * * *

4

Casper Younge

Laura Leach rose quickly, before the end credits came up, before the lights in the cinema went on. She wanted to beat the crowds of people tearing for the exits. Not that there were often huge crowds; but it was particularly busy tonight, being a new feature. She didn't like to be caught up in the crush, having bodies pressed against her, touching, brushing sleeves. Didn't like the rush of excited noise, the energetic chatting as people descended the purple-carpeted stairs to the foyer animatedly dissecting the film they'd just seen.

She could have remained behind till last, but then she'd have to sit there all alone in the revealing glare of the lights, a spectacle for people filing past. That was worse. So she was the first out of the heavy swing doors, down the stairs and through the foyer, past the closed ticket booth and kiosk. First out into the warm night air.

It was around 10:30 p.m. and had only been dark for half an hour or so. She had a coat on but didn't need it really, not with it being so warm, but without it she felt a little bit naked, a tad vulnerable. She found her car parked some way off in a side street. A blue Hillman Imp that had cost her more to repair and keep on the road than it did to buy. She could easily afford something far grander, she knew that, but that sort of thing would only attract attention and that was the last thing she wanted. The Hillman suited her needs just fine, when it behaved itself. She learned to drive whilst still at boarding school at the age of 16. Pestered her father like crazy to pay for lessons. Privately she saw it as a way of being able to drive home whenever she wanted, but of course that wasn't going to happen. She was too young to be careering around in motor cars, her father had told her. So she passed her test and had to wait a long time before she could get a car of her own. That was before she came into money. Now she didn't have the heart to trade in the old Hillman. Besides, it was familiar, trusted, comforting, had a certain homely smell. She even found she talked to it, mainly to gently chastise the thing when it got all stubborn on her. How could she replace it with a complete stranger?

Laura drove the few miles out of Langbridge to Devereux Towers. It took all of fifteen minutes. It was a straight road out, rarely busy. The Hillman's suspension struggled with the ruts and potholes of the hard-baked track to the house. She had it in mind to pay to have tarmac put down, but that would mean having builders nearby for weeks on end and she didn't feel at all comfortable with that.

She pulled up outside the main door to Devereux Towers, a huge oak-panelled affair her father had salvaged from some church or other. It had masses of studded ironwork lacing its surface, great chunky hinges, bands of metal embracing it. The thing reminded her of a chastity belt, she thought grimly. How fitting.

Once the car's headlights were turned off the entire place was plunged into darkness. There were no streetlamps here, no lamp over the door – her father felt he didn't want the faux medieval façade of Devereux Towers defaced by the modern world, and had even resisted the installation of a discreet letterbox in the wall by the door. Laura had to walk to the beginning of the track, where there was a post box on a pole, to retrieve letters.

The ivy looked like the scales on a crouching dragon, she thought, drawn to glancing up at the high walls; the shining leaves rattled in the thin breeze, sounding as if it were a faraway crowd applauding her return. She went through into the hall and flicked on the light switch. With that one simple action the joyful escapism of the evening, the last sweet residue of the memory of the film sugaring her thoughts, were washed away. Devereux Towers had her in its claws once again, smothering her with its dark corners, cold marble and cold stone.

She went into the kitchen, fixed herself something simple to nibble and then sat down in front of the TV. It was the biggest television she could find, an ITT 28-inch, and colour too. It brought a little of the cinema into her house, she felt. But all that was showing was *Appointment with Fear* – a rerun of Universal's *The Wolf Man* – so she hurriedly turned it off. Even the music during the opening credits to *Appointment with Fear* disturbed her, and the images of all those horrible, scary faces melting into each other made her shudder. And that was even before the main film began.

She turned everything off and went upstairs to get ready for bed. She still had her bedroom in the tower – Laura's Tower – but not the same room her father had prepared for her. No, not that one. Though she paused briefly outside the blue-painted door to it. At her waist, fastened to the belt of her skirt, was a key. She was tempted to open the door, to go inside, but she turned away at the last minute, a tear in her eye, her chest beginning to tighten, her breath firing out in rapid bursts.

No, not tonight. She could not go in there tonight. She could not face what was behind the blue door. She could not face her past.

So she left it locked and made her way to her bedroom. It was large, spacious, the walls curved exactly like the walls of her childhood bedroom, and it had the same long, arched window; but of course it never felt the same. It never felt warm or comforting. It always felt cold and functional, as if she were but a temporary lodger there.

She left the curtains open and got ready for bed, slipping beneath the covers. She listened to the ivy tinkling on the windowpane; the scrabbling of mice or something between the joists in the ceiling. She preferred the dark. She could get lost in the dark. Hide away, safe from curious eyes. No one could find her in the all-consuming blackness of the night.

Monday was Laura's shopping day. Most people chose Saturday, largely because that's when people didn't work and had the added benefit of the street market. But she didn't have to work so she chose Monday. Langbridge was quieter then anyway. Not as many people in the street or in the shops. So she drove her little Hillman into town and parked in one of the two small car parks. Always the same space, if she could manage it, arriving around 8.30am to ensure she secured it. She popped into the butcher's shop first.

'Morning, Miss Leach,' said the butcher. He seemed to come from the same mould as all butchers, thought Laura; large of frame, belly pushing at his white apron, pink-cheeked, looking smiling and happy even with a meat cleaver in his hand. He was hammering out lamp chops. 'Usual, is it?' He'd already wiped his bloodied hands on his stained apron, adjusted his straw hat and was piling brisket onto the weighing scales. 'Lovely day,' he said.

'Yes,' she replied, looking away to avoid his pebble eyes. 'Beautiful. Set to last, too.'

'Too hot for me though,' he admitted. I'll be glad when it cools down.' He popped the meat into a bag, hand automatically going to the sirloin. 'I hear they're planning on closing down the Empire,' he said absently, making conversation.

'Oh no!' she said, horrified. 'Where on earth did you hear that?'

'Oh, here, there and everywhere. I can't rightly remember now, as you ask. But it's been on the cards a while, I reckon.'

'Well they can't do that!' she said shrilly. 'They just can't!'

He glanced uncertainly at her outburst as he rang up the till. 'Not up to us now, is it? They can do as they please,' he said with an air of finality, taking her money and handing back change. 'Still, who needs them, cinemas? We've got telly now, haven't we? And let's face it, these days it's all a load of American rubbish they're showing. What's happened to good old British films? Where are the Norman Wisdom films? Bring back the Ealing Comedies and all that.'

'What? Ealing?' she said vaguely. 'I love America!' she cried and he smiled awkwardly at her. 'They are so – so colourful and positive!'

'Well, yes, I suppose they are, if you like that sort of thing.'

Laura wasn't really listening now. She went out of the butchers and into the newsagents, buying a Langbridge Gazette, the local paper, and hurriedly scanning the pages for news of the supposed closure. But she didn't find one solitary article about the Empire. She was in a daze throughout the remainder of her shopping, feeling she wanted to burst into tears. How could they? Whoever *they* were, she thought acidly. Petty, faceless bureaucrats making decisions in back rooms that affect people's lives. She hated them! She hated them all!

She backed the Hillman out of the parking space and there was an almighty bang, the car coming to a juddering halt as the engine stalled. Startled, she turned around to look over her shoulder and saw that she'd run into the back of another car that had also been reversing out.

'Oh my God!' she said in alarm, her hand pressed into her mouth, unsure what she should do.' Oh my God, what have I done?' She began to panic. Froze to the spot, terrified of getting out. She glanced fearfully in the wing mirror and saw a man emerging from the car behind her. 'Oh my word! This is terrible! Terrible!'

The man came slowly round to her window. She heard a light tap of fingernail against glass. Without looking up she wound the window down, expecting the worst. A loud, blazing voice, a torrent of verbal abuse.

'Good afternoon,' he said. 'We appear to have a little problem.'

Her heart crashing, her chest feeling as if someone were stamping all over it, she turned her head to look at him. It was a handsome, smiling face that greeted her. Blue eyes, blonde hair, a set of quite extraordinarily white teeth.

'I'm so, so sorry!' she stammered. 'I'll pay for it. I'll pay for everything! My attention was elsewhere, I'm so, so sorry!'

He looked back to his own car. 'Really, it's not that bad,' he said. 'And you know, I think my attention was just as far away as yours. You're not entirely responsible. In fact, I'd say it was entirely my own stupid fault. I was pulling out far too fast for such a small car park.'

'It sounded awful!' she said, hardly daring to look at him.

'Really, it's not as bad as it sounded. It rarely is. Please, come and take a look for yourself.'

Reluctantly she opened the door and accompanied the man to the rear of the car. There were pieces of broken rear light on the ground, and the bumper of his car was dented. 'Oh dear, I'm terribly sorry, really I am!' she said.

'I'm more concerned about what I've done to your lovely little Hillman Imp,' he said. He bent to his haunches. She couldn't help but notice the way the sunlight bounced off his healthy-looking hair. 'See, it's not that bad, but you'll need some minor work doing. Largely cosmetic, I'm happy to say.' He rose to his feet. 'And all my dratted fault for not looking where I was going. That will teach me not to be so impatient.' He reached into his jacket pocket and took out a notebook and pen. 'I suppose we ought to swap names and addresses for insurance purposes,' he said. He held out his hand. 'Casper Younge – pleased to meet you!' he said, flashing that warm, engaging smile again.

She shook his hand. 'Laura Leach.' The contact brief. 'I really don't want the bother of involving insurance companies,' she said. 'I'll pay for anything, whatever it costs. I can write you a cheque.'

He held up both his hands. 'Hold on there – I've said it was my fault. It's up to me to pay. OK, to save no-claims bonuses I'll stump up the cash.'

'I couldn't let you…'

'You don't have a choice!' he replied brightly. 'I insist. It would hardly be proper of me to take advantage of a lady in distress, would it?' He scribbled on the piece of paper. 'Here you are; this is my telephone number. When you've taken the car to the garage and got a quote then give me a ring and I'll settle up.' He put a finger to his lips to stem her protestations. 'I insist,' he said, thrusting the paper into her hand.

With that he gave a smile and a wave and went whistling to his car.

She stared at the phone number, her heart racing.

* * * *

5

An Elephant in the Room

They were waiting for him, their eyes button-bright, like a pack of hyenas anticipating the collapse of a wounded animal. He knew he was in trouble the minute he opened the door to the staff canteen, the conversations dribbling into quiet and all heads turning towards him.

'I need some water for my bucket,' Vince said, almost apologetically.

The cleaners were finishing off their shift, downing the last dregs of tea from their mugs, one or two of them already having bags in their hands and ready to leave. But his presence halted them. It halted everything. Something was in the air and Vince didn't like the smell of it one bit. Of course, it had to be Monica who spoke first.

'Well here he is! Here's lover boy!' She cackled loudly and the others followed suit. 'Lover boy Vince!'

He avoided looking into her nasty little eyes, but she was blocking his way to the sink. 'I need water for my bucket,' he said again.

'Water for your bucket!' she echoed and made it sound real dirty. 'I'll bet you do. My, you're a dark horse, aren't you, Vince? Still waters really do run deep where you're concerned,' she said, refusing to stand aside so he could get to the sink taps.

'I don't know what you mean,' he said.

'Didn't think you had it in you,' she said. 'Didn't think you had the inclination.'

'I'm sorry...' he said, shrugging and squeezing past her to put the bucket into the sink. He brushed against her body and didn't like the way it felt.

'That's it, Vince. Stick it in and fill it up!'

The women all laughed shrilly and he felt his damned cheeks beginning to betray his embarrassment like beacons on a zebra crossing.

'Oh, leave the young man alone, Monica; you can see he can't take it,' said another cleaner, but clearly enjoying the baiting.

'He can't take it, but he looks like he can give it, eh?' said Monica. 'What's this we hear about you having a crush on the Witch of Devereux Towers? That true, Vince? She'll eat you up and spit you out, a woman like that!'

And again everyone burst into laughter. Vince ran hot water into his bucket and squeezed in a bit of washing-up liquid, watching the bubbles froth up like his desire to get out of there. It filled up too slowly for his liking and his discomfort grew and grew till he felt he might run from the room. But he tamped it down, held onto the sink's edge with his knuckles glowing white.

'Mark my words, Vince,' Monica continued, 'you'd do well to keep away from her; she's damaged goods. I should know; I've done some cleaning for her a while ago and she's as batty as hell.'

'That's not true,' he said quietly.

'No? What do you know, lover boy?' She came closer to him and he could smell stale cigarette smoke on her breath. 'Do you want me to give you a few lessons, Vince?'

He turned off the tap and hoisted the bucket. Water slopped out and put a dark stain on his groin. He noticed how Monica's eyes widened even more in amusement. 'I wish you'd all just shut up!' he said, head down and rushing for the door. He heard them snigger at his back. Why did Edith have to go spreading things like that around, he thought? Now he was a complete laughing stock.

He was still smarting as he cleaned the doors to the projection booth. The phone on the wall rang; apparently the film delivery they were expecting that afternoon was going to be late, possibly causing problems. Vince thought he should notify Martin Caldwell at once so he hurried downstairs, threaded through the narrow corridors and went to his office. The door was slightly ajar. He knocked timidly.

'Mr Caldwell?' he said. 'I've got a message for you.'

He heard a noise from within the office so he slowly pushed open the door.

Martin Caldwell was standing in front of his desk, his trousers and underpants around his ankles, his white rump pumping back and forth. He was gripping Monica's flabby bottom and she lay slumped across his desk. She was gasping in a way Vince found most alarming, and Caldwell was grunting as if he were lifting heavy weights and about to have a heart attack in the process.

Caldwell's head swung round suddenly, his eyes glazed.

'I'm sorry, Mr Caldwell,' said Vince not knowing where to look, 'but I've got a message…'

'Get out! Get out!' Caldwell yelled, pushing himself away from Monica and scrabbling to raise his trousers.

Vince scuttled away, feeling like one of those cartoon characters whose legs seem to run for ages before finding purchase and actually going anywhere. He almost sprinted up the stairs to the projection booth, his cheeks firing up for the second time that day.

An hour later, just as Vince was getting ready for the first screening, Caldwell came up to the projection booth and closed the door after him. He asked Vince how he was; made a half-hearted attempt at discussing the weather before turning to the real reason he was there.

'Look, Vince, there's an elephant in the room…'

Vince blinked, glanced around him. 'Sorry?'

'That thing, earlier, in my office.'

'Ah…'

'She was helping me out,' he said, first looking up at a spot on the ceiling and then down to his Chelsea boots. 'I know what it looked like, but it's not that straightforward.

These things never are, are they?' Vince shook his head. Carried on inserting the anamorphic lens for the Panavision picture he was about to show. 'Doesn't mean a thing. I love my wife, you understand?' He laughed nervously. 'You know how it is, one thing leads to another and then wham! Look, we're both men of the world...' He stared fixedly for a second or two at Vince. 'Well, maybe not. Listen, what you saw in my office, it never happened, right?' Vince remained quiet, going about his business. 'What do we pay you, Vince?' he asked, and Vince told him. 'Seems you're about due for a raise. I'll put something forward to HQ. There, how's that, Vince?' Vince told him it sounded OK. 'I'll look after you and you look after me, eh, Vince?' he said, rubbing his hands down his trouser legs. 'I'm glad that's all sorted then!'

And with a clap he left a bemused Vince to finish off what he was doing and start the show.

Monica wasn't so forgiving or generous. She purposefully sought him out the next morning, pinning him against the corridor wall, her face a few inches away from his.

'You say one word about what you saw yesterday, you little toe-rag, and you're dead! Do you hear me? Dead!' How anyone could cuddle up to a woman whose clothes reeked of week-old fish and chips, Vince would never know. He didn't say anything, just averted his eyes. 'I thought as much, you wimp. Are you a fucking man or a mouse?' she said contemptuously, thumping him squarely on the shoulder.

Mr Caldwell is a married man,' he said.

'It speaks!' Monica said. 'So fucking what?'

'So it's wrong, is all,' he said.

'What do you know? Who asked for your opinion, you dozy little twerp? Get back inside your little box where you belong and keep that mouth shut!'

She left him, lighting up a cigarette as she tottered away on her too-high heels. He was tempted to call out that there was to be no smoking in this part of the building but he simply wasn't that brave.

He spent the remainder of his shift sinking into the doldrums. He felt he should have been able to say something to her, to defend himself, and even to stand up to Mr Caldwell to tell him how wrong it was for a married man to be going off like that. But he couldn't and that was that. All of which all made him feel real bad about himself.

He was glad to finish for the evening and get on his bike. But instead of going straight home he decided to ride out to Devereux Towers. He'd not been there in ages and he might just catch a glimpse of Laura Leach.

He stopped at the edge of the field. From here he could see the building plain enough, like a child's discarded building block, incongruous and a little forbidding. He decided to take a closer look, stuffing his bike into the undergrowth and making his way on foot over the barbed-wire fence and along the edge of the field. Up close he could make out Laura's little blue car parked outside, but no sign of any activity. All was completely still and quiet.

He lingered there for half an hour or so, the Sun still strong, slapping his neck with its heat. He was about to call it a day and go home when he saw a car in the distance, going up the track that led to the house. It looked like a white Ford Cortina. It parked some way from Devereux Towers, hidden from its view by a small copse of trees in full leaf. A man got out. He had a pair of binoculars through which he scrutinised Devereux Towers and appeared to make one or two notes on a piece of paper before getting back in the car and driving away.

What was all that about, he thought? Who on earth could that be, hanging around the place like some kind of spy? He felt immediately protective of Laura, concerned for her safety. After all, out here, isolated from everyone and everything, Devereux Towers must attract all manner of strange, snooping people.

* * * *

6

Double Promise

Laura Leach took her car to the local garage for a repair estimate. The mechanic bent down to survey the damage, rubbed his stubble-peppered chin, strolled around the Hillman, crouched down to the rear of the car again and gave his grave verdict.

'It's not going to be cheap,' he said. 'It will cost you at least a hundred and fifty pounds. There's a dent, a minor re-spray, that kind of thing. That's just an estimate, of course; in reality it will be more than that.'

She thanked him and booked it in to be repaired. She never once considered ringing the number of Casper Younge, though for some reason she'd hung onto the piece of paper he gave her. In case she should ever need it, she told herself.

Another two weeks passed and another Monday morning shopping trip came around. She was in the process of returning to her car with her fully laden carrier bags when a voice at her shoulder caused her to start.

'Well, good morning, Ms Leach!'

She immediately recognised it as belonging to Casper. She couldn't understand why her hand now struggled with the key to unlock the boot, or why her heart began to race as if she'd been running. 'Good morning, Mr Younge,' she stammered.

'We bump into each other yet again,' he said. 'Here, let me give you a hand with that.' He lifted the boot for her, grabbed the handles of the bags and stowed the groceries away. 'Good job you don't eat much; this little boot couldn't cope with much more.' He slammed the lid down. 'I am most disappointed in you, Ms Leach,' he continued.

'You are?'

'You never rang me to tell me the cost of repairs to your car.' He bent his head to check out the car's rear. 'And I see it looks as good as new. I insist you let me pay for the job. What did it cost you?'

'Oh no, it doesn't matter to me,' she said. 'It's all done and dusted now. Best forget all about it.'

'Absolutely not!' he said adamantly. 'You must tell me at once so I can settle up.'

'No, really…'

'Then I refuse to leave this spot until you have told me the cost. You will have to run over me with your car to get out of here. You wouldn't want two accidents in the same car park, surely?' He smiled broadly, raising a Roger Moore eyebrow.

'I certainly don't want to knock you over, Mr Younge, but I have made my mind up and that's that.'

He sighed. 'In that case I insist I buy you dinner instead.'

She was taken aback. 'I'm not sure I understand what you mean,' she said, somewhat flustered.

'If you will not let me pay for the damage done to your poor little Hillman then at least let me take you out to dinner. It is a small price to pay and it would be an honour,' he said.

An honour! The quaintness of it made her smile in spite of her nervousness. His gentle expression had her warming to him. 'I hardly know you,' she said.

'Then perhaps we ought to use the opportunity to get to know one another better.' His face fell serious. 'Forgive me, I am being overly presumptuous. I notice from the small amount of shopping that perhaps you are not buying for two. At least, it is my hope that is the case.'

'Yes, you are correct,' she said, 'I am buying for one.'

'That's settled then!' he said.

'It is?'

'I can pay for dinner in lieu of your repairs and there is no Mr Leach about to throttle me for making the suggestion!' He reached into his jacket pocket and took out a pencil and piece of paper.

'Do you always keep those things handy in case of accidents?' she said. 'Or for inviting women to dinner in car parks?'

He laughed. 'I used to be a police officer,' he said. 'Old habits die hard.' He handed her the paper.

'I have your number still,' she admitted.

'I'm flattered it wasn't consigned immediately to the waste bin. There is a lovely new restaurant opened up in Langbridge. Apparently they do a mean fish dish.' He pocketed the pencil. 'Please say yes, Ms Leach, and help quash this poor man's horrid sense of guilt.' He leant against the boot of her car. 'Otherwise I might have to lie down in front of your tyres till you say yes.'

Bemused, enthralled, frightened, Laura said yes. 'When?'

'Tonight?' he replied.

'As soon as that?'

'Why not?'

She frowned. 'I don't know…'

He put a hand to his forehead. 'I'm sorry, there I go again. It's a habit of mine, being so impetuous and always assuming other people feel the same. I understand if you don't want to go out to dinner. I mean, as you say, we hardly know each other and yet here I am badgering you as if we've known each other years!' he stood away from the car, held out his hand for her to shake. 'I'll let you go now, and if you decide – '

'Yes!' she said breathlessly. 'Yes, I'll go to dinner with you tonight.'

'You will? That's wonderful! I mean, it will be just fantastic to eat in someone else's company again.' His attractive face fell dark, then faintly sheepish. 'There I go, off on one again. My wife died two years ago. Not a great deal of fun eating on your own.' He pointed to the boot of the car. 'Sort of takes one to know one,' he said. 'But you will still come, won't you? You won't refuse me simply because I open my big mouth and make an ass of myself, will you? I promise to be on my best behaviour tonight.' He wandered over to his white Ford Cortina, pointing out the damage on his own car. 'Terribly lazy, unlike you. I'll get it fixed some time or another!' He paused at the car's door. 'Give me a ring and let me know where you live so I can pick you up. Promise?'

She said, 'Yes, I promise.'

'Double promise?'

'Double promise,' she said.

He waved cheerily, got in his car and drove away giving her a toot on the horn as he pulled out of the car park. She was aware of other shoppers looking across at the noise, then at her. She suddenly felt extremely vulnerable and shut herself away inside her car.

She looked at the scribbled number, her excitement rising. He was so handsome, she thought, whilst she felt so plain, so ugly...

She lifted the piece of paper to her nose. The faint, manly smell of him lingered on its surface. Had she really been invited out to dinner? With a nicely spoken, handsome man? Really? Was all this happening to her?

No, she couldn't go, she thought. It was madly impetuous, like he said, and she was never impetuous, not since...

She shook the horrible thoughts away. It couldn't hurt to have one little meal out. Just the once. She hadn't been out for years and years and years. It was all so nerve jangling, so utterly terrifying. And yet so deliciously beautiful, she thought. Yes, I will go!

No, I can't! Damn you, Mr Casper Younge...

Even the name was warm and inviting and rolled off her tongue as if it had been there forever.

She gunned the engine and drove home; hardly realizing she'd been driving till she pulled up outside Devereux Towers. She placed the paper bearing his number on the coffee table and made herself a calming drink of tea and sat down with it, staring hard at the paper as if awaiting some kind of response from it. Two hours went by.

She tentatively picked up the telephone receiver, her finger hovering uncertainly over the dial. With a huge inward breath she dialled the number. Casper answered. He sounded over the moon to hear her voice.

'Seven o'clock, Devereux Towers,' she said.

'The old folly?' he said. 'I know where that is. I'll be there at seven prompt. I've already booked us a table. Actually, I booked it as soon as I left you. I'm so glad you didn't change your mind.'

Laura let the receiver drop down onto the hook a little too heavily and she put a hand to her mouth. 'Oh my God,' she said under her breath, 'what have I done?' She thought about calling him back straight away to cancel things, even lifted the receiver with that intention, but then decided it was too difficult a thing to do. She could turn out the lights, lock all the doors and pretend that she was out, but he'd come knocking and knocking, and what could she do about that?

In the end she ran a very hot bath and tried to stem her escalating agitation. Afterwards, still wrapped in her bathrobe, she ran her hand across the few dresses she possessed hanging limply in her wardrobe, and she shook her head in dismay. She didn't have a thing to wear. Not a single thing. She hadn't been out in years and here was the evidence of her isolation. She was going to look drab, awful, simply awful whilst he would look so dashing. He was going to be hugely disappointed.

She wept into her palms, sitting on the edge of the bed and rocking back and forth. Her red-eyed, tousled haired reflection stared accusingly at her from her dressing table mirror. How horrible you are, she thought; how miserable, fat, frumpy, worthless and ordinary,

Thoroughly dejected she settled on the black dress she wore for her father's funeral, no longer fashionable, in fact it was a little tighter around the midriff than it had been when she'd bought it. She put it on, smoothed it down and pinned on one of her mother's brooches to brighten it up. Her shoes were plain also, flat and uninteresting. When she looked at herself in the full-length mirror she felt a fresh wave of depression swamp her. She hardly bothered to fix her hair. It defied fixing at the best of times.

Oh well, she thought, he will get what he gets and if he decides to walk away then all good and well. It's what she deserves after all. That's what her father had told her: people always get what they deserve in the end, especially bad people.

There was a knock at the front door. She swallowed hard, opened it slowly, disconsolately.

'Ms Leach!' said Casper Younge, looking dapper in a smart suit and tie. He handed her a large bunch of flowers. 'You look positively beautiful!'

* * * *

7

Funny-Peculiar

They sat at a table tucked away into a quiet corner of the restaurant. The waiter handed out menus. Laura shrank in on herself, holding the menu card like a shield to hide behind, glancing skittishly at other diners. Casper hooked an index finger over the top of her menu and teased it down a little.

'Peek-a-boo!' he said. 'Are you trying to hide from me?' His blue eyes sparkled in the candlelight.

She put the card down. 'No, of course not.'

'You look uncomfortable. Are you alright?'

She gave a jittery smile. 'I'm not used to going out,' she said. 'I don't feel as if I belong here.'

He frowned. 'You most certainly do.'

'I feel people are staring.'

He looked around. 'They are far too busy concentrating on themselves,' he said. 'Most people generally are. If you don't like it here we can leave.'

'No, that would be terrible of me after all the trouble you have gone to, Mr Younge!'

'Now then, isn't it time you stopped calling me Mr Younge? I sound like a teacher or something. Call me Casper.'

She smiled. 'Like the friendly ghost,' she said.

'Yes, that's it, a jolly old spook! Never been called that before, but it's got spirit!' He laughed and she laughed with him. 'There you are, not such a bad old place after all. You must smile more often. Your face lights up when you do.'

She lowered her head to hide her embarrassment. The waiter came to the table, asking if they'd like drinks. Laura looked across at Casper, panic widening her eyes. 'I really don't know...' she said.

'That's fine. I'll order for both of us, shall I?'

'I don't drink,' she said quickly. 'Water, please.'

'Then I'll have water too,' he said. 'A bottle of your best mountain spring water!' he said to the waiter. 'Are you ready to order yet, Ms Leach?'

'I'll have whatever you are having,' she said quietly.

'You may not like what I'm having,' he said.

'I'm not fussy, honest.'

'I might like fish tonight,' he said, looking up from his menu at her. She nodded. 'Trout, salmon or sea bass; which might I choose?'

'Possibly the trout,' she said.

'Yes, I do rather fancy trout tonight. For both of us, please,' he said to the waiter.

The waiter loped off. Vivaldi scratched the air. There was a gentle murmur of voices, the sharp clink of metal against ceramic.

'It is a nice place,' she said, looking about her, almost as if trying to convince herself. 'And please call me Laura. Ms Leach sounds like a headmistress.'

'Laura. You know, whenever I say that it sounds like someone breathing. It's a nice name.'

'You certainly didn't have to go to all this trouble,' she said. The waiter brought the water. Casper poured some out into her glass and she lifted it to her dry lips.

'This is as far from trouble as I can imagine,' he said. 'It is my pleasure.'

'Are you always such a gentleman?' she asked. 'Manners are fast becoming old fashioned these days.'

'Only in the presence of a lady,' he said, giving a mock bow. 'Perhaps that's it. Perhaps I am old fashioned. It's just the way I was brought up, I reckon. I had a rather privileged background. Educated privately, boarding school, that kind of thing.'

'Me too,' she admitted. 'I hated it.'

'They're not all Billy Bunter or Mallory Towers, are they?' he said.

She noticed a young couple walk in. The woman was terribly slim, hair flicked neatly back, blue eye shadow and heavy lashes. She sat down very elegantly, floating down like a feather to her seat. It made Laura feel uncomfortable all over again.

'What's wrong?' he asked concernedly.

'Nothing. Nothing is wrong. Why do you ask?'

He waved his fingers briefly in front of his face. 'I can tell by your expression.'

She began to colour. 'Is it that obvious?'

'To me it is,' he said.

'She's so pretty,' she said, nodding in the direction of the young woman.

'I'm sure she is, to her boyfriend. But beauty takes many forms. Not everyone likes butterflies, you know. You are beautiful.'

'I am not!' she said, shocked. 'You are just saying that to be polite. I was not fishing for compliments.' Her features hardened and she felt herself going tense.

'Please forgive me, Laura. There I go again with my big mouth. I speak what I think without thinking before speaking.' He frowned. 'Does that actually make sense?' he smiled and she smiled back. 'Am I forgiven?'

'There is nothing to forgive. What happened to your wife?' she blurted, and immediately regretted having said it. 'Oh, now you must forgive me. That was very insensitive of me to have brought that up.'

'That's fine. She died of cancer. A long illness. We had only been married six years. We were very close.'

'I'm very sorry,' she said.

'And has there ever been a Mr Leach?'

Laura shook her head. 'Only my father.'

'So you live all alone?'

'All alone, yes.'

'That's not good, to live all by yourself. I should know.'

'I am used to it,' she said.

'I'm not,' he sighed. 'I loathe being by myself.' He raised a glass. 'But tonight I am not alone. Tonight I am sitting here with Laura and we are about to eat trout together.' Their glasses clinked merrily against each other. 'Though I admit I have never eaten trout before.'

'Never?'

'Never. Not a fan of fish.'

'How do you know you will like it?'

'I don't, but I am willing to try anything once. I mean, what's the point of life if we can't stick our turtlenecks out from our shells every now and again, eh? Bring on the trout, I say!'

She gave a squeak of a chuckle. 'You are funny!'

'Funny ha-ha, I hope, and not funny-peculiar!'

'A bit of both, perhaps.' She put her glass down on the table. Studied it hard. 'Why have you brought me here, Casper?' she asked.

'Why, I told you, to repay – '

'You could have come here with any woman you liked. Someone like her,' she said, indicating the pretty one that came in. 'Instead you brought me.'

His eyes grew sober. 'Yes, I am here with you, aren't I? Do you think me so shallow that I can be turned simply by a flash of red lipstick?' he appeared faintly hurt. 'Not all men are the same, Laura. Do you really want to know why I invited you out to dinner? The real reason?' She nodded dumbly. 'Because I like you. It's nothing more complicated than that. Do you know how much parking money I shelled out waiting for you to come along in that blasted car park? It's not a fun spot, you know.' He smiled warmly. 'The man that checked the parking tickets gave me more than one suspicious glance, I can tell you!'

'I'm sorry,' she said, 'I'm spoiling your evening.'

'Not at all! Far from it. And we both really need to stop saying sorry all the time. I shall demand a forfeit every time one of us says it from here on in! Agreed?'

'Agreed.'

'All settled, then.'

Afterwards he drove her back home, walked her to the front door. She looked at him nervously but he made no attempt to kiss her like she feared, not even a friendly peck on the cheek.

'Well, Laura, it has been a wonderful evening, but remind me to steer clear of the trout next time.' He put his hands behind his back, studied his shoes for a second or two. 'I don't suppose…'

'You don't suppose what?'

He gave a shrug. 'Would you mind if I see you again?'

'I think the damage to my car is more than paid for, Casper,' she said. 'That was very expensive and you should have let me pay my half.'

'Perhaps if I crash into your car again that would give me another excuse…'

'An excuse?'

'It would be nice to see you again.'

'I don't know…'

'You're right. That was too forward of me. You have my number if you decide…Well you have my number.'

He went back to his car. She said something to him but he couldn't catch it and wound the window down. 'What's that you say?'

'I had a lovely time,' she said hurriedly and went inside and closed the door.

* * * *

8

Quiet at the Back

The summer months wore on, the heat relentless, as if there were some kind of heavenly furnace being stoked up to bursting point. The atmosphere inside the Empire became decidedly oppressive, but it wasn't only the heat that affected Vince Moody.

When he was called to Martin Caldwell's office he was surprised to see that another desk had somehow been squeezed into the cramped space and Monica the cleaner was sitting at it like she owned the place. An Adler typewriter sat unused in front of her. She had a cigarette perched between her pursed lips and she exhaled a large blue cloud of smoke towards him, her mouth twisting into a barely disguised contemptuous leer.

'Monica is my new secretary,' Caldwell felt he had to explain. 'Someone to answer my phone, do things for me.'

'Mrs Kimble...' Vince began.

'She's no longer with us,' said Caldwell. 'She'd worked beyond retirement age anyway.'

Vince thought he looked troubled, like the last thing he needed was another body cluttering up his office, but he guessed Monica had other ideas. She was sitting like a smug cuckoo waiting to be fed.

'I can make sure you're doing what you're supposed to be doing now,' she said. 'Keep a close eye on things for Mr Caldwell.'

Vince met young Edith as he left Caldwell's office; or rather she met him.

'There you are, Vince,' she said breathlessly. 'Have you been avoiding me?'

'Yes,' he said abruptly.

'Why?'

'Because of your big mouth, that's why,' he said, but of course he immediately felt he had been too harsh and began to beat himself up over it.

'I'm ever so sorry,' she said, her head bowing. She appeared genuinely upset. 'It sort of slipped out, about you and the witch.'

'She's not a witch!' he defended. 'Did you have to let it out to Monica, of all people?'

'It seemed harmless at the time. A bit of a laugh,' she said sullenly.

'Monica is far from harmless,' he said, leaving her standing there in the corridor. This was not going to be a good day, he could tell. He would be glad to shut himself away in his projection booth.

'Can we still be friends, Vince?' she asked plaintively. 'I promise to keep my big mouth shut in future.'

'I don't know,' he said. 'Friends only bring trouble.'

She tottered down the corridor after him. 'I promise I won't be trouble ever again. Cross my heart and hope to die.'

'Don't promise that, stupid,' he said, turning back to her. She came up short in front of him, nearly colliding. 'You'll make it happen.'

'So we can still be friends?'

'Maybe,' he said in the best noncommittal tone he could dredge up, and left her to go out into the yard. He had to deposit a few cans of film in the store ready for collection and was carrying the first lot out, fumbling for keys to the padlock, when someone came to his side.

'Is Martin Caldwell in?'

He was a tall, handsome man who carried himself like he knew he was good looking. Neat blonde hair, smart clothes. A refined voice, not from around these parts, he thought. Vince had been told by Caldwell never to say he was in until he was clear who was asking to see him.

'Dunno,' said Vince. 'I can find out for you. If he is, who shall I say wants to see him?'

'Tell him it's a friend from way back when. Tell him Katherine sends her love. He'll know who it is. I need to speak to him.'

Vince did as he was told. He knocked loudly at Caldwell's door, wary of bursting in on anything he shouldn't. Monica was sitting at her desk thumbing through a copy of Film Review. She glanced up and eyed Vince like a cat watches a bird at a feeding table.

'Mr Caldwell, there's a man in the yard asking to see you. He says he's a friend from way back when and Katherine sends her love. Said you'd know who he was.'

At this, Caldwell jumped up, almost knocking over his lunchtime flask of oxtail soup. He went round to Vince, grabbed him by the arm and took him outside into the corridor, closing the door on Monica. He whispered into Vince's ear. 'Did he tell you his name?'

'No, Mr Caldwell.'

'Describe him to me.' His face went ashen as Vince related the details. 'So where is he now?'

'Waiting in the yard still, by the door.'

'I'm not here,' he said. 'You go down and tell him I'm away somewhere.'

'Where somewhere?'

'I don't know, Vince! Use your initiative. Tell him I'm doing some kind of staff training. In Birmingham, somewhere far away.'

'What sort of staff training?'

'Vince!' he said, putting a hand to his forehead. 'What does it fucking matter? Just tell him. Tell him I'll be gone for a few days.'

'Your car's in the yard.'

'Bugger!' he said, squeezing his eyes shut. 'Well he doesn't know I drive an MG.' He gave Vince the car keys. 'Here, tell him what I said and then go sit in my car, pretend it's yours.'

'I can't drive, Mr Caldwell.'

'Like that matters! Just do it, will you?'

Vince shrugged his acknowledgement. 'Are you afraid of him?'

'Afraid? No, of course I'm not afraid. I'm just not ready to speak to him yet. And if he ever comes around here again you tell him I'm not in. For now, all you need to do is go out there, tell him I'm otherwise disposed and sit in my bloody car. How difficult can that be?'

Vince went back outside. The man was leaning near the rear door. 'So where is he?' he asked.

'Mr Caldwell isn't in. He's gone away to attend a staff training course in Birmingham. It's far away.'

'Yeah, right. When is he coming back?' he growled.

'He didn't say. None of my business really.' He took the car keys out of his pocket. 'Sorry, I have to go to my MG now.' He walked over to the car, feeling the man's stare hot on his back. He unlocked the door and almost fell into the car's low seat. He watched the man out of the corner of his eye as he ambled over to him.

He knocked on the window for Vince to wind it down. 'When you see him, tell him I'll be back soon and I'll ram his bloody training course up his backside if he isn't in to see me. That clear?' Vince nodded that it was very clear indeed. The man floated away like an angry black cloud looking for a place to rain on.

Vince sat in the car for a further ten minutes, unsure what he should do next. The heat inside the car became unbearable, the smell of hot leather and plastic strangely comforting. Eventually, Caldwell poked his head around the door to the yard and seeing that the coast was clear went to the MG.

'He's gone?'

'He says he'll be back though, Mr Caldwell.'

'Bastard!' he snapped. 'OK, Vince, get out now; I don't want your body odour stinking up my car. Don't you ever use deodorant?' He snatched the keys from Vince's hand and locked the door. 'Remember what I said. If he ever comes here again, I'm not in.'

He nodded, hung back as Caldwell stomped to the Empire's rear door. Vince raised his arm, sniffed under it. That comment wasn't fair. He didn't smell. He used Imperial Leather every day and that soap wasn't exactly your cheap stuff from the market.

Later that evening, Vince thought he'd go down into the auditorium to look for Laura. Edith, Ice-cream tray strapped in front of her, stepped up to him as soon as she saw him, blocking his way.

'Hello, Vince,' she chirped brightly, but with a slight tremor of concern in her voice.

'Hello, Edith. Can I get past, please?'

'You don't want to go there tonight,' she said.

'Yes I do,' he countered, but she stood her ground. 'What is it with you tonight, Edith? You're not giving me orders too, are you? Only I've got far too many people doing that already and I don't need any more.'

He pushed by her and was brought up short by what he saw. Laura was indeed sitting on the back row as usual, but this time there was a man sitting with her. And he had his arm snaked around her shoulder. They looked like they were very friendly. Too friendly for his liking. What made it seem worse was that the man sitting with her was the very same who had come into the yard looking for Caldwell earlier in the day, the one his manager appeared to be afraid of.

'I did tell you not to go,' said Edith, coming to his shoulder, 'but you didn't listen to me.' She whispered in his ear. 'I don't suppose it's her brother,' she said.

Distraught, Vince turned away. 'Of course it's not her brother, stupid! Stick to selling your Ice-creams like I've told you.' He barged through the heavy swing doors out of the auditorium and someone hissed loudly for there to be quiet at the back.

* * * *

9

Bullets to the Soul

Laura was so unbearably happy she thought she might burst with it! She could barely remember any of the film. She was wrapped in a tight bubble of nervous excitement enflamed by his nearness, the contact of his arm around her shoulder, the smell of his aftershave, the heat of his breath as he leant close to her cheek to whisper something about the film. And afterwards, when the lights went up, she didn't rush immediately to the exit; they stayed behind as people filed by on the stairs and she was so proud to be with Casper that she actually wanted people to see her with him; she needed them to see that he belonged to her.

They hung back, long after the last of the cinemagoers had left, then they wandered out of the cinema hand in hand as if they'd all the time in the world. He put his arm around her waist and pulled her close. Before they reached his car he stopped her and gave her a light peck on the lips.

'I can't believe we are here together like this,' she said. 'I am the luckiest woman alive. I feel like I am on cloud nine!'

Casper Younge laughed lightly. 'Whatever tablets you are on, Laura, I'll have some too!'

Her face clouded over. 'What do you mean, tablets?' she asked.

He was immediately aware that he'd unintentionally hit some kind of raw nerve. 'Why, nothing was meant by it, Laura. It's just a figure of speech, that's all. Have I upset you?'

'No!' she said suddenly, forcing a smile. 'How could you upset me on a night like this? It's so beautiful, so perfect. Just like you.'

'Steady on there, Laura; such things can go to a man's head!'

'Well you are,' she said. 'So loving, so attentive, so handsome too. I keep asking myself, why me? Like it's all a delightful dream that will melt away in the morning. These last couple of months with you have been the most happiest in my life.'

Casper drew her away from the car. 'Shall we take a walk in the park? It's a lovely evening and there's something I'd like to ask you.'

She didn't need persuading. The park was all but empty, the smell of cut grass and roses in the flowerbeds hung heavy in the still air. He bade her sit down on a park bench and they sat in exquisite silence for a minute or two.

'You are very quiet,' she said.

'I'm thinking,' he returned.

'Thinking about something nice, I hope. What was it you wanted to ask me?'

'Why won't you let me into your house? Don't you trust me, Laura?' His face was serious, almost a look of hurt there.

She clasped his arm. 'Yes I do! I trust you like no other!'

'But not enough to be invited into your home, it appears.'

'It's not like that, Casper. There hasn't been a man in Devereux Towers since my father died.'

'So I do not come up to the high standards set by your father, is that it?'

'No, no! Not That! It's just … well; it's just how it is. I'm very particular about who I let into my house.'

'Are you saying I am not special to you?' His eyes looked moist with upset. 'I thought…'

'Please, Casper, let's not spoil a beautiful night. Of course you are special to me. Very, very special.'

'Do you love me?' he asked quietly, earnestly.

She sighed, turned her head away. 'I suppose I must,' she said.

'Only suppose?'

'Yes, I do!' she blurted. 'I do love you. With all my being I love you.'

He smiled warmly at her. 'In that case,' he said, getting off the bench and going down onto one knee, 'Laura Leach, will you marry me?'

He produced a red velvet box as if by magic, flipped it open. A gold ring with a large diamond in its centre flashed in the lamplight.

'Oh, Casper! You can't mean it!'

'I most certainly do. Most definitely I mean it.' She began to cry. 'Oh dear, it's not that bad, is it? I mean, we can always take it back to the jewellers and change it for something else.'

'It's perfect,' she sobbed. 'Do you mean it, really mean it? You're not simply pulling my leg?'

He raised an eyebrow. 'Blooming expensive joke!' he said. 'I told you I mean every word. Laura Leach, you still haven't answered my question: will you marry me?'

'It's only been a couple of months...' she said. 'It's too fast.' He took the ring out of the box, grasped her hand and gently slid the ring onto her finger. 'It fits!' she said, staring at it.

'Not a bad guess, eh?' he said, grinning. 'So it's fast – like I say, I'm an impetuous kind of fellow. But I know instinctively when something feels right and this feels just right. Do you think you could make your mind up one way or another; my knee is beginning to hurt.'

'Yes!' she said. 'I will marry you!'

'Wonderful!' he said, squeezing her fingers tight and getting up. He leant forward and kissed her, but she looked very agitated again. 'What's wrong?'

'She pulled her hand away from his. 'You might not want to marry me when I tell you...' She fell into silence.

'Tell me what?'

'There are things about me you don't know.'

'I know all I need to know, Laura. Nothing you can say can be so bad it will stop me marrying you.' He clasped her hand again. 'You can tell me, if you wish, in your own sweet time. But let's just enjoy tonight.'

She nodded, her face sullen. 'And I cannot...' She struggled to find the words. 'I cannot...'

'You cannot what?'

'I cannot sleep with you till after we are married,' she said in a rush. 'There, you will not want to marry me now,' she said, rising to her feet. 'You will think me strange. But that is who I am, because of what has happened to me and I can't do anything about that, can I?'

His arm wrapped around her waist and he eased her down to the bench again. 'That sort of thing doesn't matter to me one jot,' he assured her. 'And I really don't care about what happened in the past. I love the present Laura. We'll take things one step at a time'

'Really? You are not annoyed or disappointed in me?'

'What a thing to say! What kind of a man do you take me for?'

'Please don't let this be a cruel joke,' she said, her eyes filling again. 'If I find you are not being serious I will die. I could not take the heartache it would bring.'

'You have my word. I love you, Laura.'

'And I love you too,' she said. 'So much it hurts me inside.'

They sat holding each other tightly, in profound silence, listening to the distant sound of cars humming on tarmac. 'Perhaps now you might let me into your home,' he said in a whisper, stroking her hair tenderly.

'Perhaps I will,' she said, her voice muffled by his jacket. She was staring at the ring on her finger, hardly daring to believe it was true.

Casper Younge smiled. 'That's good,' he said.

He felt as if someone had taken a spoon and scooped out his insides, slowly, painfully, and then left him to die a lingering, miserable death. Heartache wasn't heartache at all; it was a vile torture endured by the entire body and he didn't like how it felt one little bit. He'd never experienced anything quite like this before. Vince Moody had suffered misery in his time, but these were dark new depths he was sinking into where the immense pressure was about to crush him.

He didn't deny she deserved to be happy, just as he was destined always to be miserable and lonely, a fact given additional weight on seeing the happy couple together. Now the name that used to give him such pleasure inspired only agony every time it fired through his mind. Laura, Laura, Laura. Like bullets to the soul.

Vince switched on his Ever Ready bicycle lights and began to pedal away from the cinema yard. He'd taken his time locking up because there was nothing to rush for. Life had ceased to matter. He pedalled down the main street, heading home, and then he saw them – Laura and her new man-friend. They were strolling arm in arm along the pavement, she with her head resting snugly against his shoulder. He averted his gaze; felt embarrassed even though Laura didn't know who he was, had probably never even looked in his direction. He was all but invisible to the couple so lost in their romantic rapture.

As he drew level with them they paused by a car that was parked at the side of the road, the man unlocking the door to get in. Vince's insides got all screwed up when he saw him kiss Laura. But some way past them he brought his cycle to a halt and turned round to look at the car.

It was a white Ford Cortina. He was certain it was the very same car he'd seen that day a while ago in the field near Devereux Towers. The day he saw the man leaving his white Ford Cortina to study the old building through a pair of binoculars.

The car drove off and he was left battling a number of conflicting thoughts and emotions. He was upset, that's all. There were millions of white Ford Cortinas on the road.

But there was only one Laura Leach and now she'd been snatched away from him by another. Faint heart never won fair lady, he pondered bleakly. Why couldn't he have plucked up the courage to talk to her? Yet he never had the chance, did he? No, that's not true; he could have made the chance. That was just an excuse. His entire life was one big excuse, he thought, feeling doubly sorry for himself.

The sight of his cold, lonely home didn't make him feel any better either. So he carried on pedalling around the streets till exhaustion finally forced him inside. He went to bed without eating. He felt he would never be able to eat again. What was the point?

* * * *

10

Slippers under a Bed

One of the most dangerous jobs at the Empire had to be changing the light bulbs in the ceiling high above the auditorium. Vince remembered the time the Deputy Chief Projectionist took him on his first tour of the old building. They ascended a flight of rickety old stairs and passed through a tiny door at the top. Michael, sucking loudly on a sugared almond, flicked on his torch.

'Follow me, and be careful,' he said. He was a man of few words and every one of those was like he was spitting out something that was causing a bad taste. 'Tread only on the joists,' he warned. 'If you put your foot in the middle you'll go right through the ceiling and kill yourself.'

That alarmed Vince. That and the dark. There could be anything lurking up here – mice, spiders, rats. Michael went on to show him how to reach the units that held the bulbs in place, how to remove the spotlights and replace them. Vince remembered how Michael pointed through the hole. Way down below, too many feet to be comfortable, he saw the auditorium seats looking like they'd been made for dolls. He felt sick with apprehension and overcome with giddiness. Michael, he recalled, chuckled at his discomfort. But he had to overcome his fear, because when a bulb popped it was his job to replace it. He'd actually gotten quite used to it over the years, no longer afraid of the dark or the imagined rats. He still didn't like the feeling of looking all those feet down to the floor, so he avoided the temptation to peep through the holes when he changed the bulbs. And he was always very careful, of course, to only step on the joists.

He felt a little like the Phantom of the Opera, scuttling through the dark bowels of the ancient theatre. What he did eventually discover during these excursions was that he could access other areas of the cinema via a small door at the far end of the vast expanse of ceiling. He found most of the ceilings of most of the upper-storey rooms could be accessed in this way.

On this particular morning he heard the hum of faint voices carrying up from below. The ceilings were thin and if you listened carefully almost every word could be discerned. He'd learned an awful lot about the lives of the cleaners from snatches of overheard conversations. All about their periods and it being that time of month; about not being able to get cheap stockings to stay up; about buying tins of paint for the bathroom and where fig rolls could be bought the cheapest.

These particular voices, though, weren't discussing how to get the cheapest anything. There was some kind of an argument going on and it appeared to come from the direction of Martin Caldwell's office. Vince crept silently across the joists, bending down to where the sounds were the clearest.

'So what am I supposed to do?'

He recognised Caldwell's voice straight away. There was no mistaking Monica's shrill tones either as she responded with some gusto.

'What are you supposed to do? Well you'd better think of something because it takes two to make a bloody bargain!'

'You told me you were on the pill!' he said.

'I must have forgotten to take them!' she fired straight back.

'You dozy mare! Are you serious? You forgot to take them?'

'That's not the point,' said Monica. 'I'm up the duff and that's all there is to it.'

Vince heard Caldwell moan. 'You can't be pregnant...' he said dejectedly.

'What did you expect? I ain't no fucking Virgin Mary. You were there, remember?'

'But you weren't supposed to get fucking pregnant!' he said. 'I'm a married man, in heaven's name! You'll have to get rid of it.'

'Not a chance. I'm many things, Martin, but I'm not a murderer. You put the thing there so you can do something about it.'

'Like what, Monica? What is it you expect me to do?'

'Leave your wife.'

There was a moment's silence filled with all sorts of menace, then Vince heard Caldwell give a cough, like he was choking on a chicken bone or something.

'You can't be serious!' he said breathlessly.

'Don't come over all John McEnroe. The ball was definitely in,' she replied. 'I'm not walking the streets of Langbridge as a single mother, not for you or anyone, so you can do what's right by me.'

'And divorce my wife? No way, Monica. I love my wife.'

She snorted in a way that Vince was very familiar with. 'Like you thought about that before you had your bloody way with me, and not just the once either. You weren't loving her then, were you?' There was the sound of a cupboard being slammed shut, a drawer being opened, something clattering on a desk.

'Monica, be reasonable...'

Vince flinched when he heard something heavy crash against the wall. 'Reasonable?' she screamed. 'Are you forgetting I've also been helping you in other ways; helping you and your friends by giving you details about Laura fucking Leach?'

'Jesus, Monica – that's my bloody Oscar you've just gone and dented! That was a present from my wife. And they're not my friends...'

'Who cares what stuff you're involved in with them, friends or not. What will your wife say when she finds out about you and me? When she finds out about the other dodgy stuff you're involved in?'

'You wouldn't...'

'Oh no?'

There was the sound of the office door being yanked open.

'Monica, please...'

Then the door slammed with such force Vince felt the ceiling shudder. He thought it best he creep quietly away. He'd already heard far more than he felt comfortable with. The stuff about Laura, though – what was that all about?

Later that afternoon, as Vince was preparing for the afternoon screenings, Caldwell knocked on the projection booth's door and entered. He looked unusually haggard. His tie was undone at the neck, like someone had grabbed it and tried to mug him; the top button of his shirt was unfastened. Vince had never seen him like this. A sweet smell of some spirit or other wafted in with him. His bleary eyes looked like he'd been at the bottle some time.

'Hi, Vince,' he said, a little unsteady on his feet.

'Good afternoon, Mr Caldwell.'

'What are you up to?'

Vince frowned, then shrugged. 'Doing what I do, Mr Caldwell. I'm working.'

Martin Caldwell went over to sit on the old wooden stool by the workbench. He toyed with the handle of the film winder. He looked at the projector. 'You know, I wouldn't have the faintest idea how to lace up one of those things,' he revealed. 'I don't know much about film either. The only things I know about are balance sheets and budgets.' He shifted his attention to playing with a roll of sticky-tape. 'You're lucky, you are, Vince.'

'I am, Mr Caldwell?' He didn't feel lucky. He felt like luck and Vince Moody existed in different hemispheres of the planet.

'Your life's so uncomplicated. You're not married. You've got a mindless, simple job...' Vince was tempted to interrupt at that point but the moment passed. Caldwell sighed. 'You don't even have a blasted car to worry about.

Me, I've got it all: debts, pressure, a wife, all sorts of complications. So many fucking complications I'm drowning in them.' He sat cloaked in miserable silence for a while and then dropped down from the seat and headed for the door. 'Anyhow, good to talk,' he said, slinking quietly away. Vince heard the dull tramp of his world-weary footsteps echoing down the corridor.

One part of Vince said it was the man's own stupid fault. If you play with fire you can expect to get burned. But at least Caldwell had had the opportunity to get burned; Vince hadn't been close to lighting a single match.

At the end of the evening Vince closed down the projection booth as normal, checked the auditorium for any stragglers, turned off the lights and did the same in the toilets. He'd once locked a woman in the cinema by mistake, because she'd got caught short and had emerged from the toilets to find the cinema in darkness and all locked up. She inadvertently set off the alarms with her panicked banging on the doors and Caldwell wasn't too pleased with having to turn out again because the police had called him back to the Empire to let her out. The woman was in a terrible state and it made front page of the Langbridge Gazette.

'Get a fucking phone so they can call you next time!' Caldwell had told Vince.

Vince had locked everything up, checked the toilets for stray women and was about to leave when Caldwell came staggering down the stairs in the dark. He wobbled across the foyer.

'I thought you'd gone home hours ago,' said Vince. 'I nearly locked you in.'

'I've got keys,' he said absently. 'Tons of bloody keys.'

'Are you OK, Mr Caldwell? You don't look well.'

'It's a cold brought on by Smirnoff's,' he said, suppressing a burp. He went to the large plate-glass doors and stepped away from them in horror. He hid behind a false marble pillar. 'Fuck! He's here!' he said.

'Who is?'

'Him. The man. You know, outside…'

'The man who called the other day? The one you didn't want to see?'

'Yes, yes, that's the bugger. I'm trying to avoid him. He mustn't see me.'

'Shall I call the police?'

'What? The police? God, no! Not the pigs.' He waved for Vince to come towards the door. 'Have a look and tell me if he's still there.'

Vince did as he was told. Stared through the glass doors. 'There's nobody out there, Mr Caldwell.'

'You sure?'

'All clear. Not a soul. Are you sure you saw him?'

'Yeah, of course I'm sure!' He ran the back of his hand across his damp forehead, crept up cautiously to the doors. 'I'm certain he was there. Maybe he's waiting for me. Check out the back yard, will you? He could be round there.'

Vince said OK and came back minutes later. 'Nobody there. Maybe you imagined it. Brought on by the Smirnoff's, perhaps.'

Caldwell glowered hard at him. 'Very fucking funny, Vince. Very fucking funny. I'm going out the back way. Make sure you lock up after me.'

Vince watched as Caldwell's MG burst out of the open yard gates like he was in an episode of *The A-Team* and roared down the road headed for home. Vince mounted his Carlton Criterium. He'd found it difficult to forget Laura, leave her to her new man. The same man that appeared to be haunting his manager. It was as if his old life was like an unmade bed, with crumpled sheets so uncomfortable he didn't like the feeling of getting back into it.

There was no real reason he could furnish that excused his night-time cycling out to Devereux Towers. He just knew he had to go there. He had to see the place where she lived, to know she was in there, to know she was near. One last look then maybe he could forget her once and for all.

And that was all the reason he needed. He pedalled out to the track that led to the house. It was completely dark now, the building like a black smudge against the faintly lighter sky. He turned off his cycle lamps and trundled his bike along the rutted track till he got close enough to make out two cars parked outside. One was Laura's blue Hillman; the other was the white Ford Cortina. Both of them snuggled up close together like two pairs of slippers under a bed.

* * * *

11

The Blue Door

There was a perceptible change in the weather as the year took a steep nosedive into autumn. The field in which Devereux Towers stood had been scraped bare, the trees and hedgerows fringing the field beginning to turn amber. Despite a log fire crackling energetically in the large grate of the stone Tudor fireplace, the room could not quite shoulder away the growing cold of the evening.

The dining room was large, originally fitted out to resemble some kind of medieval baronial hall, but Laura had attempted to temper the effects of bleak stone with patterned wallpaper, uplifting pictures, thick rugs and functional contemporary furniture that sat uncomfortably in the room. They were sitting on chrome-framed chairs with cushions of brown corduroy, seated at a large oval smoked-glass table mounted on tubular chrome legs, as far from medieval as it was possible to get.

'I rarely use this room,' Laura confided. 'When you're in it on your own it makes you feel so small, so I usually take my meals elsewhere.'

'I'm honoured you opened it up for me,' said Casper, raising a glass of wine. 'Makes me feel like a regular king. The meal was lovely, Laura.'

'Now you're being facetious,' she said, glancing down at her plate.

'No, really, I love sausage and chips. How was the cod?'

'I told you I can't cook. I was never taught how to.' Her face looked despondent and her eyes about to fill with tears. 'I'm sorry, I must be a real disappointment to you.'

'I've told you, I don't care,' Casper said. 'I'm more than pleased that you feel able to let me into Devereux Towers. Sausage and chips was the icing on the cake!' He wiped his mouth on a napkin and looked about him. 'It's very grand. Your father must have poured an awful lot of money into this place.'

She nodded. 'Too much, one might say. He loved it, but as you can see it is an impractical old thing really. Too cold in winter and costs a small fortune to keep heated. The upkeep of Devereux Towers is quite something, what with all the repairs and what not. That is partly why I only use a small number of rooms; and the fact that I feel I rattle around the place like a marble in a can.'

'So why not simply sell it?' he asked. 'It must be worth a small fortune to the right buyer. Buy yourself something smaller.'

She shook her head vigorously. 'Oh no, I couldn't do that, ever. I don't want to live anywhere else.'

'But you can't afford to keep paying out for the old girl, surely?'

'I have more than enough to live on. There are no worries on that score.'

He nodded thoughtfully. 'That's reassuring. Still, if you ever get desperate you can always sell the family silver, eh?'

'I won't ever be desperate, Casper.' She set down her knife and fork. 'You haven't really spoken about your wife, even after all this time.'

His expression fell sullen. 'I'd rather not. It is still extremely painful. You do understand, don't you? When the time is right, I promise. But tonight is about us, about the future not the past. As they say, the past is a library, not a living room. I have not pushed for details of your past,' he added.

'Forgive me, Casper. It is insensitive of me. And you are correct; tonight is about you and me. When you have finished your meal I must show you around the rest of Devereux Towers. After all, one day you will live here with me.'

He blinked. 'You know, I never really thought about that. I suppose I will. I rather fancy myself as lord of the manor!' he said, grinning over his glass of wine.

'We haven't discussed a date for the wedding yet,' she put forward speculatively. 'I would like to begin to make plans. That is, if it is alright to think along such lines...' she said. 'If I am not being too forward...'

'My dear Laura, if that is bothering you why not say June? You could be a blushing June bride. How does that suit?'

'Really?' she said, her eyes lighting up. 'June next year?'

'You would prefer sooner?'

'No, June would be wonderful!' she burst. 'June would be just perfect!'

'There, that's all sorted then. We'll make a list of what we need to get arranged.' He rose from the table. 'My congratulations to the chef,' he said, picking up his plate. 'I never thought chardonnay went with sausage, but now I try it, I find it makes perfect sense!'

'What are you doing?'

'Taking this to the kitchen so I can wash up. I take it there are no servants to do that kind of thing,' he said, glancing theatrically around the room. 'No, only me, it seems!'

'You're my guest. I will see to those.'

He shook his head firmly. 'I insist,' he said, collecting Laura's crockery on the way. He paused. 'Except I don't know the way.'

She laughed and led him to the kitchen. 'Come, put those things down and I'll take you on a tour.' She linked her arm through his.

She led him through the many rooms in the main part of the house, most of them being little used, made obvious by the great many dust sheets over furniture. She casually pointed out paintings on the walls, starchy portraits of other people's ancestors, telling him that she'd no idea who any of them were. Her father had constructed something of an imaginary past, a long line of nameless dukes and nobles who bore no relation to her family but, over the years, Laura said she'd become so accustomed to seeing them that they felt almost like distant friends or relatives. He also collected a good many other things, like vases or fancy pieces of furniture, almost as if he'd been on the Grand Tour himself. He was particularly proud of his collection of tribal artefacts.

Casper was intrigued, so she took him to her father's study. Even the electric light failed to wash away the dark shadows or inherent gloom of the place. He admired the collection of weapons.

'Are they really old?' he asked.

'Oh yes, some of them extremely old. I don't like any of it. The masks scare me, the statues are grotesque and devilish, and I hate the spears and the clubs. They were made to kill and hurt people. I sometimes imagine I can still see dried blood on them.' Casper picked up a long wooden club carved all over with strange creatures and abstract forms. 'That is a Fijian warrior's war club, called a bati,' she explained.

'I'll bet this could do some real damage,' he said, testing its weight and balance.

She gently took it off him and placed it back where it belonged. 'I'm sure it could.'

'Why not sell them, if they are so horrible? I'm told such things are beginning to get very valuable.'

'I couldn't do that,' she said with finality. 'They belonged to my father.'

'Tell me about him. You never speak about you father.'

'No,' she said quickly. 'I don't want to. Come, there are more places to see.'

'All this stuff, it must be worth a small fortune,' he speculated. 'He must have been quite well-to-do, to have been able to indulge his passion to such a degree.'

'Yes, he was. We were. I am.'

She looked at him, expecting some kind of reaction, but she felt heartened when Casper said he knew nothing about antiques or their value, and hadn't the faintest interest in money. After all, there were far more important things in life than money. What point was there in collecting things when they'd all be given away to strangers when you were dead and gone? Nothing is ever really yours, he said. Even the skin over your bones has to be given up at some point. She said she agreed, but even so one day she must get a valuer in to go over things, if only from an insurance point of view. Yes, he said, being practical that would be a good thing.

'I mainly live in the tower,' Laura said, having come to the end of the guided tour of the rest of the building. She took him through a large arched door and up a circular staircase to the first floor. 'Father always called it Laura's Tower, after me,' she said, but there wasn't a hint of fondness in her voice, just a bald statement of fact. 'This room belonged to my sister,' she said, opening and pushing at a door. All the furniture, bed included, was covered in dust sheets. 'It's not been used in a long, long time. Not since she died.'

It felt cold, damp and dispiriting thought Casper. 'I was thinking of wedding guests,' he said. He saw her stiffen. 'Who will you invite from your side of the family?'

'I don't have any family,' she said.

'Not a single person?'

She came to him, touched his arm tenderly. 'I thought it might be just you and I.'

'What, no one else? A wedding without guests?' He shrugged. 'I guess I never really gave it much thought before. But what about my parents, my brothers?'

'You didn't tell me you had brothers.'

'I'm the better looking!' he quipped. He saw how agitated she was becoming. 'Look, let's talk about that some other time. If you want it to be limited to the two of us, that's fine by me. Anything to please you.'

Laura closed the door, avoiding his gaze. They passed another door on the landing, painted in blue. Casper paused and pointed. 'So what's behind here?' he said, putting a hand on the handle. It was locked.

'Oh no, you can't go in there,' she said harshly, pulling his hand away. 'No one goes in there.'

He looked surprised. 'Sorry, Laura. What have you got in there, dear? A dead body or two?' He laughed but her frosty expression didn't melt.

'No one goes in there,' she repeated, almost under her breath. 'It's not used at all. It's just a boring, empty old room,' she said, dragging him away. They ascended the stairs at the end of the landing, to the next floor, Casper casting a last, inquisitive glance back at the door. 'This room is mine,' indicating a door but not opening it. 'And this room is where you will be staying tonight. It used to belong to my mother and father. I always thought it was a little too masculine in its décor for mother, but she never complained at all the dark furniture and drapery or anything. But it will suit you, I feel.'

'Oh yes, I will feel quite the noble sleeping in here,' he said upon seeing it. 'It's really very nice of you to invite me to stay over like this.'

She looked faintly embarrassed. 'The bathroom is over there.' She pointed out yet another door further down the short corridor. 'It's basic but serviceable. The hot water is a little temperamental because the old boiler needs replacing. That's Devereux Towers for you.'

He took hold of her hands, which he noticed were trembling. 'I know how much it has taken for you to invite me into your home like this, Laura, and I really appreciate it. But if you would rather me leave because it all makes you feel uncomfortable then you only have to say the word and I will leave at once.'

'Please don't go!' she said. 'I'm glad you're here. You've made me so happy when I thought I would never be happy again.'

He smiled warmly, gave her lips a peck. 'Good, I am glad to hear it.'

Now it was his turn to look troubled and she read it immediately in his deepening frown. 'What's wrong? Have I upset you?'

Casper shook his head. 'This is hard for me, Laura, because I have something to tell you. Something I have meaning to let you know for a long time now.'

'I understand. You don't want to marry me...' she said.

He squeezed her hand. 'Not at all! It's not that. Of course I still want to marry you. Look, there is no easy way to say this so I will have to say it straight. I have been having trouble with a lump.' He prodded his chest. 'They say it's lung cancer. Please, Laura, don't look like that. Really, it's nothing. They can work wonders these days and they were quite hopeful for me. I have an appointment at the hospital tomorrow morning to pick up the results of a few tests they've been carrying out. I'll be up and leaving early tomorrow so I could be gone before you're up.'

Laura's face had drained of colour. 'Casper, why didn't you tell me? That's awful!' She suddenly felt very faint, as if her legs had turned to weak rubber and were unable to take her weight.

'I didn't want to say anything to trouble you, dear,' he said, holding her close to him. 'Not when you look so happy. Don't worry about good old Casper Younge; I'm built like an ox. I just need to get tomorrow over and done with, that's all. It's been preying on my mind somewhat.'

She wanted to collapse and burst into tears, but he made light of the entire thing. It bothered her the remainder of the evening, even though it wasn't mentioned again. They paused on the landing a few hours later and he kissed her lightly before tramping along the landing to his own room.

'Please wake me tomorrow if I am not up to see you go. I want to see you go,' she said.

'Don't you go worrying your pretty little head over me. I promise I'll come straight back after my appointment and let you know the lie of the land.'

He blew her a kiss and closed the door on her troubled face. The room was cool and cheerless, just like everything else about Devereux Towers, he thought. He went over to the long, arched window and looked out. Through the darkness he could see the twinkling of Langbridge's street lights in the far distance, but little else. A light wind whirled around the tower like a forlorn spirit.

Casper got ready for bed and lay there for a few hours, listening to the eerie noises old houses make at night. Disconcerting clicking, scrapings and scuttling sounds. Eventually he looked at his watch. It was way past midnight. He slipped out of bed, crept to the door and opened it quietly, listening intently. All was still. He padded softly across the landing, paused once to look at Laura's room, and then went down the flight of stairs to the blue-painted door. He tried the door handle again and it was still locked, as he'd expected. What on earth was in there, he thought? He bent down to the keyhole to see if he could see anything at all.

'What are you doing?' Laura said crisply from behind him.

He started at the sound of her voice, looking round to see her black, shadowy form looming over him, the details of her face lost in the dark. 'Sorry, Laura,' he stammered, 'I was looking for the dratted bathroom. I felt sure you said it was down this way.'

'That's not the bathroom door,' she said coldly. 'The bathroom is that way.'

He passed her sheepishly. 'Sorry,' he said again. 'The old memory is playing up.' He was conscious she was watching him all the way up the stairs to the bathroom door. 'I thought you must be asleep,' he said. 'I didn't want to disturb you.'

'I hardly sleep,' she said, her voice as monochrome as the gloom. 'I don't much like the night time.'

* * * *

12

The Well

The weekly visit to Caldwell's office to collect his wages had become something of a nightmare for Vince. It had been fine until Monica had pushed old Mrs Kimble out of the nest. He paused outside his manager's office door, sucked in a deep, calming breath, and knocked. There was no reply, even though he knew someone was inside. He knocked again, louder.

'Come,' ordered Monica's distinctive voice.

He entered. She was sitting as bold as brass behind Caldwell's desk. She glanced tiredly at him and pointed at a space in front of the desk which she expected him to occupy. He hesitated. 'Well, do you want your money or not?' she said smartly.

Vince went up to the desk. She didn't raise her head, rummaged around in a drawer and removed a small, square wage packet, which she tossed unceremoniously onto the desk. She slid a piece of paper over to him, slapping a pen on top of it. 'Sign,' she said.

He signed for his wages. 'Does Mr Caldwell know you're sitting at his desk?' he said, clutching the brown paper packet. He didn't dare look up at her as he said it.

'What's it to you?' she snapped. She watched him as he put the wages into his pocket.

Vince noticed Caldwell's Oscar statuette standing lopsided on the desk. It had a massive dent in the base. He knew how it had happened, of course, but couldn't resist saying something.

'What's happened to the Oscar? That was a present from Mr Caldwell's wife. She won't be pleased about it being damaged.'

Monica peered contemplatively at it from under her heavy lids. 'His wife, yes...' she said. She put out a casual hand, lifted the statue by its head, swung it over the side of the desk and dropped it with a clatter into the waste bin.

'You can't do that!' said Vince. 'That belongs to Mr Caldwell.'

'You don't know who you are dealing with, do you, squirt? Let me tell you this for nothing, your days at the Empire are numbered,' she said, a cruel twist to her brightly coloured lips.

'What do you mean?'

'Like I just said. You're not indispensable, you know.' She rested her chin on a bridge made by her hands. 'I've suggested to Martin – Mr Caldwell – that we need someone better suited to the job of projectionist if this place is ever going to improve. People like you are dragging it down.'

'That's not true!' he said, horrified. 'What does Mr Caldwell say? He's never told me I've been bad at my job.'

'So what if he hasn't? I can do as I please, Vince,' she said. She crooked her little finger. 'I have him just where I want him. You see, that's the trouble with men; they're controlled more by what's in their underpants than what's in their heads. He'll do whatever it is I want him to do.' She waved her hand, looking away again. 'Shoo, fly, don't bother me.'

Vince stifled his annoyance, felt a fire raging in his insides that he could not quench. 'That's not fair,' was all he could manage to utter as he turned about to face the office door.

'Life's not fair,' she said. 'By the way, Mr Caldwell is looking for you. You'd better go find him fast if you don't want to upset him.'

'What does he want me for?'

She grinned. 'You'll have to go and see won't you? He's down in the basement somewhere.'

He found Martin Caldwell down in the boiler room. He was rummaging through a bunch of keys, standing before a door in a corner of the room.

'You wanted to see me, Mr Caldwell?' Vince asked uncertainly.

Caldwell spun round, looking faintly agitated. 'Yes I do, thanks, Vince.'

'Have I done something wrong?'

'What? Course not. Here,' he said, handing him the keys, 'which is the right one for this blasted door?'

'That leads to an empty cupboard, Mr Caldwell; are you sure you need to go in there?'

'A cupboard? I thought it led down to the old part of the Empire.'

'The basement?'

'That's right. I have to look over a few things to do with the refurbishment, and all that,' he said vaguely. 'There's an old well in there, right?'

Vince nodded. 'Yes there is. It's basically a hole in the ground that's been covered over with an iron grating. It's medieval, they say. The Empire was built on the foundations of a much older building. Some say it was the site of a medieval tannery. The door you're looking for is this way.'

Vince led him out of the boiler room, down another flight of stairs to another door. Beside it an old fire-axe hung on rusted hooks, above a positively ancient-looking fire extinguisher. He found the correct key. They felt the intense cold from the darkened room creep up the steep stone steps to greet them.

Caldwell paused at the top of the steps, letting his eyes grow accustomed to the dark. 'Is there a light?' he asked.

'No, Mr Caldwell. Electricity doesn't come this far down.'

'So nobody ever comes down here?'

He shook his head. 'There's no need. I've been in recently to store some old films I found in the loft, but before that the last time was when someone came in about seven years ago to bolt a metal grating over the well because it was deemed dangerous.'

Caldwell took out a box of matches and stuck one. 'Let me see,' he said, treading carefully as he descended the uneven stone steps.

The walls were constructed of large pieces of stone, mossy-green in places with the damp. 'Are those the films?' asked Caldwell nodding towards a pile of rusting old cans in the corner.

''Yes, Mr Caldwell.' Vince went over to them. There were about twenty in number. 'I found them stashed away in the loft, like I said. When I looked there were a load of shorts by Laurel and Hardy, the Keystone Cops, Buster Keaton, and a few Charlie Chaplin films dated around 1915 – *In the Park* and *Work*, that kind of thing.'

He struck another match. 'I don't care what they're about, what are they doing here?'

'They're film history, Mr Caldwell, classics. There won't be many copies left of some of them. And they're on nitrate film.'

'So?'

'So it's not as stable as modern film. It's flammable, can self-combust if it gets hot. That's why I put them down here, to keep them cool.'

'What the fuck are you doing keeping piles of worthless old junk that nobody wants and might even catch fire? Get rid of it.'

'But Mr Caldwell, you can't throw things like this away.'

'Do as I say, Vince,' he said with a sigh. 'Don't argue. So, this is the well, huh?'

At the far end of the square room was a rusting iron grid about three foot square and flat to the floor. It had been bolted down with four bolts, one at each corner. Caldwell went over to it, tossed away his spent match and lit another. He bent to his haunches, holding the flickering flame over the grating. He peered down into the black hole it covered.

'How deep does this go, Vince?'

'Dunno, but it goes down a long way, I guess.' Vince picked up a small stone and dropped it down through the iron grating. They listened in silence for what seemed quite a while before hearing a faint splash echoing up the circular well. The match fizzed out, plunging them into almost total darkness except for the light spilling in from the open door at the top of the stairs.

'What are you looking for?' Vince asked.

Caldwell rose to his feet and made for the stairs. 'Hazardous thing to have,' he said. 'Before any work could begin down here they'd have to check the water table and fill the well in.'

He seemed satisfied with his discovery. At the top of the stairs, as Vince re-locked the door, Caldwell asked for the key to be taken off the ring. He pocketed it.

'Is that all, Mr Caldwell?' Vince said. 'You've nothing else you have to tell me?'

'No, that's fine, thank you, Vince.' He frowned at the young man. 'Everything OK?'

Vince said everything was just fine, but he felt disconcerted with what Monica had told him. There were precious few jobs in Langbridge, and even fewer that he wanted to do. He loved being a projectionist. He'd be lost without the Empire. It must have shown on his face because he was stopped by young Edith. She was carrying a mop and bucket and he hadn't expected her to be there at that time in a morning.

'I've just got a morning job as one of the cleaners,' she said, rather too brightly as far as Vince was concerned. He didn't know how she could get excited by the job of cleaner, but Edith seemed blessed with being able to see the best in everything. 'I'm on my way to mop out the lavatories,' she added.

'That's nice,' said Vince without an ounce of passion.

Edith nudged him with the top of her mop pole. 'What's the matter with you, you glumbum you? Things aren't that bad, are they?'

'Monica is after getting me the sack, if you must know,' he said with a desultory sigh. 'And why are you always so bloody happy?' he said.

She recoiled slightly, as if the comment had physically struck her. 'Well there's no sense in being miserable, is there? Don't worry about Monica. Things are never as bad as they seem.'

'I don't believe you!' he said, exasperated. 'You're weird.'

'You're not still mad at me, are you? Is that why you're being so horrible to me? I said I was sorry, and you can't blame me for Monica's nastiness.'

'I'm not mad at you,' he said.

'I see. Then you're still pining after that Laura Leach woman, that's what it is.'

'That's not true.'

'Oh yes you are. It's written all over that sour little face of yours.'

'So what's it got to do with you if I am or if I'm not?' He brushed past her, determined to put an end to the conversation; he didn't like where it was headed.

Edith, on the other hand, was determined to keep it burning a little while longer and followed hot on his heels. 'It's probably best you forget her anyway, knowing what I know about her.'

He stopped. 'What do you mean?'

'Not only is she at least five years older than you, which is just *ancient*, she's quite mad,' she said in a matter-of-fact way.

'That's an awful thing to say about someone, Edith,' he said, failing to hide his displeasure.

'But it's true. She's a bit crazy, they say.'

'They say? Who says?'

Edith came up close to him, keeping her voice low. 'My aunt knows all about her, because she saw her in Bartholomew Place.'

'Bartholomew Place? Never heard of it. What is that?'

'It's an asylum, you know, for people with problems up here,' she tapped her temple with an index finger. 'She was in there years and years apparently.'

'I don't believe you.'

'God's honest truth, Vince. I heard she'd been in there since she was a young girl and she's not been out long. Those kinds of places give me the creeps. I mean, they can do something to your head even if you had nothing wrong with it in the first place, they're that bad. Now you don't really want to go pining for someone like that, do you? Perhaps it's a good thing she found someone else. You had a lucky escape.'

'You are a horrible, horrible young woman, Edith,' he said, walking away.

'I was only trying to help, Vince!' she called, her lip beginning to tremble. 'I'm not really horrible. Honest I'm not. You're not annoyed with me, are you, Vince? I was only trying to help.'

Vince Moody made a determined effort to stamp hard on the steps up to the projection booth just so anyone within earshot would know how fuming he was. He slammed the door shut and slumped down at the long table.

Why must people be so continually awful, he thought? And why was life so unfair?

* * * *

13

Bonnie and Clyde

She looked good and she knew it. Someone once said she had the figure of Bridget Bardot and the face of Sophia Loren, compliments she lapped up like a cat at a bowl of cream. But she couldn't argue with them, even if she'd wanted to, because the mirror didn't lie. She was beautiful and if anyone knew how to spend the currency that is beauty then it was Katherine. Kat for short.

She applied her eyeshadow, her lipstick, pouted at her reflection, ran a combing finger through her dark, glossy hair. She hankered after slightly bigger breasts, if she had to be honest, but that was perhaps being a bit too picky. She smiled at her reflection. As Mary Poppins said, practically perfect in every way...

Katherine had always been aware of her looks, ever since she was a kid at school, and she found she had an early talent for playing the opposite sex like they were toys laid on for her amusement. Precocious, a teacher had once said. Forward, said another, older than her years. Better watch her with the boys, one had joked, perhaps a disguised warning to her parents.

She soon learned she could hide behind her prettiness – how could such a sweet thing do something like pour a full pot of paint over a fellow pupil's head? She hasn't got a cruel bone in her body. Butter wouldn't melt in her mouth. Saint Katherine.

She smoothed down her dress, hands sliding into the hollows of her waist, out across the mound of her ample hips, down to her thighs.

Practically perfect.

But in spite of her aching beauty, the army of men willing to fall at her feet at her merest command, love had been hard to find. It worried her for a time that love was a game in which she got enjoyment only in breaking other people's hearts, treating them as something disposable like plastic bags, which once they were emptied of their contents, could be trashed like so much rubbish. And she'd worked her way through a lot of plastic bags, wondering why, at the end of the day, she felt desperately lonely and unfulfilled.

Lonely till she met him. Till she met Felix – the most beautiful man she had ever seen. For the first time she knew what it felt like to experience love, not to use and abuse it. They were soul mates, if such a thing exists; shared so many things it could only have been Fate that threw her into his path. Because, for one so beautiful, he too had that same cruel streak running through him. Not with her. Never with her. But when she saw how he used his looks, his unresistingly believable charm as emotional weapons to get what he wanted she knew she had found her Mr Right. Together they laughed at the pitiable vulnerability of others, at their weaknesses, at how gloriously easy it was to eat and spit them out. He jokingly called her the Bonnie to his Clyde. United in their robbing others of their love and the murdering of their delicate emotions.

Felix would be home soon, she thought excitedly. He could still do that to her, get her excited, even after four years together; get her all worked up, like a schoolgirl. She couldn't wait to see him again.

Yes, she thought, cocking her head at the mirror; together they were practically perfect in every way

It was an anxious time for Laura. She found she could not sit still, kept gliding to the window to stare out even though she knew he wouldn't be back from the hospital yet with the results of his tests. Casper had phoned once that morning to say his appointment had been delayed by an hour or so but he'd come though to Devereux Towers just as soon as he could. He told her again not to worry, everything would be alright. But that was like telling the rain to stop falling; worrying came naturally to Laura Leach.

She attempted to fix herself something to eat but couldn't manage the sandwich she made. It sat on the plate with scarce a bite taken from it. Finally she heard the sound of his car crunching to a halt on the gravel out front, and with her nerves ripped almost to shreds Laura all but ran to the door, swinging it open as Casper turned from locking the car door. He looked at her, his face pale, serious, troubled.

'Casper, what's wrong? What did the consultant have to say?' she said, going to his side and linking her arm through his. She led him inside. He felt disconcertingly heavy against her, like he needed to be physically supported.

'How about a cup of tea, eh, Laura?' he said, managing a thin smile and squeezing her hand.

'Never mind the tea,' she said. 'Tell me what the results were. They're not bad, are they? Tell me the news isn't bad.'

Casper shook his head gravely. 'I wish I could, Laura. Truth is the news isn't good. It's not good at all. In fact it's...' He faded into ominous silence and gripped her shoulders. 'Laura, it's terminal lung cancer. They've given me six months to live.'

She felt faint, her head going all giddy, and she thought she might collapse in a heap. The words caused her mind to spin with their implication and she felt suddenly very sick. 'No, Casper, they've made a terrible mistake. You're so young, so fit and well, so healthy. Look at you! They must have mixed your results up with those of someone else. It happens all the time.'

'No, Laura, I'm afraid it's true. They've made no mix-up. We went through all that at the hospital.'

She uttered a tiny shriek and put her hand to her mouth. 'That can't be so, Casper. I've only just found you. I won't have you taken away from me. They can do all sorts of things these days, can't they? You said so yourself. There must be some kind of operation, surely?'

'It's pretty bad, Laura.' His voice was on the verge of breaking up, crisping into nothing like a dried-up leaf.

'I won't accept that, Casper! There are all manner of treatments. I've read about them.'

'Well,' he said quietly, 'there is one, but it's out of the question.'

'Why? Tell me about it.'

'It's no use, Laura, it's far too expensive.'

'That doesn't matter. Tell me about it.'

'The doctor said there was this clinic in Philadelphia. They're specialists in lung cancer and have perfected a procedure that they say has ninety-five percent success rates. It's something we can't do in this country yet. It's not even available privately, even if I had the money, which I don't.'

'That's it, then. We'll get you to Philadelphia,' she insisted.

He grasped her tighter. 'No, Laura, we won't. Don't get your hopes up. It's too far out of my reach.'

'How much, Casper? Tell me what it costs.'

'The doctor said the full treatment was around twenty thousand pounds. So you see, you'll have to put that out of your mind. We must resign ourselves to spending what time is left to us in the best way we can.'

'I have money, Casper. I can afford it.'

'I couldn't possibly take it, Laura. 'It's what your father left you.'

'Then all the better I use it for something good. What use is money to me if you are gone?' She hugged him close, burying her head into his chest and he stroked her hair tenderly. 'Please say you'll let me pay, Casper. I couldn't bear it if anything happened to you. We've been so happy together. We can still be happy.'

He kissed the top of her head. 'If it pleases you,' he said, 'I will consider it.'

'We'll contact the clinic; send them a cheque straight away, whatever it takes.'

'It would be better if we arranged something else. Perhaps a bankers' draft, or maybe even cash so I could process things faster. Are you sure about this? It's a huge amount of money. It will clear you out. We'll have nothing but each other at the end of it.'

'That's all that matters,' she said. 'I love you. We'll go to the bank today.'

'No, there really is no need to rush.'

'I'd feel a lot better if we could get things moving as fast as possible. We can't afford any delays. You have to get over there to the clinic.'

He hugged her close. 'Laura, you are a sweet angel, do you know that?' He stroked her shoulder.

She sighed in frustration. 'I forgot; I need to get my money together. It exists all over the place in various accounts and shares and what not. I couldn't do it today even if I wanted to. It will take at least a week or so to sort out. That won't delay things too much, will it?'

'It will give me time to make arrangements with the clinic in Philadelphia. A week is fine.'

She started to cry, her body convulsing with her grief. 'I love you, Casper,' she said.

'And I love you too, Laura Leach,' he returned, staring into the distance.

It was late afternoon when she heard the car pulling up outside the house. Katherine peeled back the curtains. He was just getting out. He saw her, smiled and waved at her.

She dashed down the stairs excitedly just as the door opened and he came into the hallway. She flung herself at him, kissing him full and deep on the lips. She crushed her hips against him and he grasped her bottom and held her there.

'God, I've missed you, Felix!' she said.

'So it seems!' he returned. 'You sure smell good.' He kicked the door closed with the heel of his foot and he pushed her back so that she was pinned to the wall. His hand went up inside her blouse and cupped her breast. 'Let's go upstairs,' he said.

'Let's do it here,' she said breathlessly.

'They might see us though the glass in the door,' he warned.

'So what? They shouldn't be looking.'

He kissed her arched neck, his lips travelling down to her collar bone, down to the plump rise of her breast. 'So, Kat, how has your day been?' he asked.

'So-so. How was yours?'

'Oh it's been a belter of a day!' he said. 'I've made twenty thousand pounds.'

She pushed his head back so she could look into his gorgeous eyes. 'Never! She fell for it?'

'Hook, line and sinker, the sad bitch. She's desperate to save her poor, doomed Casper.'

'Felix, you certainly know how to work women, I'll give you that.'

He grinned. 'Yeah, Kat, I know just what they like.' His hand ran up her stocking, then he inched it slowly up her skirt.

She moaned softly and closed her eyes. 'I should say...'

* * * *

14

France Sounds Good

Vince prepared sandwiches and a flask of tea and packed them into his saddle bag. Though the long, hot summer had lost its grip on the weather, there were days when it was still fine and warm. He was determined to make the most of what was promising to be a glorious Sunday. He carried out the usual routine of oiling everything on his cycle with 3-in-1 oil, a spray or two of WD-40, and then set off early for the town of Glastonbury, a good fifteen miles away from Langbridge.

The country roads were still and quiet, the tang of damp foliage in the air, birds chirruping animatedly from the hedgerows. Just Vince, the flat, unending land and his bike.

Such times of peace flushed out the soul, he thought. The energy he was expending had the effect of purging his mind of his troubles, at least for a few hours. Monica became an evil spirit banished to the night, his monotonous life something he left far behind in Langbridge. For a little while he felt free, almost as if he might snap the bonds that tied him to his dull existence if he just had the courage to keep on pedalling. Almost.

He loved Glastonbury, though it had been taken over by hippies and its streets seemed these days to smell of incense. The hippies, with their long hair and strings of bright beads, their flowered shirts, loose sexual relationships and even looser attachment to what constituted for most people an ordinary life, might well have come from another planet. And he got the impression they looked at him the same way too, pushing his bike along the high street in Glastonbury, in his un-cool clothes, sporting an un-cool haircut, wearing an unflattering pair of bicycle clips around his ankles and finishing off the geeky picture nicely. Maybe he felt envious of them, he couldn't be sure. Or maybe he felt the same pity and disdain they heaped on him.

Vince Moody chained his bicycle to railings on the edge of town and followed the sign pointing to Glastonbury Tor, his Tupperware box of sandwiches in one hand, his thermos flask in the other. This trip had become something of a habit, especially during the summer months, but even well into autumn, before the warm weather closed down for winter. It was a kind of pilgrimage, he mused, but not of the religious kind. He wasn't sure whether he believed in a God or not, part of him feeling he'd like to openly denounce the idea as mere superstition, the other part not daring to go so far in case he was wrong and end up on His wrong side, as he seemed to be doing with everyone else on the planet.

Glastonbury Tor was ancient. That appealed to him. A massive, manmade, ridged conical mound that dominated the land. You could see it for miles. Why it was made, or who made it, were the subjects of many theories. They said King Arthur was buried here, but that was a load of bollocks because King Arthur never even existed; he saw that much on telly. There were books for sale in Glastonbury that said aliens had come down from outer space and built it, but they'd write any load of rubbish in order to make a profit and there was always someone dumb enough to believe it.

But none of that really mattered to Vince. To him, Glastonbury Tor represented something personal to him and it had nothing to do with King Arthur or aliens from Mars.

It was a steady climb up the stone steps and flags that led to the summit, and after cycling fifteen miles his legs were a little weak. At the very top of the Tor were the remains of a church, a single structure, like a stone finger pointing up to the sky, called St Michael's Tower. It was a hollow shell, no roof, tiers of blank, arched windows, a couple of open doorways in and out. He paused outside it, taking in the panoramic views of the countryside as the Sun drove away the last of the morning mist. The road below had been reduced to a thin, scribbly line, people to little sticks, houses to matchboxes, and trees to tiny pieces of broccoli.

There were few people around as yet but soon the hill would be swarming with them, locals and tourists alike. For the moment he was alone, above everything, at the top of the world. Maybe that's why he kept coming here; it was the only time he felt he was lifted high, out from the depths of his insignificance and for once looking down on everyone and everything instead of being the one being looked down upon. Up here, at the very top of Glastonbury Tor, he became the person he really was. The real Vince, not the Vince who inhabited that horrible, tiny world below amongst tiny minds and tiny ambitions and its tiny capacity for goodness. He felt he could reach out and squash it all flat. All of it. The entire world. All of them – all the horrible people who infected his world and made it sick.

He was disturbed in his thoughts by voices. Someone else had invaded his kingdom. More would follow soon. With a sigh he went into St Michael's Tower and sat down on one of the stone seats. It was significantly cooler in there but he could still look out of the open archway to the sunlight outside. More people came, some pausing to look over the curious structure before going to stand and stare at the view, or to spread blankets on the grass. A radio disturbed the quiet. A woman giggled shrilly and a dog barked like mad in the distance.

Vince snapped open his box of sandwiches, poured himself a mug of tea and sat still and invisible. No one ever seemed to notice him, he thought. He might as well have been dead, or a ghost or something. He was in the process of trying to pick out a greenfly that had landed in his tea when he glanced up and was surprised to see him. To see the man that had stolen Laura from him.

He was sitting opposite, breathing heavily; he was obviously unfit, Vince thought, in spite of his good looks. He was busy lighting up a cigarette like they'd just had the two minute warning and this was the last thing he ever wanted to do before the bomb dropped. He didn't notice Vince straight away, not until he was pocketing his cigarettes and he happened to look in his direction. For a split second he appeared to be grappling with the idea that he'd seen Vince before, somewhere, but he quickly gave up trying to think and went back to smoking his cigarette. Vince had become invisible again.

He wanted to go across to him, tell him what a bastard he was for taking Laura from him, but of course that would never happen, not like the movie he played out in his head where they'd argue, they'd fight, Vince would beat the shit out of him and kick his sorry arse all the way down Glastonbury Tor.

His appetite having collapsed, Vince closed the lid on his box. His day had been ruined, he thought. He didn't need to be reminded that everything he'd ever wanted seemed to be enjoyed by everyone else but him. He was about to leave when he saw the man rise to his feet, a smile on his face. A young woman came up to him; she held out an ice-cream, which he took.

'There was a queue at the van,' she said.

She had to be the prettiest woman Vince had ever seen. She oozed sensuality from her slim, perfectly formed frame. Her dress clung to her like a jealous lover, the neckline low and revealing a good deal of enticing cleavage. Vince was shocked when the man grabbed her arm and kissed her full on the mouth.

'You taste sweet,' he said.

'You've smudged my lipstick,' she complained with a smile. 'Eat your ice-cream before it melts.'

'I'd rather be eating something else,' he said into her ear, low enough to emphasise its suggestiveness but loud enough to overhear.

She glanced awkwardly over at Vince. 'Keep those filthy thoughts to yourself,' she said, taking him by the arm and leading him out of the tower.

Vince stood up to look at them as they walked away. They were talking, the man's arm wrapped tightly around her waist. They kissed again and then stared at the view, silently eating their ice-creams. Vince's heart rose – the man had obviously finished with Laura, had found someone new! Laura could still be his! He had another chance and this one he wouldn't cock up. This one he would grasp with both hands.

Vince went outside and looked up to the blue heavens. That's what God could do for you if you believed in Him, he thought. Thank you, God!

'So how long, do you reckon?' she asked, her tongue licking at a dribble of ice-cream running down the cone.

'I reckon it could be a couple of weeks, tops. Maybe less. Got to give her time to get everything together.'

'Twenty fucking thousand!' she said. 'I thought you said it might be ten this time.'

'When I got to take a look inside Devereux Towers, talked to her, I knew she'd be good for much more. I suggested twenty but I didn't think she'd bite. She didn't even flinch. If she'd had the cash she'd have given it me there and then, no questions asked.'

'She must really have it bad for you,' she said.

'Kat, I reckon I could squeeze her for another five thousand if I wanted.'

'Don't get too greedy, Felix.' She crunched on the cone, eased crumbs into her mouth with her fingertip. 'You didn't sleep with her?'

'God, no!' he said. 'That gives me the creeps.'

'But you would have done, if you needed to, like you've done with the others?'

He shrugged. 'Course. You don't have to look at the mantelpiece whilst poking the fire,' he said. 'I reckon it's precisely because I didn't push to sleep with her that helped convince her. This has got to be the easiest trick yet. And all thanks to your friend Caldwell. I don't think even he realises how wealthy the fucking bitch is.'

'How is he these days?'

'Keeps trying to avoid me. He wants out. Said he's finished doing that kind of thing. Got a wife now – seen her, a bit tasty, she is. He's settled down, he says. Guess he thought he could shrug you off once and for all, eh? Still, he came up trumps by pointing out Laura Leach.' He tossed the half-eaten cone down to the grass.

'He was good in his day,' she said.

'You still got the hots for him?'

'I never had the hots for him, Felix. It was strictly business. He'd do the birds, I'd do the blokes. Anyhow, after what he did to me I like the fact he's squirming.' She snuggled up close to Felix. 'But with you it's different. We've got something special.'

'Sure do, Kat. You and me we're special.' He chewed over his thoughts for a while. 'Laura's got this one room she keeps locked up, doesn't allow anyone in.'

'So?'

'So maybe she's got something special in there. In fact, I know she has.'

'Like what?'

'I dunno. She gets all worked up if you get anywhere close to it. She's a weird fucking bitch, Kat, I tell you. Not sure what's going on in that screwed-up head of hers. You think I should check out what's in the room?'

'I don't want you pushing this too far, that's what I want. Take her money and run, like we've done with the rest. Don't treat this trick any differently. Don't make any mistakes now, not when we're so close to twenty thousand pounds. That's going to change things for us.'

'Yeah. How about France?' he said.

'France sounds good.'

'A villa.'

'A fucking big villa, with a swimming pool.' She fell thoughtful too. 'Maybe this could be the last one for us. Maybe we could settle down too.'

He lit up another cigarette. 'Maybe,' he said, his eyes on some faraway place. 'Could be paintings, antiques, something like that. Maybe even a safe. Places like that have safes.'

'What are you talking about?'

'In the room.'

'Stop going on about that bloody room!'

He said OK, but he couldn't get it out of his head. Then he suddenly remembered where he'd seen that runt of a kid, the one in the tower. It had been in the back yard of the Empire cinema, trying to make out Caldwell wasn't at home. The thought bothered him for a minute or two and then he dismissed Vince altogether and settled back to thinking about the locked room.

What the hell did she keep in there, he thought?

* * * *

15

Drops of Blood

Martin Caldwell was all in a dither. It was almost as if he'd sensed Vince was walking down the corridor past his office. He flung his door open wide and called out.

'Vince, come here!'

Vince thought the worst. 'What is it, Mr Caldwell?'

'Have you seen Monica this morning?'

He shook his head. Not seeing Monica was classed as lucky, in his book. 'No, sorry.'

'Damn her hide!' he said. 'She's not turned up and she knows there's a ton to do this week, what with the refurbishment stuff. I've got paperwork coming out of my ears.' He rubbed his tired eyes. Tired and it was only ten o'clock in the morning. 'Well, when you see the woman you tell her to get her lazy arse in here at once.'

'Maybe she's sick,' Vince offered.

'Sick?' He rolled his eyes. 'Yeah, I should say she's sick.' The phone on his office desk was ringing insistently and they weren't about to hang up. 'Get out of here, Vince, and do something you're paid to do.' Vince turned to leave and Caldwell called to him again. 'Been meaning to ask you - where's my fucking Oscar? Have you seen it?'

'Monica threw it in the waste bin. It's probably been taken out to the bins.'

'Go dig it out for me.'

'The bin men have already been and collected the trash. Sorry.'

'The bitch!' he said, going into his office and slamming the door shut. He lifted the phone. 'What?' he said, rather brusquely.

'Hi, Martin. You're sounding on edge this morning. Caught you at a bad time?'

'What the fuck are you doing bothering me, Felix? I told you I don't want anything more to do with you or your schemes.'

'Kat sends her love,' he said. 'We were only talking about you the other day. You know, we can't thank you enough for pointing us in Laura Leach's direction.'

'Like I had a choice,' Caldwell said. 'Don't expect anything else. You've had all you're going to get from me. I've told you, I've finished with that game. I've moved on.'

'Good for you. Some of us haven't. I just need to ask you a few things, that's all. No need to be uncivil.'

'Like what?'

'That cleaner woman, the one that worked at Devereux Towers, gave you the heads up on Laura…'

'Monica? What about her?'

'She ever tell you about a locked room at Devereux Towers, one that Laura's particularly precious about? A blue door?'

'Not once, why?'

'You're not keeping anything from me, are you, Martin? I wouldn't take too kindly to that.'

'Go fuck yourself, Felix. I wouldn't tell you even if I knew, which I don't.'

The man gave a chuckle. 'Bit touchy today, aren't we, Martin? Something preying on your mind?'

'Always, and you're not making it any easier. Now when I put this phone down I don't ever want to pick it up and hear your voice at the other end. I also don't want to see you hanging around the Empire, even at a distance, you hear?'

'That a threat, Martin? Well listen up, wanker, I've not finished with you yet. If you think you can ditch me that easily you're dumber than I thought.'

'What is it you want? I don't know any more rich birds for you and Kat to screw over. There are precious few of those in Langbridge. Take yourself elsewhere, like fucking

America. It's full of them; you'll have a field day,' he said, making no attempt to hide the derision.

'I reckon the Empire turns over a few bob these days, since you took over.'

Martin Caldwell began to sweat, wiped his forehead on his sleeve. 'What're you getting at?'

'Seems to me you might be able to cream a little off the profits, send it my way in return.'

'In return for what?'

'In return for me keeping quiet about aspects of your past you'd very much like to keep quiet. Kat has been so – what's the word? – informative.'

'That's blackmail,' he said.

'You know, you're probably right, Martin.'

'You'll only bring yourself down with me. You're not exactly clean, are you?'

'Think about it, Martin. Me, the most I'd get is a few years for fraud. What's the going rate for murder?'

Caldwell swallowed hard. 'You don't have proof.'

'Want to risk that? Look, be sensible, you've a lot more to lose than me. Nice wife, nice house, nice car, cushy new job in the country. Do you really want to risk all that?'

Caldwell slammed the phone down and stared hard and unforgiving at it. He sank down into his office chair, shaking, seeing his world unravel before him and unable to do anything about it.

He'd watched out for her every evening but she'd not turned up. He'd go down to the auditorium and check out the back row but always he'd climb the stairs to the projection booth bitterly disappointed.

Vince had expected this evening to be exactly the same. He'd left the projector running and descended from the booth with little hope in his heart. The cinema was only half full tonight. Martin Caldwell, even more on edge than usual, had commented upon it, saying that they really had to get more people inside or the place would sink into its own shit. It's only a weekday, explained Vince in order to try and buoy the man up; Wednesday, half-day closing in Langbridge. Nobody ever did anything on Wednesday afternoons. It was like having half a Sunday in the middle of the week. But that failed to appease Caldwell who did what he usually did and hid away from sight in his office.

Vince wasn't prepared for seeing Laura Leach on the back row. His heart almost popped with excitement when he saw she was sitting on her own again, same seat, quietly watching the film.

Do it, he thought. Go over to her, say hello. What, interrupt her during the film? Say you're checking things out, that's all. Tell her you're the projectionist – no, the *Chief* Projectionist – and you're checking to see if everything's OK. Like a fucking survey? She'd love that, you idiot! Think of something else, quick, because you'll have to get back to your box soon. Don't screw up your chance. Think, man!

Except he didn't have to worry at all. There wasn't any point. The man – that same man – was here. He'd been down to the kiosk to get her something and was making his way down the line of seats holding out a bag of Minstrels for her. He bent, he kissed, he coiled his arms around her shoulders, did all those things that caused Vince's heart to freeze stone cold with loathing and hatred and every nasty bit of emotion he could dredge up from the deepest, blackest parts of his soul.

Vince's insides collapsed. The bastard, he thought! The two-timing skunk! He was seeing two women, cheating on them both, but most importantly cheating on Laura. The slimeball!

He envisaged going up to them, telling him how wrong that was and he must be a real lowlife to do that to someone as lovely and as perfect as Laura. He'd tell her he loved her more than this scumbag who couldn't control the insides of his underpants. They'd fight, naturally, and it didn't matter if he lost because he'd come out of it looking good whichever way it went.

But of course he didn't do any of that. He slipped quietly away, back to his projection booth to allow his anger to ferment.

'The name's Casper Younge tonight,' he said.

Martin Caldwell had obviously been drinking again. His face was flushed and there was a slight wobble to his head. He was sitting in his desk chair, arms folded. 'I don't care what fucking name you're using. I told you never to contact me again. You shouldn't be here. Who showed you my office?'

'One of the ladies from the kiosk. Charm, Martin. Works every time.'

'Get the fuck out of my office. Out of my life.'

'Now, now, Martin, no need to act like that. Let's sort this amicably.'

'There's nothing to sort, Felix. Look, you saw how many people were in the cinema tonight. The takings in this place are piss-poor. It's barely hanging on. I'm not making enough to hide even a little top-slicing. So you're wasting your time. You and Kat can go and fuck yourselves, because I can't help you. Now take the hint and leave me alone. Go back to taking that poor bint for a ride. It's what you do best.'

Felix smiled. 'I'll take that as a compliment, particularly as it comes from an old master. You don't know what you're missing, Martin. We're screwing Laura for twenty thousand pounds.'

Martin's eyes widened. 'You're pissing up my back!'

'No pissing. She's all over me like a rash, believes everything I tell her. She's waiting for me, out in the car. I said I'd lost my wallet, had to come in and find it. Gives me time to talk things over with you.'

'You're taking her for all that money and yet you're bothering trying to cream a few measly quid from the Empire's takings? Why is that, Felix?'

'Because I can,' he said matter-of-factly, checking his manicured nails, picking out a smidgen of dirt.

'Well you can bugger off, because I'm not playing ball.'

'You'll regret it, Martin.'

Caldwell leant forward, his fists on the desk. His face twisted into angry lines. 'Don't fuck with me, Felix, or you're dead!'

Felix raised an eyebrow. 'Would you believe it – the little dog has got teeth!' He grabbed Caldwell by the tie, yanked him forward. 'Say that once more, Martin, and you'll be the one who's fucking dead!' He released him, flinging him back as he did so. 'You've got until the end of the week to come to your senses.'

He smoothed his jacket, passed Caldwell a last, lingering look, and then left the office. He made his way down to the foyer. Everyone had left the cinema now, apart from Edith who was stowing away ice-cream trays and sweets behind the kiosk; and Vince, who had just said goodnight to the ticket lady and was preparing to lock up the cinema doors for the night. He was taken aback at seeing Felix descending the stairs, fastening his coat. He glanced at Vince as he approached. Vince was still boiling inside, a great, intolerable pressure that was building up like a head of steam as Felix strolled up to him. As they drew level with one another Vince casually closed the plate-glass doors.

'I need to get out,' said Felix, eyeing the young man. 'Open the door.'

'I know you,' said Vince. He was aware of Edith looking curiously at him.

'Really? Well I don't know you,' said Felix. 'Open the fucking door.'

'I saw you up on Glastonbury Tor kissing that woman.'

Felix's eyes narrowed, then recognition flooded in. 'The runt, yeah, I remember you. So what?'

'So you shouldn't be seeing both her and Miss Leach at the same time. It's not right, and it's not fair on Laura.'

Felix studied him coldly. 'Are *you* telling *me* what I should or should not be fucking doing?' He smiled and shook his head. 'Get out of my fucking way.'

'If Laura found out about you and that other woman...'

'She won't find out, will she?' said Felix, his voice low and menacing.

'I'm going to tell her. She has a right to know.'

In a flash, Felix had Vince by the collar. He tumbled him backwards and he almost fell over with the force. Felix pounded a hefty, balled fist into his stomach and Vince doubled over, winded and in pain. Then he was punched squarely in the face and Vince crashed against the popcorn cabinet. Edith screamed and ran from behind the counter.

'Leave him alone, you brute!' she said.

Felix bent down to Vince, who dabbed at a bloody nose. His cheek and mouth were beginning to throb terribly. 'Listen to me, you fucking shite; don't you tell Laura anything and don't tell me what to do. Nobody tells me what to do. One more word from you, one tiny little squeak, and I'll fucking kill you. Do you understand?' Vince moaned softly, drops of blood splashing on the tiles. Felix slapped him hard across the cheek. 'I said, do you understand, moron?'

Vince nodded weakly and Felix rose, straightened his coat and casting a meaningful, smouldering look towards Edith who had her tiny hand in her mouth. As soon as he'd left the cinema she ran over to Vince who was struggling to get up.

'My God! Who was that horrible man? Shall I call the police?' She saw the blood streaming down Vince's nose. 'Oh, Vince – you've been wounded!'

Well that didn't go according to the plan he had in his head, thought Vince, allowing Edith to help him to his feet.

'I told you to forget that Laura,' she said, taking her handkerchief to staunch the blood. 'She's nothing but trouble.'

'I don't need reminding,' he said shakily. 'Not tonight.'

* * * *

16

A Wounded Dove

'What have you done to your hand?' she asked.

He was running it under the cold tap in the bathroom. His knuckles were split and dribbled blood. 'Nothing,' said Felix. 'I thought you'd be fast asleep.'

'Have you been in a fight?' She could read his face like a book. He was tight-jawed, steely-eyed, looked as if he were seething underneath. 'Christ, what have you done?' She went over to a cabinet and took out a small tub that held a variety of medicines and tablets. She opened a box of sticking-plasters.

'Just some poxy, meddling kid at the Empire.'

'What were you doing there?'

'Thought I'd take Laura along to see a film, quiz her about how she was doing getting the money together. Then I thought I'd go and see our mutual friend.'

She sighed heavily, taking the top off a tube of antiseptic cream. 'I told you to leave him alone. We don't need him now. Don't screw things up, Felix; we're so close to clinching it. Martin's a nobody. We've used him and there's an end to it. Why are you so obsessed with him?'

'I ain't obsessed.'

'You are. You can't let it rest, can you? Are you jealous, is that it?'

He scowled, drying his hands on a towel and squeezing cream from the tube. 'I had to wear gloves so Laura didn't see the blood,' he mused, smearing on the cream. 'Me? Jealous of that fucking loser?'

'You are, aren't you? Christ, it was a long time ago. He didn't mean anything to me. I told you what he was like. How he treated me. What he's capable of. Forget him. It's been nice to see him squirm, like he made me squirm, but now's the time to dump him.'

'You brought us here, Kat. You suggested we use him.'

'Only to get back at him, no more than that! It was business.'

'Really?' He grabbed the sticking-plaster she held out and slapped it over his cuts. 'You sure about that, Kat?'

'You moron!' she said, punching him on the arm. 'I love you, not that loser. I never once loved him.' She kissed him on the lips, stared into his unconvinced, sullen eyes. 'You do believe me, don't you?' He nodded reluctantly. 'So just leave him alone, eh? Let's take the money and run. Forget Martin, forget this goddamn backwater. I hate renting this place in Glastonbury. I hate Somerset. We can have a real good life from here on in, so don't screw this up for us, not when it's almost in the bag.' Kat held his hand, looked at the grazed knuckles. 'So which kid was this you floored?'

'He's the projectionist at the Empire. He saw us on top of Glastonbury Tor. He could be trouble. I was warning him off because he threatened to tell Laura. I think he got the message.'

'He won't spill the beans, will he?' she asked with some alarm. 'I told you to avoid that place.'

'He's a frightened little runt. He'll not be saying anything.'

'You don't go to the Empire again, you hear?' she said firmly.

He shrugged. 'Yeah, whatever.'

'I mean it, Felix. So, when will Laura have our money?'

He smirked. 'At the end of the week. All sorted by then. I managed to persuade her to get the cash and I'll be picking it up on Friday. I've persuaded her I'm away on business for a few days, and I'm busy sorting out the clinic in Philadelphia, flights, that kind of thing. She still thinks we'll be getting married after I've had my operation.'

'That's good,' said Kat thoughtfully. 'Till then we keep low. No more visits to Caldwell, no more flooring little runts. You and me we're going to London to do some serious shopping. I've booked us flights to France for when all this is over. I've also got appointments booked with French real-estate agents to look over a few villas.'

'You don't hang around,' he said, clutching her to him and kissing her.

'A week from now and we'll be sitting pretty,' she said.

'You're already pretty,' he said.

'Cut the smarm, Felix; it doesn't work on me. I'm no Laura Leach.'

No one likes to see a police car. It makes people feel really uncomfortable, thought Vince as he answered the rear door and saw the two police officers standing there, and the car parked like some kind of striped beast of prey behind them in the yard. Their silver buttons gleamed against the dark of their uniforms.

'Is Mr Caldwell in?' said one of them, hardly bothering to look at Vince.

'Yes, he's in his office,' he said. He led them down dark corridors.

'Always amazes me, these places,' said one officer to the other. 'How they're all so dolled-up on the outside and yet as ugly as sin on the inside.'

'Like a tart,' observed the other.

Vince knocked at Caldwell's door, was told to come in. 'Police to see you, Mr Caldwell.'

Martin Caldwell jumped out of his seat as if he'd had a few hundred volts pumped through it. 'Police?' The two officers swamped the room with their presence. Caldwell looked at Vince. 'That will be all, Vince. Close the door behind you.'

'Martin Caldwell?' said the bulkiest of the officers. A man bred for the police force, thought Caldwell, like there was a farm somewhere that churned them out.

'That's right. What's wrong, officer?' His voice was thin and insubstantial. He blinked nervously.

'You're manager here, right?'

'Yeah, sure.'

'We understand Monica Andrews works here. Is that correct?'

He nodded quickly. 'That's right. What's the matter?'

'She's been reported missing, sir.'

'What, as in missing missing?' Caldwell lowered himself into his seat. 'She's not been into work for some days now.'

'When did you last see her, sir?'

Caldwell thought about it. 'About a fortnight ago now, I think. She never came into work. Thought she had a cold or something at first.'

'Did you contact her to find out why?'

'She doesn't have a phone in the house. Who reported her missing?'

'Her sister.'

'Maybe she's visiting someone.'

'Did you notice anything unusual about her behaviour when you last saw her?'

He shook his head. 'Not that I can say.'

'Anything that might be upsetting her?'

He shrugged. 'Like I say, nothing that I noticed. She was a cleaner – we didn't talk about personal things.'

'Was?'

Caldwell cleared his throat. 'Slip of the tongue. She was a cleaner, then she got promoted to the office. I sort of thought she'd decided to pack her job in.'

The officer nodded slowly. The other was disconcertingly quiet, surveying the small room. 'Maybe you're right. Perhaps she is visiting someone,' he said, smiling that pasted-on smile police officers always carry with them. 'If you hear from her, or hear anything about her whereabouts, please contact us straight away. It might be nothing to worry about but we have to check. If you don't mind we'll question other members of staff.'

'Please, do what you must,' encouraged Caldwell. 'I hope you find her soon. She was a valued member of the team.' He rose from his seat as they made to leave the office.

Then the police officer stopped and turned at the door. 'Were you aware that she was pregnant, Mr Caldwell? She'd been to the clinic the day before she went missing.'

'What? Pregnant? No, she didn't tell me that. I mean, she's hardly likely to, is she?'

'She's not married,' said the other officer, his first words of the meeting.

'I know,' said Caldwell.

'I know it's highly unlikely, but would you happen to know who the father is?'

Caldwell felt his insides being scrunched up. 'Is that important?'

'Maybe she's with him. Or he might know where she is, that's all.'

He shook his head vigorously. 'I don't know who the father is, or if she's been seeing anyone. Like I say, we didn't talk about her private life.'

'But she was a valuable member of the team,' observed the officer.

'Manager-speak,' said Caldwell. 'Can't help it. You know how it is.'

The police officer nodded sagely. 'Yes, of course we understand. We're all getting to be like Londoners these days. Anyhow, any news please let us know, sir.'

Vince Moody crept down from the roof-space of the Empire, stealthily so as not to be heard through the ceiling. He'd managed to overhear the last few dregs of the conversation though the thin ceiling of Caldwell's office. He allowed a smile of self-satisfaction to spread sweetly over his lips.

The letter lay open in her lap like a wounded dove. She had read it and re-read it, at first thinking it was some kind of perverse joke, cruel and sick in its intentions. She was reminded sharply of all those evil little pranks thought up by the girls in boarding school, terrible memories being dragged up from the stinking silt of her past. But whoever wrote this anonymous letter knew far too much for it to be a simple, spiteful prank. But still she could not believe it entirely. How could she doubt him, her dear Casper? It simply could not be true, that he was a cheap fraud, doing all this, lying through his teeth to her so that he could get his hands on her money. That his love was a complete sham.

Laura Leach sat for a full two hours with only her crashing emotions for bitter company. In the end she put her coat on and grabbed the keys to her car. She drove in a half-daze into Langbridge, parked in the very same spot she'd been pulling out of on that fateful day she met Casper, not wanting to think that it hadn't been chance at all, that he'd planned everything down to the last little detail.

She went into the local jewellers. The elderly man behind the counter knew who she was, knew she had money and greeted her accordingly. She twisted the engagement ring off her finger and handed it over to him.

'Can you tell me how much this is worth?' she said, her voice on the verge of breaking up.

His eyes widened when he saw the large, flashing stones. He twirled it between his fingers, stared at it, frowned, took out his eyeglass and spent all of five seconds studying the ring under it.

'If you're looking to sell it, Miss Leach, you're going to be very disappointed. It's gold plated and the stones are made of glass.'

Laura uttered a tiny squeal, her face falling alarmingly pale.

'Are you alright, Miss leach?' he asked concernedly.

She grabbed the ring and threw it onto the floor. She stormed from the shop, the bell above the door tinkling frantically.

* * * *

17

Dead Space

Vince watched idly as a breeze toyed with a small cloud of dead leaves and stirred them into a disconsolate-looking pile in a corner of the Empire's yard. Vince could appreciate how miserable they must feel. If leaves could feel, that is. Normally he'd view them as just another tiresome chore on his list, to be swept up, bagged and thrown away. How many times he wished they'd cut the trees down. They didn't need them – there were trees everywhere in Somerset – and they just added to his labours. But today he saw them in a different light. He felt like them, like a leaf; tiny, crumpled-up, dried to a shrivelled husk and waiting till someone came along and tossed him in the trash without sparing a single thought for him.

Eating cheese and pickle sandwiches today wasn't easy. His mouth still hurt. One of his teeth might have to be pulled but he was reluctant to go to see the dentist. Vince was sitting on the old stone steps at the back door, looking out to the world beyond the open gates. Cars passing, people filing by. Tiny snippets, there and gone in an instant, and all he could do was look at life from a distance, trapped here in the yard by some cold wind of fate and hoping another such breeze might waft him back out again.

He heard the door open behind him. The sound of leather soles on stone.

'Hello, Vince,' said Edith, smoothing her skirt under her legs and sitting down beside him. 'Having your lunch?'

He scowled at the pointless question, put the sandwich back in the box and snapped the lid on. 'You going home?' he said shortly.

'Yes, I've finished my cleaning shift for this morning. I'll be back again tonight to stand the kiosk and do the intervals.'

They sat in silence for a minute or two. 'Don't you ever get bored, doing what you do?' he asked.

She gave a chiming laugh. 'Oh, no! I love it here. It's so exciting!'

'No it isn't exciting, Edith,' he countered dully. 'It's the Empire.'

She nudged him with her shoulder. 'You misery, you! I thought you liked being here.'

'What do you know what I like and what I don't? You're just a silly young girl with fancy notions in your head. Life's not like that at all; it's not exciting.'

Edith looked momentarily stung by the words. 'I'm not a young girl, Vince. I'm a young woman. I'm seventeen, going on eighteen.' She held up her chin. 'And you, Vince, are a bad-mood-bear!'

Vince looked at her from the corner of his eye. He shook his head. 'What do you want, Edith?'

'Nothing. Just sitting here with you, is all.' She turned to look at him. 'How is your nose?'

His hand went up to the bruising automatically. 'It's OK,' he said, the memory more painful to bear than the actual bruises.

'At least it's not broken,' she said. 'It could have been broken very easily and then you might have looked like one of those rugby players, or boxers or something, and I don't think that would have suited you, because you don't have the build for it. It would have spoilt your nice face.'

'Yeah? Well who cares?' he said, turning away. The pile of leaves shivered.

'You were very brave to stand up to that nasty bully,' she said.

'Or very stupid,' he returned. 'I think it's downright awful, that man seeing another woman at the same time he's seeing Laura.'

Edith breathed heavily down her nose. It was almost a snort. 'You ought to forget that woman, Vince. I told you she'd bring trouble and I was right.'

'That's none of your business, Edith,' he snapped brusquely. 'Haven't you somewhere to go, like the toyshop?'

Her face became overcast, her lips quivering ever so slightly. 'There is no need for that attitude towards someone who likes you, Vince Moody,' she said, getting to her feet. 'And I am most certainly not a little girl who needs to go to a toyshop, you tiresome, bad-mood-bear!'

He watched her stomp out of the yard, instantly regretting what he'd said, feeling the cold water of guilt douse him till he was soaked through with it. 'Shit,' he said, all appetite gone.

Two suited men entered the yard, looking very stiff and official. They greeted him without warmth.

'We're here to see Mr Caldwell,' said the slimmer and younger of the two. He wore glasses and held a clipboard in his hand.

'Who are you?' Vince asked.

'He's expecting us. Just take us to him,' said the other abruptly, as if he were batting away a troublesome fly.

Vince said OK. They didn't look like policemen this time, he thought; more like stuffy little council officers. He led them through to Caldwell's office, feeling the more he had to do this the more he felt like a bloody butler. Upstairs fucking Downstairs, that's what the Empire had become.

'Make us a cup of tea, Vince,' said Caldwell flatly without looking up.

'Yes, milord,' said Vince.

Caldwell frowned, but shook the two men's hands as Vince clattered down the corridor.

'This is Mr Cross, the architect' said the man with glasses and clipboard. 'I'm Mr Forster, your surveyor for the day.' His smile revealed an uneven set of teeth.

'Right,' said Caldwell, 'tell me what you'd like to see.'

'Shall we start with the basement, like I mentioned on the phone, and work our way up?'

Caldwell unhooked a set of keys from a board on his office wall. 'Follow me.'

They filed down the corridors, down flights of stairs, every now and again the two men pausing to look over something or exchange professional judgements that didn't make any sense to Caldwell, nodding in unison before urging Caldwell to move on. Eventually they reached the door to the basement. Forster had come prepared. He produced a small torch and lit their way down the stone steps, his face serious as he looked around the damp walls, shining his torch beam over the stone flags of the floor and illuminating the metal grating that covered the old well. He went immediately over to it, and shone the torch into the black hole, but it didn't penetrate all the way down.

'My, that is a deep one,' he said. 'You can't see the bottom. Is there water in there?' he asked Caldwell.

'Yes, as far as I know.'

Forster bent to his haunches, his finger touching one of the nuts that fastened one corner of the grating to the floor. It came away smeared with oil. He smelled it. 'WD-40,' he said. 'Has this been taken off recently?'

Caldwell shook his head. 'No, not at all. Why should it have?'

Forster got to his feet. 'What are those?' He pointed to a corner of the room.

Damn Vince, thought Caldwell; he was supposed to have gotten rid of those film cans. 'Nothing. Just some old junk. They should have been removed.'

Forster nodded. 'Not sure yet whether we can use this room to create another smaller auditorium,' he mused. He looked speculatively at a far wall. 'Might be able to knock that through. Whatever, you'd have to cap off that well and re-concrete this floor, putting some kind of dampproofing in. I reckon the water table is quite high and there might be the risk of flooding if we don't do something soon anyhow.' He made a few scribbles on his clipboard and exchanged words with the architect. He glanced at Caldwell, who was sweating and looking decidedly pale. 'Are you feeling alright, Mr Caldwell? You don't look at all well.'

'I've got a cold coming on,' he admitted. He had to shove his hands into his pockets to stop them shaking. He needed a stiff drink, he thought.

'Shall we move on up?' urged Forster. 'This one's a maybe. Would take a bit of work and thought to incorporate it into the overall design, though.'

'How many screens are they after creating?' said Caldwell.

'Five at least,' he said. 'To make it viable.'

'And if it's less?'

Forster smiled an ambiguous smile. 'Shall we?' he said, indicating the steps. 'Let's take a good look around first before we come to any definite conclusions. We've only just started. This is not going to be an easy job. The trouble with all these old places is that there's only so much you can actually do with them. They were designed for what they were, not for what they might become.' He looked back from the top of the steps into the dark basement below. 'In my opinion – and it is only *my* opinion – this area is dead space,' he said.

'Meaning?' asked Caldwell.

'There's no life in it,' he explained.

* * * *

18

It's only money

Friday evening. It looked like it might rain, she thought, staring out onto the bleak fields. Her misty reflection stared back at her, like some kind of lonely ghost wanting to be let inside. She returned to dicing the carrot, the silvery blade flashing in the harsh glow from the kitchen light bulb.

She had a recipe book lying open before her on the worktop. To Laura, cooking wasn't instinctive. In fact it was all but alien to her. But she could follow instructions to the letter. She could follow rules. She had spent so long doing that she never thought to question them, never deviate from what was expected of her, even in a recipe book. Everything measured to the exact ounce, timed to the exact minute. Cooking – or trying to cook – was a good way to channel the myriad streams of thought that gushed unchecked through her troubled mind. It demanded attention to detail. She could become absorbed in it, even though it was all fearfully new to her.

She sniffed, paused in her chopping, blamed the onion for her stinging tears. She scooped up the diced carrot and dropped in into the casserole dish. Next she removed the stewing steak from the fridge, took a sharp carving knife and cut the red and bloody meat into neat little chunks and tossed them into the water after the carrot. She looked thoughtfully at the slimy pink stain the blood left on her fingertips.

Casper's white Ford Cortina pulled up outside, blurred by the condensation spreading over the window pane. His familiar form emerged from the car. He glanced up at the window, saw her and waved energetically. He had something in his hand but she couldn't make out what exactly. The doorbell rang and she wiped the blood off her hands, walking almost mechanically to the door.

'Hello there, Laura!' Casper piped up. He held out a bunch of flowers for her. 'Flowers for my flower,' he said.

She took them. When he leant forward to kiss her she stepped aside to let him in. 'Please, go straight through,' she said.

'Can I smell onions?' he asked.

'Casserole,' she said blandly.

'Is everything alright, Laura? You look – well, you look awfully tired.'

'I haven't been sleeping well,' she replied. 'Please, go on in,' she said again.

He studied her for a second or two, smiled broadly and went through into the living room, taking off his jacket and flinging it over the back of a chair. Laura lifted the flowers to her nose, breathed in their scent, and then threw them outside onto the wet gravel. She closed the door and turned the key in the lock. She slid the key into her apron pocket.

'I've got everything sorted,' he called. 'The clinic is booked. Mind if I fix myself a drink?'

'Go ahead,' she said evenly. 'Make yourself at home.' She went through to the kitchen and picked up the carving knife from the worktop. She set about slicing up a turnip. She heard him come into the kitchen behind her.

'You wouldn't believe the trouble it took, though,' he said. 'Lots of technical and legal things to sort out.'

'I'll bet there were,' she said.

'Then of course there are the flights and hotels to get lined up.' He took a swig from his whiskey glass. 'This is really good stuff,' he said.

'It belonged to my father. I don't drink. My father only liked the best.'

'He could afford to, I guess,' he said, feeling a tad uneasy. 'You sure you're OK? You sound rather distant. Not your usual self.'

'Thank you for thinking of me, Casper. It's so reassuring to know that there is someone there who cares, looking after my best interests. You don't know how that makes me feel.'

He saw a smear of blood on a wooden chopping board. Observed how unnecessarily aggressive she was being with the carving knife. 'Careful,' he warned. 'Has that turnip done something to annoy you? You'll end up cutting yourself.' He came to her side, attempted to slide his arm around her waist but she pulled smartly away.

'I'm very busy,' she said.

'Fine,' he said, holding up a hand. He went to lean on the worktop, scrutinising her. He took in a breath, let it out casually. 'Have you...' He took a drink. 'Have you sorted things out at the bank, Laura?'

She turned to him; she tapped the tip of the knife against the worktop, a regular, irritated pattern, almost like Morse code. 'Oh yes, Casper. It's all sorted. Who is Katherine?'

The name took him by surprise, almost as if someone had fired a gun in the small room. But he recovered quickly. 'Sorry – who?'

'You heard. Katherine.'

'I don't know anyone by the name of Katherine,' he said. 'Look, what's all this about? What's going on?'

'Who is KATHERINE!' she screamed at the top of her voice.

He put his drink down, took a step away from her. She had the knife held out in front of her; she was breathing heavily, her eyes like two marble balls.

'I don't know what you're getting at, Laura. Calm down, please. You're scaring me. There's obviously been some kind of mistake here, some kind of misunderstanding.'

'I thought you loved me, Casper. I trusted you with everything, even my heart, and nothing is more precious than that.'

'But I do love you, Laura!' he said.

'Don't lie to me, Casper!' she shouted again, then calmed herself down, closing her eyes tight and squeezing a solitary tear from her lid. It traced a silver line down her reddened cheek. 'Don't lie to me,' she said, every single word painfully drawn out. 'I thought we were going to get married.'

'And we will get married,' he assured.

'I thought you were going to die.'

'The operation will save me,' he said desperately.

She took a step towards him and he backed off a little. 'You were never going to die, Casper. You don't have cancer. You're not the least bit ill. And you're not going to Philadelphia with my money for an operation. You never were. You never intended to marry me. The cancer, the operation, the clinic, everything a lie. You planned it all. We didn't meet by accident. You didn't fall in love with me. You never had a wife who died. The only thing you were after was my money.'

'That's not true, Laura,' he said, shaking his head. 'Where have you dredged all this up from? Christ, Laura, I'm your Casper - I love you!'

'You're not my Casper; you're someone else's Felix.'

His mouth fell open. 'I...I...' he stammered, looking for a way to retrieve the situation.

'Why? How could you be so heartless?' she asked plaintively.

'It's someone's idea of a big joke, that's all...'

'I'm the real joke, though, aren't I? That's what you thought, you and that girlfriend of yours, your Katherine, your Kat. I'll bet you've had a real good laugh at my expense. I should call the police.'

He held up both hands. 'Now hold on, Laura, let's not be too hasty. This is all a lie!'

She removed the letter from her apron pocket. Held it out. Her hand shook. Gingerly he reached out, took the letter from her and began to read. His face went pale.

Laura shook her head slowly, the knife now flat against her chest. 'You're the lie, Casper – Felix, whatever your real name is. Preying on lonely, vulnerable, susceptible women like you do. You're vermin, do you know that?'

Seeing the game was well and truly up he dashed out of the kitchen, down the corridor to the main entrance hall. He turned the handle of the door but it was locked. When he spun round she was right there behind him.

'Open the door,' he said. He swallowed hard when he saw she still had the knife in her hand. Her face was impassive, eyes frosty and lifeless. Her lips worked at something, almost as if she were reciting a prayer to herself, or silently chanting some verse or other.

'Why?' she asked. 'All I need to know is why?'

'Put the knife down, Laura,' he said.

'Why?' she asked again.

'No harm was meant.'

'No harm was meant,' she repeated. 'You clearly don't know how much I am suffering inside,' she said, the knife point almost penetrating her blouse. 'You don't know how much all this hurts me. I loved you. I thought you loved me. I'd have done anything for you. But it was all a sham. Like the false diamonds you gave me, it was all worthless. You deserve to suffer, too, as I have suffered.'

'Open the door, Laura!' he said firmly, his voice tinged with escalating fear.

'I opened the door to my heart, a door that had been locked shut for years, a door I thought would stay forever locked, but gave it freely to you and you abused it.'

'In heaven's name, Laura, it's only money!' he said. 'Put the fucking knife down!'

She stared hard at the blade, as if she hadn't realised she had it in her hand. She lifted her head, gazed into his terrified eyes. 'You deserve to suffer,' she said.

* * * *

19

Issues

For the first seven days she didn't worry unduly that he hadn't phoned her. That was the nature of the game they played. It took time and patience, they both knew that. But when the first week bled into the second and still Kat had not heard a single thing from Felix she began to get edgy. Usually he made time for a quick update, to snatch a phone call, if only for a second or two. It was their unspoken rule. By the end of a fortnight she knew something was dreadfully wrong.

She became frantic with worry. She didn't know what she should do for the best. She started at every noise outside on the street, her hope rising with the passage of shoes on concrete, only to be dashed when they walked on by. She tramped the streets of Glastonbury, scanning faces, searching for his familiar form amongst the shoppers. She went to the top of Glastonbury Tor, where they'd stood to take in the views, and she grew increasingly despondent at the sight of autumn scorching the land and shrivelling the leaves. In the end she could stand it no more.

There was a biting crispness to the air, a portent of the chill to come, he thought, unlocking his MG. He loathed winter, even though in this part of the country the weather could be quite mild. He grabbed a chamois leather to wipe away the condensation from the windscreen.

'Martin.'

His insides froze on hearing her voice. He threw the leather into the footwell, slammed the car door shut. He glanced awkwardly up to the windows of his house. 'What the hell are you doing here, Kat?' he said, anger flashing across his features. He grabbed her by the arm and all but dragged her down the street, away from his house in case his wife should see her. 'What do you think you're doing? You never come near me, near my house, near my wife, you understand? I told Felix I'm finished with your fucking schemes.'

'Where is he, Martin?'

'What?'

'You heard me; where is Felix?' She yanked her arm free of his grip, rubbing the point where his fingers had grasped her.

'How the fuck should I know? I don't care where he is. He can go to hell for all I care.'

'He's gone missing,' she said.

'None of my business,' he said abruptly.

'I've not seen him for weeks.'

He gave a casual shrug of his shoulders. 'So? Like I care.' He moved close to her face. His breath pumped out in clouds. 'You keep away from me and my wife. You come round here again...'

'And what? You'll beat the shit out of me like you used to?'

His jaw set hard. 'I'm different now.'

'A leopard and its spots, and all that,' she said. 'Like fuck you're different. Let me tell you, Martin, you're involved in this whether you like it or not and it's me that's calling the shots this time. I'm not afraid of you any more.'

'Why do you care about him anyway? He doesn't love you. People like that are incapable of it.'

'You should know. Have you laid into her yet?' She nodded towards Caldwell's house. 'Does your wife know what you're really like, what things you've done in the past? Does she know about your relationship with our friend in the north, Ray Steele, and his part in things? How he helped you out of a tricky situation? Or have you fed her a load of bollocks, created a different kind of Martin Caldwell that isn't a violent, murdering bastard?'

He held up a fist but thought better of it. 'Get out of my sight, Kat, or I swear you'll be sorry.'

'Just as I thought; the old Martin isn't far away, is he? All your stories, your false past, your bogus qualifications, your supposed new life, it can't cover who you really are.'

'Have you ever thought that Felix might simply have taken Laura's money and run? Yes, he told me how much he stood to gain. He could buy ten of you with that amount of cash, Kat. Your kind is cheap. I know it from past experience.'

'He wouldn't do that. He loves me. That's not something you'd know anything about, Martin, love.'

'You really think he loves you? You're as deluded as that bitch in Devereux Towers. Felix drove a white Ford Cortina, right?'

'So what?'

'So the police found a white Ford Cortina abandoned in Langbridge a fortnight ago. Appears it had been stolen from Coventry. They'd no idea who it belonged to or why it was there, but we both know, don't we?'

'You're lying.'

'Am I? Check out the Langbridge Gazette. It was mentioned in there. Seems like he simply upped sticks and left. He's probably sipping cocktails at some fancy fondue party in Capri, whilst you're here pining for a twofaced slimeball.' Caldwell sneered. 'It's not nice, is it, Kat, being on the other side of the fence? Being the one who's shit upon instead of doling it out. Face it, he's dumped you.'

'If you've done anything to him…'

'That a threat, Kat?' He laughed hollowly. 'You made your bed, so now you can lie on it.' He pointed a rigid finger at her face. 'You never come near me again, and if any of this ever gets out, I swear I'll kill you.' He stomped away, but stopped, turned and came back. 'I don't care if he's lying face down in some ditch or other; truth is that's what I'd like to hear. He deserves all he gets. You both do. You want my advice? I'd start with that crazy bitch he was screwing.' He grinned. 'Shame he didn't know everything about Laura Leach before he went in there all guns blazing.'

'What do you mean everything?'

'Let's say she's not the most level-headed of women is our dear Laura. She's got issues. Fucking big ones. And do you know, I sort of forgot to tell him how fucked-up she was. That must have slipped my mind for some reason.' With that he turned on his heel and left her, sliding into his car and smiling at her as he drove past.

It was evening, the end of another long day. Vince unlocked his bicycle and flicked on his lamps. Caught in its beam was a smoky cloud of drizzle. He trundled the bicycle across the uneven stone flags of the Empire's yard to the open gateway and was startled to see a thin shadow separate from the wall.

'Edith!' he said. 'You scared the living daylights out of me. What are you still doing here? You should be on your way home now.'

She stood in the lamplight, her hair already damp from the light rain. 'Sorry, Vince,' she said. 'I was waiting for you.'

'For me – why?'

Edith jerked her shoulders. 'Would you walk me home, Vince?'

He frowned. 'Why?'

She looked up at the night sky. 'It's dark,' she said.

'It's never bothered you before. Anyhow, you only live ten minutes away.'

'It's not out of your way,' she observed. 'I'd feel a lot better if you walked me home tonight.'

He felt he had no choice. And she looked so helpless, frail and wet. 'OK,' he said resignedly. 'But we'll have to walk fast or we'll get soaked.'

They left the Empire behind. There was the hiss of the odd-car passing them on wet roads, hardly another soul on the streets. They spent a few minutes lost in private thoughts.

She asked out of the blue, 'Do you like Mr Caldwell?'

'I don't know,' he said and then he shook his head. 'Not really. Do you?'

'He's got a handsome face, sure enough, but I don't think he's a nice person inside. Where do you suppose Monica is?'

'Dunno,' he said quickly. 'Don't care either. Why?'

'I heard rumours about Mr Caldwell and Monica. She used to brag to the other cleaners about stuff. Dirty stuff.'

'Well she's not here now so she doesn't matter anymore, does she?'

'You didn't like Monica either, did you?'

'So?'

'She was nasty to you.'

'Monica was nasty to everyone. That's just how Monica was.'

They ambled along in silence. Vince tried to hurry Edith along but she seemed to be dragging her heels. He was getting very wet.

'Vince, do you think I'm pretty?' she asked rather sheepishly.

Vince's sense of unease went up another notch or two so that it flashed an amber warning. 'I guess so.'

'You're just saying that to please me.'

'No I'm not,' he protested. 'Yes, I suppose you are pretty.'

She smiled. 'So you think I'm pretty?'

'Just said so, didn't I? What's with you tonight, Edith? Is everything alright?'

Edith stopped. The water glistened on her face. 'This is my street, where I live,' she said. 'Thank you for walking me home.'

'You're welcome,' he said. 'You'd better get inside; you're wet through.'

'You can kiss me if you like,' she said, stepping closer to him. Lamplight sparkled in her large eyes.

'What?'

'You can kiss me. I'll let you.'

'Why?'

'You said I was pretty.'

'Well yes, but – '

'You did mean it, didn't you?'

'Yes, I meant it,' he said, getting all flustered.

'So why won't you kiss me? I like you, Vince. I like you very much.'

'I must be ten years older than you, Edith...'

'That doesn't matter. I'm not a little girl. I'm a young woman with a young woman's feelings.'

'You shouldn't go around throwing yourself at men like this. You never know where it might lead.' He put on his cycle clips and sat astride his bicycle.

'I only said you could kiss me,' she said. 'I thought...'

'You thought what, Edith?'

Her smooth brow furrowed. 'You're still obsessed with that Laura woman, aren't you, in spite of what I said? What has she got that I haven't? Is it because she's rich?'

He didn't know how to respond. Her full, red lips pouted enticingly and he felt urges he was afraid of. 'Go home, Edith,' he said, pedalling away like mad and aware of her stare hot on his back. He didn't dare turn around.

* * * *

20

The Dark Patch

The dry reeds made a strange, enigmatic rustling sound as the wind passed through them, their ragged dark head swaying languidly, almost as if they bent over in sadness. Water gurgled over rocks, sounding to Laura like a strangled scream that went on forever. The slow-moving stream caused the pennant-like leaves of underwater weeds to fidget, not unlike a drowning man's groping fingers, and the spectral, shadowy shapes of melancholy willows lined the bank opposite, posing as ethereal guards that watched studiously over everything.

'This is the place Ophelia came to drown herself,' said Laura's father, staring at the oil-like surface of the restless stream. 'At least, this is just the sort of place I imagine it to look like.'

Laura, the little girl, held his hand tighter and snuggled up close to him. His sombre words scared her, and a shiver of dread ran icily through her as she too stared into the liquid depths.

He did so love Hamlet, Laura thought. She almost felt her father's presence beside her, but that could not be, because he was long dead and she didn't believe in any kind of afterlife, aware that it was merely her imagination being stretched on the rack of her emotions. He could no more be sitting beside me today, she thought, than Ophelia had drowned in this stream.

Yet she was, admittedly, drawn to this spot, to the softly spoken water that seemed to beckon her, tease her. A sad, lonely place she purported to own along with Devereux towers, but which in fact appeared to own her.

She so wanted to cry, but there were no more tears left inside, only a fiery anger that she could not tamp down. Her entire frame shook with it.

'You are an evil, evil young woman!' her father had said. 'You are not my daughter. My Laura could never have done such horrid things. My Laura must be dead to me.'

And he had turned away from her. That was the last time she remembered seeing his face whilst he was alive. When she came back to Langbridge to see his body before its burial his expression was still the same; one of disappointment and shame.

'He's at peace,' reassured the undertaker.

He did not look at peace, Laura thought. And she hoped he'd be restless for all eternity. She hoped he never found peace.

'Your father had already made the necessary arrangements for his funeral. I can show you the casket he chose,' the undertaker began, taking her through to another room. He pointed it out. 'The best, of course.'

'That will not do,' she said. 'Put him in the cheapest you have,' she said.

He was momentarily lost for words; he knew how wealthy she was. 'It has all been paid for, Miss Leach. It was your father's wish...'

'And that is my wish. Do as I say. You can keep the money, don't worry; I'm not after a refund.'

'Grief is a terrible thing,' he pointed out. 'Perhaps you need time to reconsider. After all, your father had a certain high standing in Langbridge society, being an important councillor, Chair of the Langbridge Civic Society, a leading light, one might say; it wouldn't be fitting to have him sent off in our most basic model.'

'I don't need any time,' she said. 'The cheapest. No flowers, no frills. Just burn him and send me the bill.'

'But he stipulated burial, in the family plot at Devereux Towers.'

'Do as I say,' she said.

'And the ashes?'

'I don't want them. Throw them over the roses in the crematorium grounds.' She thought about it. 'Perhaps not; I don't want to kill them. Do with them what you will, I don't care.'

Ophelia was mad, thought Laura, but drowning herself was the sanest thing she did. And the bravest. As much as Laura detested this world she could not do what Ophelia did. She did not have the courage to end the torment the way she did.

She twirled the bloodied knife before her eyes. Make the hurt go away, she thought. Please make it go away. The sharp edge tinged with scarlet was but a couple of inches away from her eye. She gave a tiny shriek and tossed the knife into the water. It sank instantly into the murky depths, disappearing into a clump of waving weed fronds.

She rose to her feet, left the stream and the brooding willows behind. Ahead, Devereux Towers stood like a dark block of stone, all by itself in its empty field, the onset of autumn making its stark form even more pronounced. Rolling clouds pregnant with rain appeared to brush by the single tower.

Laura became nervous when she saw a strange car parked outside the main entrance. She approached it warily and as she drew close the door opened and a woman stepped out. A pretty woman. A beautiful woman. All smiles and neat hair with a body that had curves in all the right places. Laura felt her blood begin to boil a little.

'Good afternoon,' chimed the young woman. 'I'm sorry to bother you. Are you Laura Leach?'

Laura hesitated. Studied the woman. 'Yes,' she said moving swiftly to the door and pressing a key into the lock.

'I wondered if you might be able to help me.'

Laura dropped the key. Scrabbled in the gravel to retrieve it. When she reinserted it into the lock her hand was all jittery. 'I doubt it,' she said flatly, swinging open the door.

'I'm looking for someone,' she said insistently, coming up to her. 'You might know him.'

'I'm extremely busy,' said Laura. 'I have to go.'

'His name is Casper Younge. He's my brother,' Katherine lied. 'He's gone missing, you see, and I don't know where he's got to.'

Laura's eyes steeled. She looked the young woman up and down. 'So you're Casper's sister, you say?'

Katherine smiled, but it felt as if the wild-eyed woman was snooping about inside her head. 'That's right. He wrote to me from Langbridge, but that was weeks ago. He hasn't called like he said he would and now I'm beginning to get worried.'

'What makes you think I might know this Casper of yours?'

'He mentioned Devereux Towers in a letter to me. Mentioned your name.'

'I can't understand why. I don't know anyone called Casper,' she said shortly. 'I can't help you.'

'Are you certain?' said Katherine. 'Please think; it's important.'

'I've never heard of him.' She stepped over the threshold, turned back. 'If you're worried, perhaps you ought to contact the police.'

She said it in such a way that it made Katherine doubly unsettled. 'Maybe it's just me, fussing over nothing,' she admitted. 'I don't want to drag the police into this unnecessarily.'

Laura nodded slowly. 'That's right. No sense in going to the police in a hurry, is there?' She closed the door so there was only the tiniest of cracks to peer through. 'Good luck with the search for your brother. I'm sure he'll turn up somewhere.'

The door closed with a solid thump of finality and Katherine heard the sounds of bolts being slid into place, then the key being turned in the lock. It had been a risk, confronting Laura. But she was running out of options.

Her denial of ever knowing Felix only increased her suspicions and her anxiety. Something was dreadfully wrong and this strange woman was at the heart of it.

She went back to her car and sat inside for a while, in the cold shadow of Devereux Towers. She put her head in her hand, her worst fears – fears that she'd managed to keep a lid on – were rising to the surface. Something terrible had happened to him. It was the only explanation. She was confident in her heart he wouldn't simply have taken the money and run; they were far too close a couple. That notion was only Martin's vindictive way of getting back at her in the same way she had tried to get back at him for all the hurt he'd caused her in the past, both physically and mentally.

She thought she caught sight of someone at a window but couldn't be certain. As she gunned the engine, part of her wished she'd never ever brought Martin into this in order to help satisfy her petty revenge. That Laura had discovered their plans was now without a doubt, she thought, glancing up at Devereux Towers as she eased the car down the gravel drive. If that were the case and Felix had been confronted by Laura the plan was always the same; claim ignorance no matter what, scoot back to base and then they'd both get the hell out of there and find somewhere new to start all over again. Unless Martin was right and Felix really had taken the money and run…

No, she refused to believe that. Why would he dump his car in Langbridge? It didn't make any sense, none of it did. What she couldn't quite grasp was how it went wrong so fast. One moment Laura was a fish on a hook and all but in the keep-net; the next everything was in tatters. She had to have been tipped-off by someone. That was the only explanation. Someone took it upon themselves to warn her. So was it Martin? No, she felt he had too much to lose, no matter his show of empty bravado. There was only one other she knew about and that was the young projectionist from the Empire, the one who Felix had to beat up; the one who threatened to tell Laura. He'd be the most likely. He'd be smarting after his beating. He'd nothing to lose.

Katherine resolved to confront him, pump him for information, and if anything had happened to Felix because of that interfering nobody he'd pay dearly for it.

As she left Devereux Towers behind, jolted her way down the uneven track, the distance shrinking the melancholy old building, her mind wandered to what Martin had told her about Laura. That she was crazy, unstable. She wasn't your average woman in the street; Katherine knew that much for sure. There was something weird going on in that head of hers and you didn't have to be any kind of shrink to read it in her demented eyes.

Christ, what had they gotten themselves involved in, she thought?

Laura leach sat in the dark, rocking slowly back and forth in the chair, a plaintive little mewl issuing from her dry lips twisted by despair. She ran a clawed hand through her messed-up hair, her eyes saucer-wide and unblinking.

She looked down at her arm, carefully rolled up the sleeve. The blood-sodden bandage needed changing, she thought, touching the dark, oozing patch.

And though the searing pain shot up her arm and into her skull she did not wince.

* * * *

21

Incarnations of the Past

When he saw the woman stood behind Monica's desk he almost gave a shriek of alarm. He hadn't expected anyone to be in his office.

'Edith, what on earth are you doing here?' he snapped, taking off his coat and hanging it on the back of the office door.

The young woman looked awkwardly about her for a second or two. 'I'm cleaning your office, like I usually do, Mr Caldwell,' she explained.

'Cleaning it?' he repeated brusquely.

'Yes, sir; cleaning it. It's what I do.'

'Oh,' he said, his index finger tracing one of the fine lines on his forehead. 'Yes, sorry, I understand. You startled me.'

'You startled me too, Mr Caldwell; you're in much earlier today than normal.'

'I am?'

'Nearly a full hour or so.'

'That right? Yes, well I have work to do. Have you finished here?'

'Yes, sir.' Edith scuttled around the desk, picking up her duster and can of Pledge furniture polish and made a hasty retreat.

Caldwell shut the office door, hung his keys up on the board on the wall filled with a multitude of other such keys. The place reminded him of a jail, he thought. He slid open a desk drawer and took out a bottle of vodka. He didn't bother with a glass, took a hefty, breath-sponging swig from the neck. He wiped a hand across his mouth, was tempted to take another drink but resisted and screwed the cap back on. He'd stuffed the bottle back in the drawer when a knock came at the door.

'What is it now?' he said harshly.

Edith poked her head round the door. 'Sorry, Mr Caldwell, but there's a man from the Langbridge Gazette to see you.'

'Send him to Vince. He takes care of all that crap.'

'He specifically asked to speak to you. Says it's very important.'

'It always is. Send him in.'

A young man entered, probably just sneaking into his twenties, thought Caldwell. He was dressed in a cheap suit that was too long in the arms and a tad too short in the legs. The knot of his tie did not cover the top button of his shirt; a sin Caldwell found unforgivable. To top-off the sorry-looking picture his hair was far too long and badly cut. Caldwell groaned inwardly as the young man dashed out a hand to shake.

'Mr Caldwell? Good morning!'

Caldwell gave it a half-hearted shake. 'And you are?' He didn't invite the man to sit down.

He didn't reply. He was looking animatedly about the office, giving an enthusiastic nod as he did so. 'I love cinemas,' he said. 'The glitz, the glamour of Hollywood and all that.'

'Oh yeah,' said Caldwell, 'lots of glamour here.' He took out a packet of cigarettes from his jacket pocket, flipped the top and popped one out. He offered one to his visitor who declined. 'So who are you exactly and what's so urgent?'

'Oh, sorry, please forgive me! Leonard Kimble, pleased to meet you.' He plonked himself down in a chair opposite Caldwell.

'Kimble – as in related to Mrs Kimble, my admin assistant?'

'Ex-admin assistant,' he corrected. 'You sacked her.'

'We came to a mutual understanding,' he said, lighting up the cigarette and blowing out smoke. 'What's all this about?'

'She's my grandmother, if you must know,' he went on.

'You came here to tell me that?' said Caldwell. 'I'm pleased for you but very busy…'

Leonard Kimble fumbled in his ill-fitting jacket for his wallet, and fumbled inside this for a business card. He showed it to Caldwell. 'I'm from the Langbridge Gazette.'

'That much I know already,' he said. 'What is it they say about that local rag? That's it – tomorrow's chip paper today.' He sucked on his cigarette. 'So you're a reporter, if the Gazette has such a thing.'

'That's right, Mr Caldwell – features reporter,' he said proudly.

'Features, eh?' he said. 'How thrilling. The last review your paper gave of my cinema it said it smelled of damp and suggested people ought to bring hot water bottles.'

'That wasn't me, Mr Caldwell. I like the Empire, though admittedly it can get a trifle cold in winter.'

Caldwell sat back in his chair. 'What is it you want, Kimble? I'm a busy man.'

The young man took out a notebook and pen. Flicked paper. 'Can I ask you a few questions?'

'You've got exactly five minutes.'

'It's about Monica Andrews.'

The cigarette was removed from his lips. 'What about her?'

'Well, she's still missing.'

'No shit, Sherlock. Look, that's not something I'm going to talk to you about. I've already had the police in here asking about her. Go ask them.'

He grinned disarmingly. 'Already have, thank you.'

'Then there's nothing else to say, is there?'

'Do you think Monica had any enemies?'

'Haven't you articles on missing cats and dogs to write about?'

'My grandmother said that Monica was, let's say, not the friendliest person she's known.'

'She would, wouldn't she? Monica took her job.'

The man nodded. 'Yes, she did. I understand Monica's background in admin was limited. So limited as to be virtually nonexistent. I couldn't help but wonder what special something she possessed – as she obviously lacked certain charms and people skills as well as a distinct lack of practical ability – that a woman of thirty-five years experience in the trade did not possess.'

'What's with all this Columbo stuff, Kimble?'

'I'm writing an article, hoping we can help in our small way to trace her, jog people's minds, that kind of thing. Her sister has asked us to and we thought we'd oblige.'

'Fine,' said Caldwell, stuffing the cigarette back into his mouth. 'What's that got to do with me?'

'My grandmother said Monica used to do the odd-bit of cleaning for a number of folk around Langbridge, besides here at the Empire.'

'Your grandmother knows a lot. Best ask her.'

'Did she tell you of some of these other places?'

'Sometimes.'

'Care to tell me?'

'Not really. I've told the police all I'm going to say on the subject of Monica Andrews and I'm not about to repeat myself to a second-rate arse-wipe of a newspaper.'

It didn't faze Kimble. 'Devereux Towers ring any kind of bell?'

Caldwell stared hard at the young man. 'Maybe. Maybe not.'

'Ah, the Witch of Devereux Towers,' said Kimble with a smirk.

'I hear some people call her that,' said Caldwell. 'Some people can be quite horrible when they have a mind. Have you finished, Mr Kimble? I believe your five minutes are up.' He indicated the door with the flat of his hand. 'Talk to Monica's friends – if you can call them that. She has a few here. Wait until their shift is finished; they'll use any excuse to down tools as it is.'

'Will do, thanks, Mr Caldwell.' He got up, went to the door, stopped and turned. 'One more thing…'

'Now you really are sounding like Columbo.'

'Are plans still going ahead to redevelop the Empire? Multi-screen and all that?'

'Yes. Is that all?'

'I don't suppose you'd like to show me around, give our readers an indication of what it's going to look like.'

'You suppose right. Some other time perhaps, when your readers can actually read.'

Leonard Kimble smiled, stowed away his notebook. He thanked Caldwell profusely for his help and left. Caldwell stubbed his cigarette out into an ashtray, crushing it into an unrecognisable stub of paper. He put his head in his hands. 'Fuck!' he said. He took out the bottle of vodka and downed a couple of good measures. This time he didn't put it away.

She was supposed to go to the fucking police, he thought. Why hadn't she done that? When he'd written the letter to Laura Leach telling her all about Felix and Katherine's plans to screw her over, even telling them details like where they lived in Glastonbury, he expected her to go straight to the law. That would have been enough to frighten them off and he'd have been shut of them, possibly for good. But no, the stupid bitch didn't play game and now it was all turning into an even bigger mess. The last thing he wanted was some dumb hack reporter making even the slimmest connection between him and Laura fucking Leach. This thing with Monica – it was running away with itself. Christ, he wished he'd never gotten involved with the woman. It was his own stupid fault.

He'd raised a hand to his wife, struck her. He'd been drunk, of course, but that wasn't an excuse. He desperately wanted to believe he had changed but in a foolish instant all his illusions were swept away and his wife had temporarily kicked him out of the house. Not for long, but long enough for him to hit the bottle again and seek solace where he could find it. Monica just happened to be the wrong woman at the wrong time and it soon became apparent that she was as ruthlessly manipulative as he had been in the past. He also bet the pregnancy wasn't an accident either. Bitch.

He had to get out. He couldn't stay in Langbridge. He thought that by coming to this out-of-the-way place he'd be able to lose the old Martin and reinvent another to stand in his place. Start afresh. But you can't shake off the past that easily, he thought grimly. It was always with you, waiting to spring out at you when you least expected it.

There could never be a future, just various incarnations of the past.

* * * *

22

Where there's Smoke

He'd never felt so thoroughly dejected, so mind-numbingly depressed, and Vince had had his fair share of such episodes in his short life. But this was a black level of despair new even to him.

He went down to the auditorium during features, stared his desultory stare out of the projection-booth window, but Vince hadn't seen a glimpse of Laura for weeks now. He expected, logic told him, that the longer this went on the more he'd grow accustomed to her absence, but that, sadly, wasn't the case. It was the opposite, frighteningly so. Was that love or was that obsession? And where did the two part company, if indeed they ever did? Questions he never once expected to be asking himself.

Some people enjoy wallowing in self pity the same way pigs like to wallow in mud, his mother said dismissively when he found himself being chastised for having such a sour expression. He didn't tell her the reasons, of course, but her all-seeing eyes looked as if she knew the reason. Was it possible his mother had actually been in love once, had suffered at its velvet-gloved claws? He found that hard to believe. Hell, he didn't even want to believe it.

He heard the door to the projection booth open. He looked up from his work and saw Edith standing there. She looked different and he couldn't figure out why at first.

'What are you doing in here?' he said, aware it must have sounded curt. 'No one is allowed up here during the running of a feature, except Mr Caldwell,' he added, to try and soften the blow.

'I came to see you,' she said, her pretty eyes looking nervously at him.

Then he realised what was different about her. 'What have you done to your face?' he asked. Her eyelids were smeared with blue eyeshadow, and her cheeks had been rouged in that inexperienced, ham-fisted way that made her look like she'd been too close to the fire. Her lips were coated in red lipstick.

'This? It's only a little makeup,' she said. 'Don't you like it?'

She always made him feel uneasy, he thought. He turned away. 'It's OK, I guess.'

'I thought it would make me look older,' she explained.

'Well it doesn't; it makes you look...' He stumbled into silence.

'I put it on for you,' she admitted, her gaze planted on the floor at her feet. 'I'm sorry if I upset you – you know, that night...'

'You didn't.'

'I did, I know I did. I didn't mean to.'

'Look, Edith, can this wait? I'm busy...'

'Yes, sorry, Vince.'

She backed away. 'Edith,' he said. She stopped. 'You look better without it, is all.'

'Thank you, Vince,' she said, her spirits lifted.

At the end of the evening shift Vince was once more trundling his bike out of the Empire's yard, feeling emotionally drained and needing to get home and lick his never-healing wounds, when he was unexpectedly hailed by a woman on the street.

'Hello. Are you the projectionist here?' she asked, coming up to him.

He nodded dumbly. 'That's right. I'm Vince.' At first he thought it might have been Edith again, and he didn't know whether he was disappointed or not to see it was a stranger. The woman was pretty, though, he thought, and he could smell strong and seductive perfume reaching out to caress his nose. She looked familiar but he couldn't place where he'd seen her. 'Can I help you?' he said, feeling at once uncomfortable in her beautiful, perfect female presence.

'You and I, we have a mutual friend,' she said.

Vince shook his head. 'I don't know what you mean.'

Her attractive features appeared to melt away like a waxwork dummy's before a fire, and in its place was an angry, grimacing mask twisted by some kind of inner hate. She moved close to him, close to his face. He knew something was wrong and he backed away.

'My name is Katherine,' she said. 'You met my boyfriend, Felix, some time ago. He introduced you to his fist, as I remember.'

Then it dawned on him. She was the same woman he'd seen on top of Glastonbury Tor, the one with Laura's new man-friend, or rather the thug who had beaten him up in the Empire's foyer. 'I don't want to talk to you,' he said quickly, walking away.

She grabbed hold of his collar. 'Oh, no? Well I need to talk to you. You told Laura, didn't you? You told her all about the plan.'

He shook his head vigorously. 'No I didn't tell Laura anything!' he said, feeling the woman's talon-like, manicured nails digging into his throat through the thin material of his shirt.

'You fucking liar!' Katherine snarled. 'You went and ruined things, you know that, you little runt?' She slapped him hard across the cheek and his mouth dropped open in shock. He'd never seen such a pretty woman act with such aggression. The two didn't seem to go together, but he was learning all sorts of new things these days. 'What's happened to Felix?' she said.

'I dunno,' he said, rubbing his cheek. 'I haven't seen him since he beat me up.'

'Tell me the truth or I'll make your miserable little life even more miserable.'

'I told you…'

Katherine lashed out with her foot and caught Vince full in the groin. He gasped and bent double as the pain came flooding in. 'If you're lying to me…'

He couldn't speak. He shook his head again, clutching the point of contact. He couldn't believe how much agony he was in. 'You're crazy…' he said.

'Talking of which, what do you know about this Laura Leach? You had the hots for her, isn't that right? You've gotta know something about her. Is she really as mad as they say she is?'

'No! That's just a vicious rumour!'

'Where there's smoke there's fire,' she said, bending down to him.

'You leave Laura alone,' he said breathlessly.

'Your fucking problem, Vince, is that you're blinded by love. Don't be fooled by her; she's away with the fairies. I heard she's been in some kind of mental asylum. You know if that's true?'

'I think it's another lie.'

'You'd like to believe that. Do you know which asylum?'

'Someone told me it was called Bartholomew Place, but it's just people who can't stop being horrible. They're everywhere,' he added, staring defiantly at her.

'So where is this Bartholomew Place?'

'Dunno.'

'What's the reason she was in there? Why was she admitted?' She shook him by the shoulder. 'I need to know if she's crazy enough to have done something to my Felix!'

'What? Laura? No, never!'

She got to her feet, exasperated, her eyes blazing. 'What do you know about a room at Devereux Towers she keeps locked up? A blue door.'

'Why would I know about such things?'

She stepped closer to him again and he flinched. 'Because dirty little perverts like you get your kicks by spying on women like Laura, that's why.'

'But that's not true!' he defended. 'I'm not a pervert!'

She put a hand to her blouse and ripped it open. A white button popped and clicked on the pavement. 'Oh no? Try telling that to the police when I tell them you attacked me and tried to rape me.'

'You wouldn't do that!' he said, struggling to his feet. 'They wouldn't believe you.'

'Really? Let's see - my sweet little word against a sad loser of a projectionist who keeps himself locked away in his little box all night wanking to X-rated films; a lonely little creep that lives all on his own, doesn't have a girlfriend and never has? The jails are full of your kind.'

'Then I'll tell them all about you!' he said. 'You and that boyfriend of yours. I knew you were up to no good.'

'I'll simply tell them we were in on it together. You told us all about Laura, helped set things up for us. Whichever way you look at it, Vince, you're fucked, so don't mess with me. For the very last time, where is Felix?'

'I told you, I dunno! I can't help you!'

Her eyes narrowed into venomous slits. 'Yes you can, Vince. You said someone told you about this asylum, Bartholomew Place. I want you to go back to this someone and find out all you can about it and why Laura Leach was in there. Got that, Vince?'

He nodded, grateful that the pain in his groin was subsiding and wasn't going to be permanent like he'd feared. 'I'm not sure where to start,' he admitted.

'That's your problem. I'll meet you here at the same time two days from now. Don't let me down, Vince. You're involved in all this whether you like it or not.'

'But I haven't done anything wrong!' he said.

'Tough. That's not how other people will see things. In two days, Vince,' she said. She stamped down with her foot, three times, onto the front wheel of his bicycle, denting the spokes and buckling the rim. Katherine sauntered away down the empty street.

Vince lifted his cycle and inspected the damage. Double-butted spokes, he thought – they cost a fortune to replace. And they'd not be able to straighten the rim. He'd need a complete new wheel really. Shit. He groaned at the pain between his legs, groaned also at the pain of embarrassment he felt, being floored by a woman. What is it with these people, he thought? Had everyone gotten it in for him?

Katherine drove back to Glastonbury, still anxious about Felix's whereabouts but feeling a whole lot better for having taken it out on someone. By the time she'd parked her car outside the house they rented her temper had cooled off somewhat. She went inside and stared at the phone, willing it to ring, but of course it didn't. In the end she went upstairs, set a hot bath running to try and relax.

She was about to draw the bedroom curtains when she caught sight of a figure stood on the pavement opposite, apparently looking up to her window. She peered harder, trying to separate out the features from the deep shadows. Her heart almost stopped when she realised it looked like Laura Leach.

Without hesitation she ran downstairs, flung open the front door and stepped outside. The dark street was empty, both ways. Had she imagined it? What the hell would Laura be doing here anyway – and how on earth did she know where she lived?

She waited a minute or two and then went back inside, making sure the door was locked. She attempted to shrug off the unsettling feeling it left her with, but it hung around her shoulders like a damp shawl for the remainder of the evening.

* * * *

23

Irreparable Damage

'I see you've had a bit of trouble,' said the milkman, handing Katherine a pint of gold-top. She was on her way out, just as he was bending down to the step. She flashed him an uncomprehending glance. He indicated with his thumb to the road. 'Your car,' he explained.

The windscreen had been smashed in. 'What on earth...?' she said, treading the short path to the gate, the milkman at her heels. The bonnet was covered in a sprinkling of glass, and it lay on the pavement catching the early-morning sunshine.

The milkman wandered over to the passenger side and peered in at the window. 'That's the culprit,' he said. 'There's half a brick on the passenger seat. No respect for anything these days, some people.'

Katherine opened the car door and lifted the brick, scrutinising it as if the identity of the vandal lay in its ragged form. She dropped it to the ground. 'Bastard,' she said.

'Probably some cider-head or other, on their way home drunk. It happens,' the milkman surmised. 'You ought to telephone the police. There's Doble's garage down the road,' he added. 'He'll be able to fix it for you.' Then he shook his head sorrowfully. 'Long-haired yobs, they're everywhere. They bring their football-terrace hooliganism onto the street.' He abandoned Katherine and clambered aboard his milk-float. It rattled away down the street, its electric engine moaning soulfully.

Katherine drove the car to Doble's garage and arranged for them to order in and fix a new windscreen. She was stopped on the way out of the garage by one of the mechanics. 'It's a good thing you brought this in today, miss,' he said, his face falling serious even for a garage mechanic. 'Here, let me show you something.' He led her back over to her car parked in the forecourt and crouched down to the rear wheel. 'You see this puddle?'

'Yes. What is it?' she asked, hardly interested in the ramblings of some local grease monkey.

'That's brake fluid. I had a quick check underneath and, if I'm not mistaken, it looks like someone's taken a pair of snips to the brake pipe.'

'Someone did it deliberately?'

He screwed up his nose. 'Well it doesn't look like natural wear and tear to me. You can even see the scratches in the old copper, new copper showing through where they've been at it. It's not quite severed but even so it wouldn't have been long and you'd have lost some braking power and maybe even had a nasty accident. I'll check the other wheels, just to be safe, and we'll fit a new pipe, drain the system of brake fluid and refill it with fresh.' He stood up.

'Could it have been the same person who smashed my windscreen in?' she said, her heart beginning to race a little.

'Bit of a coincidence otherwise. Can't have been done long otherwise you'd have noticed the loss of braking power. My advice would be to go straight to the police with it. Even if someone were playing a prank it's a stupid and dangerous thing to do.'

That was the second time that morning someone had mentioned the police. 'Yeah, I'll think about it,' she offered.

Her mind in a bit of a daze, Katherine left them to their work and went out onto the main street of Glastonbury. Morning shoppers were steadily filling the pavements as the town didn't so much spring to life as pull down the blankets from its sleepy face a little at a time. As she made her way back through town she saw a blue Hillman Imp crawling slowly towards her. She stopped dead when she realised it was Laura Leach sitting behind the wheel. As it drew level Laura turned to stare fixedly at Katherine, her expression stony, her dark, gimlet eyes unblinking. Katherine felt her chest tighten beneath the woman's strangely uncompromising glare. The car all but came to a halt beside her before suddenly speeding up and leaving Katherine to watch as it shot away into the distance.

It was Sunday and it was early. Normally at this time of year Vince would have a long lie-in on his only full day off work, but he was due to meet with that woman Katherine on Monday evening and so far he had nothing to tell her. He remembered that Edith had an aunt who had seen Laura in this Bartholomew Place and he'd asked Edith whether she might take him to see her. Strangely, she jumped at the opportunity. So he found himself sitting beside Edith, taking one of only two buses to run that day to the small village of Blaxton where her aunt lived. And Edith, as usual, was full of beans. She was humming a song to herself, the last in a long line of such songs.

'Are you never quiet?' Vince asked.

'I like music,' she said. 'I've just bought the album *An Evening with John Denver* Do you like John Denver? I just *love* John Denver. Have you heard *Annie's Song*? It's *so* romantic!'

Vince frowned. 'He's OK, I guess. I don't listen to the radio much,' he admitted. 'I don't have many albums either.'

'That's no problem,' she said. 'I can borrow you some of mine, if you like?' He didn't respond either way. 'This is really nice, Vince,' she said. 'You and me going out together.'

'It's only a visit to your aunt,' he reminded. 'It's hardly a date or anything.' Though he had to admit he was warming to her by the day, in spite of himself and his resistance. She could be quite infectious. 'Are you sure your aunt knows something about Bartholomew Place?' he asked, thinking of his meeting with Katherine and not looking forward to it at all.

'Yes, she does. Though I only know what she told me, which wasn't a lot. You'll meet her soon enough anyway and then perhaps you can put this Laura-thing to rest.'

'Maybe I don't want to put it to rest,' he retorted shortly. 'Maybe I want to find out it's all been a pack of lies. And anyway, even if it was true and she had been in that place, it wouldn't stop me feeling the same way about Laura, if that's what you think.'

'I didn't think that at all. You asked me to take you to see my aunt and that's what I'm doing. I thought we were enjoying a nice day out at the same time. Nothing wrong with that, is there?'

This time he was sorry he'd upset her. He tried to study her profile without her noticing and thought that she really was a pretty young thing. She'd avoided putting on any makeup and he thought she looked better without it.

'I'm sorry,' he said. 'I'm a little bit on edge, that's all. I find I tend to snap without thinking about it. I never used to, but a number of people have been on my back recently.'

Her clouded expression was wiped away instantly. 'That's alright, Vince. Look, I have something that will cheer you up later.' She lifted up a carrier bag and rested it on her lap. She took out a foil-wrapped pack. 'They're cheese and pickle sandwiches for lunch. I know how you so like cheese and pickle.'

'Cheddar?'

Her eyes looked troubled. 'Red Leicester,' she said.

He smiled. 'I love that as well,' he said, and was pleased when she smiled too. 'You shouldn't have…'

'I wanted to.'

'That's very kind of you to think about it, I guess.'

She beamed with pleasure. The bus gave a lurch on the country road, her arm coming into contact with his. She didn't make an effort to remove it and he let it stay pressed against him. He rather liked the feeling. Together they stared pensively out of the dirty bus window to the vibrant colours of autumn, the few remaining leaves, tenuously clinging to branches that whipped close by them, dressed in their autumnal livery of acid yellows and rich ambers.

They arrived at Blaxton, a sleepy little place tucked out of the way, populated by people who tended to tuck themselves out of the way – mainly farmers and the like. A trip from Blaxton to Langbridge was the equivalent of a trip from Langbridge to London. They took a side lane that led to a few desultory-looking cottages burdened by heavy blankets of moss-covered thatch. Edith brought Vince to a halt beside one of them.

'Before we go in to see her I just wanted to warn you,' she said.

'Warn me? Of what?'

'My Aunt Elizabeth – Aunt Liz – she can seem a little strange to those who don't know her.'

'Strange? In what way?' he asked uncertainly. 'You never told me about her being strange.'

'That's because I didn't want to alarm you as you seem to have your mind set on wanting to see her and I didn't want to spoil us having a day out together. There's something you should know about her. My aunt knows about Bartholomew Place because she was in it.'

'As a worker?'

She shook her head. 'She was admitted for a time.'

'You could have told me earlier! Is she safe?'

Edith smiled at his sudden disquiet. 'Oh yes, perfectly harmless now. She's been a lot better since they changed her medication. She used to hear voices – mainly God, Mary and Joseph, sometimes Marilyn Monroe, but I never knew how she fitted into the scheme of things. They told her to do various acts and she'd do them – steal things from shops, walk naked up the street, set fire to the vicarage...'

'I think I've changed my mind. You didn't tell me she was mad!'

'She's not mad!' she defended. 'Not now at least. But she's still a bit eccentric.' She grabbed his hand and held him firm. 'We're here now, aren't we? She's not going to attack you or anything – she might preach a bit of the gospel if she's in the mood, but that's no more mad than going to church and hearing it, is it?' She led him meekly through a gate, down the weed-strewn path and to a battered old door. She took out a key and unlocked it. 'She always locks it against Jehovah's Witnesses,' she explained. 'She's terrified of them because they tend to come in pairs, like policemen or bailiffs; no one should be trusted if they come in pairs, she always says.' She pushed hard at the door but it hardly budged. 'You might find this a bit of a squeeze,' she said apologetically, easing her way through the narrowest of openings.

Vince followed and was amazed to see the entire hallway, small as it was, stacked high with cardboard boxes, heaps of bulging carrier bags, skyscraper-like stacks of newspapers and magazines. Empty tin cans and bottles were everywhere. He noticed every last step on the stairs leading up to the bedrooms was piled high with every conceivable object; mounds of neatly folded clothes, rows of spent light-bulbs, empty bleach bottles, blackened old pans, cracked ceramic jugs, dented metal ones, threadbare cushions and moth-eaten blankets. It would have been near impossible to get up the stairs, he thought. He heard a soft mewling, and two cats leapt from out of nowhere to scuttle over the precarious piles like agile mountain goats on a steep-sided rock face to sit and cry plaintively at him. He saw at least two more scoot away to hide as they pushed their way down the clutter-strewn hall.

'It's like the worst junk shop I've ever seen!' said Vince, half appalled, half fascinated. 'Don't tell me the entire house is like this.'

'I'm afraid it is. That's Joseph's fault – told her to keep everything as he and Mary might need it if they had another baby and had to move to a bigger house.'

'She believes that?'

'It's real to her. She can't throw anything away. All this makes sense to her – she says she's even got it organised. Every now and again we manage to persuade her to clear some of it but she gets upset if we go too far. It's a case of doing what we can.' She paused and put a hand to her mouth. 'Aunty Liz!' she called. 'It's only me, Edith. I've brought someone along to see you!'

'Are you definitely sure this is safe?' he asked nervously. One of the cats looked desperately thin and hungry and ready to take a bite out of him. 'How many cats has she got? They're all over the place.'

'About ten, at one point. And five dogs. She had a time when she started to collect two of everything, you know, ready for the flood. Langbridge had a rather terrifying one in 1947 which convinced here that was a warm-up to the real thing. So we had dogs, rats, mice, budgies – you name it. Most of the twos became threes and fours and more; you know how it is when you get male and females together. The amount of kittens and puppies we've had to take to the RSPCA! Thing is, you turn your back and she takes another one in.'

'Christ, Edith, I hope none of this runs in the family, for your sake!'

A woman burst unexpectedly out of a doorway; her eyes were wide, and with her unruly, matted hair it gave her such a demonic appearance that it caused Vince to start. He tripped over something on the floor and fell onto a mound of cardboard boxes. His heart pumping like mad he stared up at her.

'Do you want a cup of tea?' said the woman calmly. 'Hello, Edith – is this the young man you were telling me about?'

'Hello, Aunty Liz. Yes, this is Vince.'

She bent down and held out a scrawny hand. 'Good morning, Vince,' she said. She shook her head dolefully. 'Can you not sit all over my work? You have no idea how long it took me to organise all this, and now you're sitting in it and messing it all up.'

Vince scrabbled to his feet. 'I'm sorry,' he said, looking down at the crushed boxes. 'I'll pay for any damage done.'

Aunty Liz put a hand to her forehead. 'That's far too late, young man; the damage is irreparable. Right, let's have that cup of tea, shall we?'

Edith stifled a chuckle and Vince scowled at her.

* * * *

24

Miracle Baby

'She used to be married,' Edith whispered. 'It was her husband who had her put into Bartholomew Place when he couldn't cope. She was there more than two years, I think. They divorced.'

They were sitting scrunched up together on a small sofa; on either side of them a pile of clothes in carrier bags. The living room, if anything, was worse than the hall. Vince could just about see the corner of a television poking out from behind a pile of wooden tea chests that appeared to be filled with nothing but old copies of The Radio Times. You could hardly move – *breathe*, even – for crap, he thought.

'And you say she's better now?' he asked incredulously. 'I would have hated to have seen her when she was worse.' He nodded towards a door. 'What's she doing? She's been in there ages. It's only a pot of tea she's supposed to be making, not the pot itself.'

'You're so impatient!' she chastised lightly. 'Nothing's that simple with Aunty Liz. There are all manner of rituals to get through, all in a set order, and if she misses one or screws it up, she has to begin all over again.'

After what seemed an age Aunty Liz came in bearing a tray, which she carefully put down on the edge of a coffee table before them. Vince automatically went to move a pile of paperback books out of the way.

'No!' she cried, and his hand jerked back as if stung. 'Leave all those just as they are; it's important they stay that way – can't you see, young man?'

He nodded quickly. 'Yes, I can. Now that you mention it.'

She sat down on a padded chair, which was in the in the slow process of losing its padding from various rips and tears. A cat jumped up onto her lap and stared an unforgiving stare at Vince. 'He's a bright boy,' she said to Edith as if Vince weren't in the room. 'Where did you find him?'

'He works at the Empire cinema, Aunty Liz, as a projectionist.'

'Really? Does that kind of job pay enough to get married on?'

'Aunty Liz!' said Edith, her cheeks at once flushing the brightest pink. 'We're not getting married!'

'What? Oh dear! You're not going to live in sin, are you?' She wagged a finger at Vince. 'That's not the way to behave, young man. You must make an honest woman out of her. You do know she's a miracle baby, don't you, Vernon?'

'Vince,' he corrected.

'He doesn't want to hear that, Aunty...' said Edith.

'But you *are* a miracle, darling! You shouldn't be here! And miracles deserve better treatment that this.' She glowered at Vince. 'My sister couldn't have a baby, they told her, but Edith here was born against all the odds. She is a bona fide miracle.'

'I'm not, Aunty, really...' said Edith.

'Don't argue, dear, I know a miracle when I see one. Barren, she was, your mother. Unable to bear children. God smiled on her and gave us you, our little Edith!' She turned to Vince. 'So you will marry her.' She began to look around the room.

'What are you looking for, Aunty?'

'My hat, of course!'

'Which hat, Aunty?'

'The one I shall be wearing at your wedding, silly! It's here somewhere.'

Edith passed Vince a cup of tea. She caught more than a glimmer of alarm in his eyes. 'Don't worry about the hat just yet, Aunty Liz, there's plenty of time. I'd like to ask you a question or two, if I can?'

Her attention snapped back. 'Yes, dear, fire away.'

Bartholomew Place,' she said. 'You do remember that, don't you?'

She smiled sweetly and forgivingly. 'Do you think me dotty or something? Of course I remember it.' She bent closer to them both, her voice lowered by an octave. 'It's where they put people who were not quite right in the head, dear.'

'Where is it, Aunty Liz?'

She sat back. 'Oh, it's over the border in Dorset. Not far outside Dorchester. Such a dreary old building. Some say it used to be a former workhouse and whether that was true or not it looked the part. It had high walls, like a prison, you might say, in case any of the nutters escaped. You wouldn't want that, would you, mad people running like crazy all over the town?' She gave a chiming little chuckle.

'Do you remember being there, Aunty?' she probed gingerly.

'Yes, like it was yesterday. I was posted there in a governmental advisory capacity,' she said with authority. 'I was brought in to sort things out, to bring a bit of order to the place. That's what I was doing there. It wasn't an easy time for me, mind, being amongst all those crazy people, dribbling, moaning, screaming or wetting themselves all over the place. But one had a job to do.'

'Do you remember anyone called Laura Leach being inside Bartholomew Place?' Vince asked.

'Most definitely. Laura had been in a long time before I went there, and she was in when I left.'

Vince's heart sank. 'The same Laura Leach who lives out at Devereux Towers?'

'The one and the same. Her father was instrumental in having her committed, they say; pushed for her to be sectioned.'

'Why? What was so wrong with her?'

'Ah, I don't rightly know. Some really terrible thing had happened, that much was obvious. I mean, you wouldn't be in Bartholomew Place all those years without something being dreadfully wrong. One minute she'd be as placid as a little lamb – never talking, mind you, all blank eyes, that kind of thing; and the next thing, well, screaming so much that you feared her lungs would pop with it, a regular banshee, tearing at her hair and arms in a most frightening way. They'd sedate her and lock her away in restraints when she was like that. Then you'd never see her for ages. They tried all sorts to cure her of whatever was wrong with her – ice-cold baths, electric shocks, all the most modern treatments, but she never got any better whilst I was there.'

'That's so sad,' said Edith, glancing at Vince's crestfallen face.

'The screaming fits were the worst thing,' Aunty Liz continued. 'At those times she'd call out someone's name over and over again.'

Vince's ears pricked. 'Whose name?'

Liz had to trawl through her fogged memories. 'Gosh, now there's a thing. Who was it now?' She fell into what appeared to be a semi-trance-like state and Vince was on the edge of getting concerned for her when she said, 'Alan! That's who it was – Alan. Over and over and over, till they put her to sleep.'

'Have you any idea who this Alan was, or why she'd be calling his name?' Vince asked.

'No, hang on...' she said. 'It wasn't Alan, it was Alex, and it wasn't just Alex she called; she used to shout, *Alex, I'm sorry...*' She smiled a self-congratulatory smile. 'That's what she used to say.'

'What was she sorry for, Aunty?' Edith pursued.

'For whatever terrible thing she'd done to Alex, what else?' said Liz.

Vince felt decidedly uncomfortable now. He lowered his gaze and studied his hand on his lap. 'I'm sure she's better now,' he ventured. 'She has to be, hasn't she? I mean, they wouldn't have let her out otherwise, would they?'

Aunty Liz swung her head slowly. 'No one as bad as that can ever truly get better, can they?' she said, her eyes sombre and inward-looking. 'It's always there, just below the surface, like flowing water beneath a crust of ice. You never know when the ice will crack and the water will come gushing out again.'

* * * *

25

Blood

The man from the fire brigade was not very happy with the situation. The Empire was undergoing its annual fire check and, as far as he was concerned, things were not looking good. The fire officer had dragged Martin Caldwell out of his office to go through a list of possible fire hazards and things that ought to be in place that simply weren't in place. It was an accident waiting in the wings, he'd prophesised in a deep, doom-laden voice.

Caldwell felt like a school kid all over again, remembering his father standing with his school report in his hand and going through the shocking grades and comments one by one. The fire officer was doing the same, in the same manner – blunt, not a hint of humour.

'Death by burning isn't a nice prospect, Mr Caldwell,' he warned, leading him through corridors, into rooms, pointing out what seemed a mountain of minor problems that needed to be addressed before the Empire would get issued with a fire certificate. They eventually reached the basement. 'What's behind this locked door?' he asked, trying the handle.

'Nothing,' said Caldwell. 'There's a flight of stone steps leading to an empty room, and there's a well in one corner, that's all.' He didn't mention the pile of nitrate-based films Vince still hadn't shifted. Films that might combust.

'You don't use it for storage, anything like that? Nothing combustible?'

He was like a fucking mind reader, Caldwell thought uncomfortably. 'Nothing in there except fresh air.'

The officer went over to inspect a couple of rusting hooks in the wall near the door. He looked at a list on his clipboard. 'What's happened to the fire-axe that used to hang here, near the fire blanket?' he asked stiffly.

'No idea,' he admitted. 'It appears to be missing.'

'Find it or provide another,' he said shortly, making a note on his sheet. 'It's there for a reason.' He handed Caldwell the sheet of paper. 'Take care of all these things otherwise you won't get your certificate.'

'Sure,' said Caldwell walking the officer to the rear door and bidding him goodbye. 'I can do without this shit,' he said under his breath. He went up to the projection booth to find Vince. He handed him the sheet of paper. 'Here, see to this lot, will you?'

He took the sheet. 'This really isn't my job, Mr Caldwell. Mrs Kimble, she always saw to the fire checks…'

'Fuck Mrs Kimble. There isn't any Mrs Kimble and I can't get anyone to come and replace Monica, even temporarily. Just take care of it.'

He stormed from the room leaving Vince in a daze. The man was getting too edgy, he thought, and more than that his bleary eyes was a dead giveaway to his constant drinking. If head office caught him doused up like that he'd be for the chop, no mistake.

But Vince had other, more pressing things on his mind. His meeting with Katherine for one, and what he ought to tell her. The trip to see Edith's aunt had really unsettled him. What if it were all true about Laura? There again, could you really trust the word of a woman who had spent time in Bartholomew Place herself and took orders from Marilyn Monroe? And though he had been fighting against it, he was starting to like Edith in a way that began to conflict with his love for Laura. It was like he was being unfaithful to her by allowing the feelings room to grow.

Vince hung back after everyone had left at the end of the day, waiting in the yard till he was certain he was completely alone. He sat there in the dark, growing tenser by the minute till he heard a car pull up outside the gates. He went out to meet Katherine who came to stand in the entrance to the yard.

'Well, Vince, what have you got for me?' she asked.

He wasn't certain, but some of the swagger had gone from her voice. 'Laura was in Bartholomew Place for years,' he said.

'So? Is she crazy?'

'She's not in the institution now,' he defended.

'What put her there?' She sensed his reluctance. 'Tell me, you little squirt, or I'll make it bad for you.'

'It sounds like something she did. Nobody's certain what that was but it sounded serious enough for her to be committed to Bartholomew Place.'

'What else, Vince? Come on, you're holding something back.'

'She used to cry out someone's name – someone called Alex. Alex, I'm sorry, she'd say.'

'Who's Alex?'

'Dunno. Can I go now?'

'Where is this Bartholomew Place?'

'In Dorset, near Dorchester, but it's not used for anything anymore. It's been closed down years. You don't seriously think Laura had anything to do with your boyfriend's disappearance, do you?'

'That bitch seems crazy enough to do anything. So, is that everything?'

He nodded. 'Can I go now?'

'You never spoke to me, right?' she said, taking a step towards him. 'Me, my boyfriend, all of this, you don't mention it to anyone, you got that?' She rolled up her coat collar against the fine rain that had begun to fall. Vince reckoned she didn't look half as pretty as she did when he first saw her. It was almost as if she'd aged prematurely, or the bad inside her was leaking to the surface and contaminating her skin.

Katherine left the young man and got into her car. She sat there a few seconds, thinking things over. With every day that passed with no news of Felix she feared the worst; she feared him dead.

She drove out of Langbridge, headed towards Glastonbury. Something inside her was telling her to forget Felix and get the hell out of Somerset. That's probably what he'd have done, if she were honest with herself. But another part of her refused to let him go. She'd never had these kinds of feelings for anyone before and she didn't want to lose something she never thought she'd have. When she arrived home something made her check out the empty street after she'd parked and locked the car. This entire thing had made her jumpy as hell. Tiredly she unlocked the front door and flicked on the light. Nothing looked out of place, but something felt wrong. Something didn't look right.

The door to the living room was open. She'd closed it when she'd left for Langbridge, she was certain. It was a habit of hers.

Someone had been inside the house.

'Felix?' she said. 'Is that you?'

She moved cautiously to the living room door, pushed it wider. The room was empty. Next she went into the kitchen, checked over the back door and windows. Everything was in order, no sign of a break-in. The only other people who had keys were Felix and the landlord, and the landlord always arranged a visit. He wouldn't simply turn up unexpectedly to let himself in, and never at night.

Her heart was beating a tattoo. She opened a drawer and took out a knife.

'Felix, are you there?' she called at the foot of the stairs, one hand steadying herself on the banister. She turned on the light. All was silent. 'I've got to warn you,' she said, 'I have a weapon.' She spoke to make herself feel braver, but it didn't work. She crept up the stairs, the knife before her. Her bedroom door was also ajar, and that had definitely been closed when she left.

She pushed the door open further, reached in for the light switch.

The room was in a complete mess, as if a tornado had swept through it. All her clothes had been taken out of wardrobes and drawers and flung carelessly all over the room. The bedcovers had been thrown to the floor and lay in a crumpled heap.

She gasped when she lifted one of her dresses. It had been slashed repeatedly with a blade of some kind. Everything had. Every piece of clothing had been shredded. Even the bedcovers had been slashed violently into ribbons.

'Oh, my God,' she said under her breath, grasping the knife even tighter. But it was the sight of words written in her red lipstick, in great, angry, angular capitals all over the wall above the bed that caused her blood to freeze.

YOU'RE HATEFUL. I'LL KILL YOU FOR WHAT YOU DID.

Katherine felt suddenly very sick. It had to be Laura. How had she gotten inside? How? There was no sign of a break-in.

Then, amidst the carnage, she saw Felix's jacket hung over the back of a chair. She went over to it, lifted it carefully from off the chair. He was wearing this the last time I saw him, she thought.

But what made her legs buckle were the savage, jagged smears of blood on the jacket sleeve.

* * * *

26

Releasing the Soul

'If you want to go far, you have to be prepared to reach far,' the editor had told him.

Leonard Kimble didn't need that kind of encouragement. He was born with the urge to go far, but not for a poxy, small-town newspaper like this where the majority of people who read it turned to the births, marriages and deaths section for their world-news fix. He couldn't wait to dump the job in which they treated him more like an office boy than a trainee reporter. He made tea more than he made news. And let's face it, he thought as he made tea yet again, this time for his grandmother, there was no news to be made in Langbridge. The Big Flood of 1947, in which three people, five cows and thirteen sheep died, was the last time they made the nationals, and that event, plus the 1966 World Cup Final, were the only two highlights anyone in Langbridge ever talked about. Since then it had to make do with the turning on of the Christmas lights in the town centre for anything approaching excitement.

He measured tea into the china teapot, called out to his grandmother: 'Won't be long!' That's another thing about Langbridge, he groused in his head; all they seem to do around here was make tea.

'There are some custard creams in the cupboard by the fridge,' she called back from the living room.

The nearest thing that had come to big news recently was Monica Andrew's disappearance, but no one seemed to be treating it as such, not even the police. That's because the local pigs were half-baked morons; the same half-baked morons that'd refused him entry into the police force when he'd left school. That's where his heart lay; that's what he wanted to pursue as a career, like his Uncle

Phil. Become a police officer. Uncle Phil loved the job. He took two holidays abroad a year and was set to retire early on a decent pension. Moreover, Leonard Kimble had been soused in a heady cocktail of police dramas on telly since he was a babe-in-arms – *Z-Cars, Kojak, Hawaii Five-O, The Sweeny, Police Woman, Starsky and Hutch.* They got the birds, they got the cars and they got respect.

But as yet it was a career that lay on the other side of a door currently closed to him. So until he managed to find a way through that door he was stuck with the Langbridge Gazette, running around the town hunting out stories on blind terriers, vandalised parsnips down at the allotment and horses that could tell your fortune by counting their snorts. Stuck with all that and making tea for the office.

What he needed was a lucky break. A story that proved he had what it took to become a police officer; something that had taken investigative journalism to its limits; something that required brain power, acute reasoning, faultless deduction and sheer determination – basically your average Sherlock Holmes kind of thing that lifted him above your average PC Plod down at Langbridge police station. Something he could take as proof of how good he was the next time he applied to the force. He'd slap it on their desks and tell them how lucky they'd be to have him. Well, maybe not the last bit…

'One custard cream or two, gran?' he shouted. She could be a little deaf, except when she heard something she shouldn't be listening to, in which case her hearing improved miraculously.

'Just the one,' she replied. 'I'm on a strict budget since they finished me at the Empire.' She did not attempt to hide her vitriol. 'Did you speak to Martin?' she asked as Leonard brought in her tea and biscuit.

'Yes, gran,' he said.

'And?'

'He didn't say much, really.' He dunked his biscuit into his tea and stared at it disconsolately. 'Like he says,

Monica is probably off seeing friends somewhere and forgot to tell anyone.'

Mrs Kimble gave a sneer and forced a tiny snort of disdain down her nose. 'Monica doesn't have friends; she has various grades of enemies. Her mother was the same when she was alive. Her sister's just as bad. It's in the blood. I tell you, Leonard, there's something strange going on at the Empire and has been for a long while. Ever since Martin Caldwell took over the place. I never did trust him.'

'Look, gran, I know he gave you your marching orders, but in fairness you were at retirement age. There's no legal obligation...'

'That's his excuse,' she said cuttingly. 'Don't dunk, dear; it's so working-class. Things are not well in the state of Denmark, Leonard,' she said cryptically. He looked querulously at her. 'Hamlet, dear. Hamlet. That man Caldwell is not all he appears. It wouldn't surprise me in the least if he hadn't had a hand in Monica's disappearance.'

'Gran!' he said. 'You can't go around accusing people of those kinds of things.' He sighed. She'd reached that age when lately any inhibitions or tact had lost all relevance. She spoke her mind freely, which was disconcerting as it wasn't exactly a mind basking in robust health. Her being angry didn't help, either. It poisoned her thoughts. And what's more he got the impression she was trying to use him to get back at Caldwell any which way she could.

'You want a good story, don't you? Something to get you noticed? Don't squander this opportunity, Leonard.' She looked furtively to the window, as if someone was likely to be in earshot, which, of course, was highly unlikely but he guess it added drama for her. She leant closer and said quietly, 'I met Martin's wife a couple of times when she came into the Empire. She's a pretty thing. Nice woman – skirts just the right length. Well one day, when she comes in to the Empire to see Caldwell, I notice she's got this black eye, a real shiner. She'd tried to cover it up with makeup but you could still make it out. She also had bruises on her wrist, as if someone had grabbed her.'

'Maybe she had an accident. These things happen,' he offered.

'That's right, and maybe she walked into a door, like I've heard so many women do over the years. Woman, it seems, are very careless – something to do with special awareness being a particularly male ability.' She raised her eyebrow tellingly. 'I've met many men capable of hurting women in my long life, Leonard, and I tell you, Martin is one of them.'

'Even if it was true, gran, and he beats his wife up, you can't jump to the conclusion that he did something awful to Monica.'

'No? Well there's plenty more I know about Mr Smarmy. I know he and Monica were an item.'

'He's married!'

'Leonard,' she said patiently, 'you've a lot to learn. He was seeing her regularly, in the Biblical sense, I mean…'

'He was having sex with her?'

'If you want to put it so crudely, yes.'

'Why didn't you tell me before? Do you have proof?'

'It's hardly likely there are going to be any soiled sheets lying around the Empire, now, is it?'

He was shocked by what she was saying. More shocked she even knew about such things; he never thought his gran capable of, well, physical stuff. 'Still, it's one thing to be having – you know – and another to link it to her disappearance.'

'There's something else as well. The books were never quite right for a long time. A discrepancy between takings and bankings, if you get my meaning? It wasn't a great deal, I suppose, but when I questioned the odd-thing he made me balance the books so they looked OK.'

'Fraud? You were involved in fraud?'

'Don't be so crude, Leonard. It was a case of tidying up the kitchen that had gotten into a bit of a mess, that's all.'

'Why didn't you refuse, or report it at the time?'

'And lose my job?' She pointed a harsh finger at him. 'That bit stays out of the news, you hear? I only said it to provide context.' She sipped her tea. 'The thing is, I'll bet Monica's disappearance is all wrapped up together with his other dodgy dealings somehow. We had strange people coming and going, not your average reps. I reckon he was in debt up to his eyeballs – I've seen similar cases before – and he drank like a fish, too, as a result of all the stress. There's a story here, Leonard, a big one, if you only got your finger out and dug a little deeper. Don't you want to help your old gran?'

'Of course I do,' he said. His soggy custard cream broke in half and plopped into his cup of tea. He fished in the hot liquid to try and retrieve it before it sank but to no avail. It disappeared from sight, like a fish escaping the keep-net and diving deep into muddy water.

'So what are you going to do?' she asked insistently, her brows lowering disapprovingly as he sucked tea from his fingertips.

'I'm going to ask around first; you know, go to people who might know her. I've already talked to her sister. I'm also going to ask at the other places where she used to do a bit of cleaning. One of them is Devereux Towers – she did work for them some time ago.'

His gran gave a tut-tut. 'The Leach place?' Her face fell thoughtful for a moment. 'It's strange you should say that. I remember taking documents to Caldwell's office one day, and on his blotting-pad was a piece of paper that wafted accidentally to the floor as I put the files down. I picked it up and couldn't help but read it. It was in Monica's handwriting – such a distinctive, almost illiterate scrawl,' she added with a screwing-up of her nose. 'Anyhow, it was Laura Leach's name, address at Devereux Towers and phone number. I remember at the time thinking how odd that was. I mean, she's not the sort of person Martin would be contacting. Not Laura.'

'Perhaps Caldwell needed a reference from her for Monica,' he said.

She shook her head. 'Monica had already been at the Empire ages; it would have been far too late to be asking for a reference. Still, I never paid it much heed. Who knows what Martin Caldwell is up to? My one piece of advice is to be careful when approaching and talking to Laura Leach.'

'Why? She's peculiar but harmless, is what I hear.'

Mrs Kimble folded her arms as if to fend off the cold. 'I'm not so sure about that. I knew her mother and father, as much as anyone could know them. I was working for the town council when Mr Leach sat as a councillor. A strange man, quiet but determined but very domineering with it. He used to look at you as if he didn't trust you. I don't think he particularly liked women. His wife was the same; fragile, reserved, distrustful of everyone and everything, a regular reed of a woman, but we saw even less of her. For the most part they kept themselves to themselves, locked inside Devereux Towers. Closed books all, you might say. They were very suspicious of anyone, unless they came from London, and even then only from select parts of the city. A queer old bunch, the Leaches. Did you know Laura Leach had been sent away to an institution?'

'I heard something, yes. I don't know any details. I thought it might just be a tall story to embellish the old tale of the Witch of Devereux Towers and all that.' He gave a little laugh but his gran didn't crack the faintest of smiles. 'What are you saying, that she's loopy?'

She gave a twist to her head and raised that knowing eyebrow again. 'She was involved in the death of someone, what does that say about a person?'

'Laura Leach? I've seen her; she's a quiet, harmless little thing.'

'Nothing about the Leaches is straightforward, Laura in particular. Her father tried to disguise the fact she'd been sent away, but things get out in a small town like this. And I heard it from a reliable source,' she continued. 'The man that died was a driving instructor, and because of it Laura was put into a mental institution for years. Work it out for yourself.'

He shook his head in disbelief. 'Are you saying Laura actually killed someone?'

She shrugged. 'Whatever happened she's free now, isn't she? But just be careful when dealing with her. I never did trust Londoners. All that prolonged exposure to traffic fumes has got to have an adverse effect on the senses, hasn't it?'

It was here, in his study, where she felt her father's presence was the strongest. She could almost hear his breathing. He had a distinctive, whining sound to his exhalations.

Everything in the room was exactly as he had left it. His large mahogany desk by the window, still laid out with pens and paper; his night-black telephone with its thick, brown cord; his family's photographs lined up so that they faced his luxuriously padded chair, forever under his scrutiny. The bizarre and often grotesque wooden tribal masks watched her suspiciously from their place on the walls, as if they stood guard over the room in his absence. Statues, many carved in wood so black they looked like coal, stood in serried ranks on cabinets and above the fireplace, like an army of goblins from some mythical underworld. And interspersed amongst all this was her father's collection of ancient weapons, both practical and symbolic. His Fijian war clubs, Zulu assegais, Australian aboriginal spears, South American obsidian knives, all designed to stun, to kill or to maim.

She shuddered when she remembered her father lifting down a Zulu assegai, purported to have been used at the battle of Rorke's Drift in 1879. He held the leaf-like blade close to her eight-year-old face.

'See, Laura, this had special significance to the Zulu. Each of these objects is significant in its own way. Did you know that the British soldiers found massacred after the battle of Isandhlwana had been eviscerated – that is, disembowelled – by such weapons? Naturally, our Victorian forefathers put it down to an expression of extreme barbarianism on the part of the Zulu, evidence of their inherent savagery. But they did that to be kind. They slit open the bellies of the dead in order to release the souls, so that they could pass freely to the next life.'

Laura shrank back from the weapon. 'Has that spear killed a man?' she said, terrified.

'Undoubtedly,' he said matter-of-factly as he hung the short spear back on the wall. 'The war clubs have staved-in people's skulls, and the black obsidian knives have been used by the Aztecs to slice open the chest and remove the still-beating hearts of sacrificial victims.'

'That is so awful,' she said. 'To kill...'

'Sometimes people believe it is alright to kill, when if fulfils a greater object, a spiritual need, for instance.'

'God says we must not kill,' she pointed out.

'And what if you do not believe in God?'

It was a concept she found difficult to grasp. 'That's plain silly!'

'Not to some of these people,' he explained. 'They do not believe in our God. They do not abide by the teachings of our Bible, so to them it is not wrong. But it was right by their gods, by their beliefs.'

'So if someone does not believe in God it is alright for them to kill?' It was a logical conclusion for a child to make.

'It is never as simple as that,' he said. 'There are times, even when we believe in God, when there is no option but to kill. At times of war, for instance. Or if someone is seeking to harm us.'

Laura Leach shook away the childhood memories, as best as she could because they seemed to hover around her head like a smoky cloud. She went over to his desk, sat in his chair. She looked at the short line of three framed photographs facing her. There was one of her mother. One each of Laura's dead sisters. But there wasn't a photograph of Laura on the desk.

Her father had taken every image of Laura from the house and put them in a pile in the garden and burned them.

* * * *

27

Granite Cold

He hadn't expected to feel jealousy. But Vince felt something cold scrape his stomach as he walked down the stairs with an empty waste-paper bin in his hand. He stepped down into the foyer, and he saw Edith chatting away with a young man. She had been busy re-stacking the sweets in the kiosk but was obviously finding the young man's attention infinitely more rewarding.

Vince recognised him – Leonard Kimble had been to the Empire a few times, trying to secure free cinema tickets so he could write a movie review for the Langbridge gazette in return. Caldwell didn't give out tickets that easily, but Vince reckoned the old place could do with all the publicity it could get so he'd give Kimble one or two of his own freebies. But in the end the reviews weren't well written, and in fact were perhaps the worst thing he'd ever read in the Gazette and that said something. Leonard Kimble, Vince heard later, had only managed to land the job because his mother was related to the paper's editor. Everyone in Langbridge was related to everyone else, he thought, in one way or another.

'Hello, Vince,' said Edith. 'This is Leonard. He's a reporter now. How exciting!'

'We know each other already,' said Vince unexcitedly.

'Lenny was in the year above me at school, isn't that right, Lenny? He was spotty then.'

Kimble's face said he would have preferred to have kept that to himself. 'Hello, Vince. How are things?' he greeted.

'On the scrounge for tickets again?' said Vince.

'Not today,' he returned. 'I need a bit of information.'

'He's writing an important article for the Gazette,' said Edith, quite enthralled.

'Important, huh? Have more chickens gone missing?' said Vince. 'Wait, don't tell me – the swimming baths in Glastonbury will be having a change of water? Mercy me, whatever next?'

'Very droll,' said Kimble, brushing off the swipe. 'There's more to the job of Gazette reporter than reporting on missing chickens. Like there's more to being a projectionist at the Empire than changing light-bulbs and emptying bins.' He looked down at the bin in Vince's hand.

Edith looked from one to the other of them. 'I thought you two were friends.'

'Acquaintances,' Vince informed. He didn't like the way Leonard Kimble had been eyeing-up Edith, staring at her chest, small though that might be. 'What do you want, Leonard? We're very busy here.'

'What do you know about Monica's disappearance? I talked to Caldwell and he's not saying much.'

'That horrible woman?' said Edith. 'Why do you want to write something about her?'

'She may not have been your cup of tea,' he said, 'but she's missing. I'd like to help find her, write something for the Gazette to jog people's memories, that kind of thing.'

'Well she can stay missing for all I care,' said Vince.

'That's not very nice, Vince? Did you have something against her?'

He said bluntly, 'I didn't like her. End of story.'

'Is that so?' he raised an eyebrow.

'She was going to try and get rid of Vince, get him sacked,' interjected Edith. 'She was a nasty woman. No one is sad that she's gone.'

'Had it in for you, did she, Vince?' said Kimble.

'Monica had it in for everyone, not just me.'

'But you're glad she's gone?'

'What's that supposed to mean, Leonard?'

He shook his head. 'Doesn't mean a thing. My gran tells me Monica and Caldwell had a thing going on. You hear anything like that?'

'None of our business is it?' said Vince. 'He can do what he likes.'

'Imagine if his wife found out. He wouldn't want that to happen, would he?'

'Leonard, who do you think you are – Dixon of Dock Green or something? Leave it to the police.'

'But that's what all investigative reporters do, isn't it, Lenny? Snoop around,' Edith enthused.

Vince gave a grunt. 'Not for the Langbridge Gazette they don't.'

'Monica used to do some cleaning work for the Leach family at Devereux Towers,' said Kimble unperturbed. 'One of the cleaners said you had a crush on Laura Leach.'

'What has that got to do with anything?' said Vince, flashing a smouldering glare at Edith. He saw her shrink back to the Mars Bars she'd been stacking.

'Just thought you might give me a few tips on how to approach her, that's all. I hear she's a bit strange.' He laughed. 'They used to say at school that she'd murdered her family and had them all walled-up somewhere. Maybe she's done the same to Monica, who knows?' He laughed again but no one was laughing with him and it petered-out into an embarrassed croak. 'Just a joke,' he said.

'Well it's not funny,' Vince remarked caustically. 'She's a normal, nice woman, and I wish people would just leave her alone. Why do people always have to be so spiteful and vindictive?'

'Where there's smoke…' said Kimble with a wink at Edith.

'Meaning?' said Vince.

'She was closely involved with the death of a driving instructor years ago. That's why she ended up in Bartholomew Place. You know what that is?'

'Yes, I know!' Vince snapped. 'So she's been ill, why must everyone assume the worst? A driving instructor's death? That's ludicrous! You don't even know her – how can you say those kinds of things?'

'I know her as much as you do, Moody,' he returned. 'You only know what you want to know. Anyhow, I managed to trace someone who actually worked there as a nurse. I'll be speaking to her.'

'I thought you were looking into Monica's disappearance?' said Vince. 'Now you're snooping into Laura's past. What's the connection?'

Leonard Kimble smiled. 'One never knows what dirt one will dig up once one starts digging. You have to admit, it all sounds juicy, doesn't it? Very Daily Mail.' He deliberately turned his back on Vince and faced Edith. 'Maybe we can go out for a drink together one night. Talk about old times.' He made no attempt to hide the fact he was taking in the mound of her breasts.

'Old times?' scoffed Vince. 'Like life in the nursery?'

Edith glanced at him. She turned to Kimble and said that would be nice and she'd think about it. Kimble left the Empire, whistling confidently to himself.

'I really don't like him,' said Vince.

'He's harmless,' Edith said. 'He said he always fancied me at school. Said I looked pretty now, just before you came down the stairs. He didn't know I was working here.'

'You're not falling for that, are you?'

''I never really liked him myself. He's always been a bit strange and creepy. He got expelled from school for a while for groping the girls. After that I avoided him. All the girls did.'

'You're not going to go out with him then, are you?'

'I wasn't going to, and certainly not if you don't want me to, Vince,' she said, her large eyes blinking.

Vince said, 'He's all talk. He's no more an investigative journalist than I am manager of the Empire. He's full of hot air and wind, is all. I'd avoid people like that.'

She reached out and touched his hand. 'But you will be manager one day, Vince.'

'I'm a nobody,' he said, snatching his hand away and putting it in his pocket. 'I'll never be anything.'

'You've never been a nobody to me, Vince. You'll always be a somebody to me.'

Her words stirred strange emotions within him, and he swore he could still feel her hand on his, as if she'd left some kind of exquisite scorch mark there.

There was a heavy pounding at the door, which shattered the silence and made Laura start. Her heart crashed wildly as the noise continued. She closed the door to her father's study and went into the grand entrance hall. The *thump-thump-thump* didn't abate and echoed the sounds of her thumping heart.

'Who is it?' she asked.

The knocking stopped for a second or two at the sound of her voice. Then it cranked back up again, more furious than ever. Laura unbolted the heavy oak door and swung it open.

'Where is he, you bitch?' Katherine screamed. She looked positively manic, her hair plastered down by the rain, her clothes already soaked through. Her mascara had run, and coupled with her bright-red lipstick it gave the impression of a half-drowned clown. But her eyes were livid, wide, blazing orbs of sheer hatred. 'What have you done to him?' she cried.

Laura closed the door on her but Katherine stuck her foot in the gap, stopping her. 'Get away from me!' said Laura. 'Leave me alone!'

'Not until you tell me where he is!'

'I don't know and I don't care,' Laura said.

'I know it was you who damaged my car, who broke into my house and slashed everything up. You're stalking me, aren't you? Trying to scare me off. And you left me this!' She held up the blood-smeared jacket. 'What have you done to Felix?'

'Felix?' she echoed. 'I know that's his real name,' said Laura. 'Just as I knew you weren't his sister either. I knew that much when you first came to see me. You must both think me entirely stupid.' Laura's expression had hardened. 'And you must think me totally helpless, too.' Her tone was granite-cold.

'You don't scare me, you crazy bitch! I know you've done something terrible to Felix and you won't frighten me away till I find out what you've done.'

'He said he loved me,' said Laura flatly. 'He made me think he was telling the truth, and all along he used that to get money from me. I loved him, and I believe I would have done anything for him. How could you have been so cruel?'

'Look at you, Laura,' Katherine sneered, 'do you really suppose a man like Felix could ever love a woman like you? He told me how he was glad he never had to sleep with you to get the money. He said he'd rather sleep with a pig!'

Laura screamed loudly and launched her full weight at Katherine, grabbing her by her slender throat, forcing her back so that she fell awkwardly onto the puddled gravel. Katherine's eyes bulged; her tongue was forced slug-like from between her red lips as she struggled to breathe. She beat at Laura with her fists but could not dislodge her. Laura's face was twisted with rage, her teeth bared as she squeezed her fingers around Katherine's throat with all the strength she could muster.

But then she released her. She stood up, her chest heaving. Her hair wet and matted, her eyes fierce. Katherine gasped for breath, holding her throat and raising herself onto her elbow. 'You're fucking crazy!' she said, the effort painful.

'If I ever see you again,' said Laura breathlessly, 'I will kill you.' She went to the door, was about to close it.

Katherine struggled to her feet. 'What's behind the blue door, you bitch?'

At this Laura grabbed one of her father's walking-sticks from a stand by the door, a stout oak affair topped with a silver handle in the shape of a bull. She cried out shrilly and ran to Katherine, raising the stick high and swinging it down across Katherine's face. Blood gushed from a long cut on her cheek. She raised it again, this time savagely hitting Katherine's shoulder. The woman ran back to her car crying out in agony, Laura close behind her, swinging the walking stick wildly, managing to land a couple of blows onto Katherine's back as she swung open the car door. She flung herself inside and locked the door on Laura's manic screaming. The walking stick's silver handle crashed against the side window, smashing it and showering Katherine's bloodied face with glass. The car tyres threw up gravel as Katherine sought to get away as quickly as she could, the stick coming down on the car's roof, denting it. Laura took one last swing at the speeding vehicle but missed. Laura cried out at the top of her voice till she could cry no more, watching Katherine's car bouncing down the track in the distance. She threw the walking stick away.

Sobbing, Laura turned and went inside. She thought she heard her father's breathing again, close at her shoulder. Heard him say that sometimes it was alright to kill someone, especially if they sought to hurt you.

Yes, she thought, tears stinging her eyes, sometimes it is the only way...

* * * *

28

As Frail as Feathers

The café – *The Friendly Butty* – had seen better days, thought Martin Caldwell, though he guessed the better days can't have been up to much. He'd never seen this high-street café with any more than two or three people sitting at the tables, and this morning he was the only one in the place apart from the surly-looking woman behind the counter, who had managed to serve him coffee and toast without uttering a single word. With nothing else to do she'd made herself a cup of tea and was sitting in a far corner of the café near the window, reading a dog-eared copy of *Exchange and Mart*.

He looked at his watch. She was late. She always used to be. It was one of the things he used to hate about her, used to get him all riled-up. His head hurt like the blazes and even the tink-tink of his spoon against his cup cut into his skull like a pick-axe. He knew he'd drunk too much yesterday. And the day before. And he shouldn't have touched the bottle this morning either but he couldn't help it. Things were getting out of control and if there were one thing he hated more than anyone being late it was losing control over anything. He felt his blood beginning to bubble with the thought.

The bell over the door tinkled loudly and he looked up to see Katherine walking towards him. Christ, he thought, she looked rough! She wasn't wearing any makeup, her hair was a mess, and her clothes so creased that it looked like she might have been sleeping in them. But the thing he noticed straight off was the large sticking-plaster on her cheek and the significant area of bruising around it. Though he didn't show it he was smiling inside as she pulled up a chair and sat opposite him. He saw how stiff her movements were and how she grimaced as she eased the chair closer to the table.

'Morning, Kat. You look like shit.'

She glowered at him. 'You look marginally better. Have you been at the Gordon's again?'

'Been in a fight with a bulldog?' he said. 'And lost, obviously.'

'Fuck you,' she said.

'Can I get you a drink? Toasted teacake, maybe? You look like you haven't eaten properly in ages. Anyone would think something was troubling you.'

'Cut the crap, Martin. I'm not in the mood for it. I need you to help me.'

'Ever thought I don't want to help you?'

'Ever thought you had a choice?' she said. He noticed how her hand was trembling. She looked back over her shoulder to the woman in the corner. She wasn't taking the slightest interest in them. 'Why here?' said Katherine.

'Not as easy for you to make a scene.'

'Don't bet on it, Martin. She's going to kill me...'

His eyes widened. 'Hang on, who's going to kill you?'

'She is. That fucking Laura Leach.'

He gave a low chuckle. 'You're off your rocker, Kat.'

'She's the one with a screw loose. She's out to kill me, I know she is. The same way she killed Felix.'

He held up his hand for her to calm down. 'Keep it low, Kat.' He leant forward, over the tomato sauce bottle. 'Maybe you're overreacting.'

'She broke into my house in Glastonbury, slashed up all my clothes and then tampered with my car's brakes so I'd have an accident. She almost beat me to a pulp - look at my fucking face! I don't call that overreacting!' She wiped her tired eyes with the back of her hand. 'She's done something to Felix, I know she has. She left me his jacket and it had his blood all over it. I thought she was going to kill me too last night. I think she would have if I hadn't managed to get to my car in time.' She pulled down the polo-neck of her jumper to reveal fierce red welts around her throat.

'Laura did all that?'

'The bitch is fucked-up, Martin. I need your help with two things.'

He sat back, arms folded. 'Two things? Fuck that, Kat. I told you...'

'The first thing is to help me find out what's behind the blue door.'

Caldwell unfolded his arms and leant forward again. 'Felix did mention that. What's so special about that room?'

'That's just it, I don't know, but I'm willing to bet there's a connection between what's in there and Felix's disappearance. He was intent on finding out, and maybe that's what went wrong. I've got to know, Martin. I love him. I'm going to fucking pieces without him!'

'What makes you think I can help you on that score? And, like I say, maybe I don't even want to help you.' He lifted his cup to his lips. 'You made this mess, Kat; you can get yourself out of it. I don't give a damn about what happened to your precious Felix.'

'We've gone through this, Martin. I know too much about you. I could fuck your life up real bad if I put my mind to it. Don't mess with me.'

Martin's face stiffened. He eyed her through the steam swirling from his coffee. 'What is it you want me to do?'

'You've got connections with people who could break into Devereux Towers, snoop around the place. You've used them before.'

'No longer my game,' he said patiently.

'Make it your game, Martin. I need to find out what secrets she's hiding. I need to find out what happened to Felix, one way or another. And the second thing on my list – I want you to have Laura Leach taken care of.'

Caldwell glanced at the woman in the corner. She was still absorbed in her paper. 'That's murder you're talking about, Kat,' he whispered.

'It never bothered you before. Since when did you develop a conscience?'

'That was years ago. I'm different now.'

'You can't shrug it off so easily, Martin. I won't let you.'

He sighed heavily, his eyes flitting agitatedly. 'It'll cost you plenty.'

'I don't care what it costs,' she said. 'Make it happen.' She rose from the table, wincing at a pain in her shoulder. 'You've got one week. If I don't get results I'll make it bad for you.' She leant on the table, putting her bruised face close to his. 'I don't care what happens to me anymore. Without Felix I'm nothing. So don't think for a minute I won't make good on my threats; I've nothing to lose. Find out all you can about Felix and then kill the bitch.'

He could tell she was deadly serious. She'd been so smitten by this guy Felix it was like a rampant disease that was eating her up. 'I'll do my best,' he said.

'You'd better,' she warned, leaving him and slamming the café door behind her.

The woman looked up from her reading. 'Wanting something else?' she said.

'Got any aspirin?'

She sat in the dark, in her father's leather chair, as she had done so many times. The moonlight from the window fell onto the three framed photographs. Everyone smiling. Everyone happy. Only she wasn't there amongst them to share that happiness, if that's what it really was. It looked happy, and to an outsider perhaps it even appeared so, but Laura knew it was far from that.

Rain dashed itself against the window panes, the noise startling her. Strange, but it had been raining on and off now ever since she'd found out about Casper – Felix.

Almost as if the weather were crying for her, mimicked her tears.

Why did she sit here? What did she hope to gain by it? Was it to try and see things from her father's perspective, to reach behind his motivations? To see things how he must have seen them all those long years ago?

She remembered how he'd never said a word as they drove through the night. His eyes were fixed, staring straight ahead, as if he couldn't bear to look at her.

'Where is Alex?' Laura said from the back seat of the car.

He didn't reply. The windscreen wipers batted away fat drops of rain, the rubber blades squeaking.

'I need to see Alex!' she cried.

'You'll see Alex again soon,' assured the nurse sat beside her. 'That's where we're taking you.'

'But where is it we're going?' Laura asked tearfully.

The doctor sitting on the other side of her spoke. His voice was not as comforting as the nurse's. 'Somewhere where we can better look after you.'

'I don't need looking after,' she said. 'I'm not ill!'

'We'll be the judge of that,' said the nurse.

'I want my mother!' said Laura.

'You'll see your mother, too,' said the doctor.

Laura bent forward to try to speak to her father. 'Where are we going? Why don't you speak to me?'

'He's busy driving the car,' explained the nurse. 'It's night-time and it's raining. Let him concentrate, there's a good girl.'

'I'm not a girl! I'm seventeen and a half!' she protested.

'Keep calm and quiet, please, Laura,' said the nurse. 'You'll only get distressed and you're not well as it is.'

'I'm perfectly fine! Where is Alex?'

'We've already told you,' the doctor interjected. 'Now if you can't be quiet we might have to sedate you again. You don't want that, do you?'

She shook her head and remained quiet till they passed through a set of massive double gates and pulled up outside a dark-looking building. The doctor grabbed her firmly by the arm and all but hauled her from the car. She was taken by him up a flight of stone steps, flanked on the other side by the nurse. Laura turned around to try and look over her shoulder. Her father followed silently a little distance behind.

There was a small light burning over a plain-looking desk on which sat a telephone and little else. The nurse picked up the phone and spoke quietly into the receiver.

'Father...' said Laura, the doctor's grip on her arm firm. 'Why are we here?'

'To make you better,' said the nurse, coming over to her. Laura could see in the light that she was quite elderly and had a friendly, warm face that smiled reassuringly.

Laura didn't like this place; it was cold and gloomy and had a strange, uncomfortable smell about it that make her stomach feel queasy. 'I'm not ill,' she said.

'Don't worry, Laura; we're here to help you.'

Laura pulled away from the doctor. 'Where's Alex? Take me to Alex, like you promised. Father, what's going on?' But he stood immobile, his face impassive.

'There, there, Laura, don't get hysterical again,' said the doctor, stepping towards her.

There was the sound of footsteps hurrying down the corridor towards them. Two more men dressed in white shirts and trousers. They appeared out of the dark like twin spectres.

'Father!' Laura pleaded, fending off the doctor's groping hands. 'Tell them to leave me alone!'

'You've done a terrible thing, Laura,' her father said. 'It is a sign of a diseased mind and you're here to have that disease cured. Until you are better my daughter remains dead to me. I'm not sure she shall ever come back from the dead.' He turned away from her.

'Father!' she yelled. The doctor grabbed her, the two other men also holding firmly onto her, though she struggled with all the strength she had and lashed out with her foot, landing one of the men a painful blow on the shin.

The doctor nodded at the nurse. 'Nurse Bradshaw, if you please...'

Her warm expression had melted to one of sorrow, and bearing that same look of sorrow she produced a syringe. 'Hold still, please, Laura,' said Nurse Bradshaw. 'This is for your own good.'

'Get that thing away from me!' she screamed. Her arms were now held rigid by the men and she felt the heat of the needle passing into her flesh. 'What are you doing to me? Why are you doing this to me?'

'You know why, Laura,' said the doctor. 'But we can help you. At Bartholomew Place we help all manner of people.' He glanced at Laura's father.

They dragged her away, already her senses beginning to blur, making her feel giddy and light-headed. 'Father' she called again, trying to look back at him. He had his back to her. He didn't turn around. He appeared to be signing something on a clipboard.

They passed quickly down insipidly-painted corridors lined with featureless doors, her legs now buckling beneath her and the men having to half carry, half drag her along. Her eyelids felt as if they were made of lead and she was hardy able to keep them open. Then she heard the harsh clink of keys in a lock, was vaguely aware of a door being thrust open. She was tossed like a sack of grain into a small, darkened room. She fell to the floor and before she could scramble to her feet the door was slammed closed and locked.

Laura beat at it, terrified. 'Where am I? What are you doing to me?' she said, her words slurring. She felt so, so weak. Her legs as frail as feathers, so she sank to the floor, sobbing as the black ink of unconsciousness began to cloud her mind.

'Alex, I'm sorry,' she said. 'I'm so sorry…'

* * * *

29

A Certain Kind of Freedom

He never thought he'd ever have to come back here again. Not to this gritty northern town where he'd spent so many of his younger years. Years he was not proud of. Foolishly he'd assumed he'd left it all behind. It was a life that belonged to a different person, these narrow streets with their dirty-brick back-to-back houses, the coal mines, the heaps of spoil that looked like hills. He guessed it was true what they said: you can't shrug off the past like it never existed. It's always there.

And testament to that past was the Eddleston Working Men's Club. Martin Caldwell stood in the dark car park, staring long and unforgiving at the dilapidated old building, watching people filing in, hearing the strains of an electric guitar floating out of the open doors. As he approached the club he could smell beer in the air, strong and familiar. A flood of memories accompanied it.

In the doorway an old man was sitting at a wooden table. 'You a member?' he asked, his voice gravelled by years of smoking. He had a fag planted between his lips now, ash drifting down to an open book on the table.

'I'm here to see someone,' Caldwell said.

'Which someone?'

'That's OK, Ralph,' said a voice. 'He's with me. Sign him in.'

A thick-set man in his forties came up to them. He had a mess of long, black hair going grey at the temples, and sported a handlebar moustache. 'Hello, Martin,' he said. He nodded for Caldwell to follow him.

They went into the club, cigarette smoke hanging in a thick pall; the fuggy outlines of people huddled around small, wooden tables. There was a band up on stage doing a bad cover of a Bay City Rollers' number and some of the crowd were giving them hell. The man paused at the bar.

'Drink, Martin?' he asked.

'Later,' he replied. 'Let's get on with it.'

'Fine.' He led them through a door into a short corridor and held open another door, 'My office,' he said. He shut the door after Caldwell.

'Nice,' he said, looking around him at the dingy wood-clad walls, the stack of cardboard boxes, the shadeless light-bulb, the photograph of a topless woman tacked to the back of the door. 'I like what you've done with the place, Ray,' he said.

Ray Steele smiled. 'Long time no see, Martin. I never thought I'd ever see you back in Eddleston again.'

'Never wanted to be back,' he said. 'You haven't changed.'

'Can't say the same for you, Martin. Look at you now – regular dandy, eh? Life must be treating you good.' He sat down on a chair behind a flimsy-looking chipboard desk, opened a drawer and pulled out a bottle. 'Fancy a snifter?'

'I need a favour,' said Caldwell seriously.

Steele's smile faded and he put a glass on the desk, poured out a good measure of Jack Daniels. 'I'd like to help you, Martin, for old time's sake, but things have changed. Look at me, I'm going straight now.'

'Going straight isn't doing you any favours,' he observed.

'I get by.' He downed the alcohol in one. Smacked his lips. 'Whatever it is you're wanting, Martin, I ain't got it no more.'

'I need a job doing.'

He shrugged. 'Like I said.'

'Are you forgetting something, Ray? Forgetting what you did for me?'

'That was then, Martin; this is now.' He poured again. 'What are you getting at? This isn't some crude attempt at blackmail, is it?' He bent forward. 'I could have both your legs broken before you reached your car in the car park, you know that?'

'Nice to see that the old Ray Steele hasn't disappeared entirely.' He took in a deep breath, licked his lips at the sight of the drink. 'Ray, I need your help. I'll make it worth your while. You look like you could do with an injection of cash anyhow.'

'OK, let's say I was interested, what exactly do you want? No promises, mind, but because we're friends I'll hear you out.'

Caldwell ran his hand through his thick hair. 'I need someone taken care of,' he said.

'In what way, taken care of?' he asked warily. 'There are different levels, you know.'

'Taken care of in the same way you took care of a certain someone else for me.'

'You mean when you needed to silence a certain woman, who found you out and who threatened to spill the beans on one of your scams? That certain someone?'

'That's the one, Ray.'

He sucked in a breath that hissed over his teeth. 'You know what you're asking here?'

'Course I fucking know.'

Steele shook his head. 'I don't know, Martin. Things are different now, like I said. A man would need one hell of a financial incentive to climb back on that old warhorse.'

'Whatever it takes. Cut beating about the bush, Ray; are you going to help me out or what?

'I'm not saying I am, and I'm not saying I'm not. We need to talk over particulars first. Man or woman?'

'Woman.'

He smirked. 'You never learn.'

'I didn't come here to be preached at, Ray,' he said sullenly. 'There's this place, some kind of Georgian folly or something. A woman lives there all alone. It should be easy for you. She's loaded too. There's also this room that I need you to get inside.'

'And what's in this room? Anything for me?'

Caldwell cocked his head, his lips tight. 'I wish I fucking knew. Maybe there is, maybe not. Look, I'll go through the details if you decide to take this job on. If not I'll go elsewhere, in which case the least you know about this the better.'

Steele tut-tutted. 'Don't you trust me, Martin? An old friend?'

'Never did, Ray; and we were never friends.'

His eyes narrowed in thought. 'So, a break-in and a woman to be topped. All in a day's work, eh?' He swigged at his glass, put it down hard on the table. 'Say I decided to take this on for you – this has got to be the last time.'

'You have my word,' said Caldwell.

'Which we both know is worth shit. I mean it, Martin, we never meet again, and we never speak again. You got that? You never, ever come back here.'

Caldwell nodded. 'Deal. Got a spare glass?'

With Caldwell out of the way for a day or so Vince felt a certain kind of freedom. He'd never really been left fully in charge of the Empire, and the sudden responsibility filled him with excitement and dread in equal measure. Whenever Caldwell had taken holidays, they shipped in someone else to cover. He'd been surprised when Caldwell had called him into his office, his mood as black as the stormy weather outside, and asked him to deputise.

'I'll be gone all day, maybe two. You're manager till I get back,' he said.

'Are you sure, Mr Caldwell?' asked Vince.

'Who else is there?'

'What about head office sending someone?'

'HQ doesn't need to know I'm gone. Whilst we're on that, if anyone calls make some excuse or other for me and tell them I'll get back to them. It's only one day, for Christ's sake, surely you can manage that, Vince!'

He'd said yes because he didn't have a choice, but now he was enjoying the feeling. He even sat in Caldwell's chair, spun it round a few times, picked up the phone and made a pretend call.

'Just do it!' he said brusquely to static. The office door opened and Edith came in. He slammed the phone down hard.

'It suits you,' she said.

Embarrassed, he rose to his feet. 'What does?'

'Sitting there. Being manager. It's where you should be, Vince. You should be in charge.'

'Don't be ridiculous. I couldn't be manager,' he said. 'What do you want?'

'Keys,' she said, nodding at them hanging on the office wall. 'And to clean your office.'

'It's not my office, Edith.'

'It could be. One day. You'd do a far better job of it than Martin. He's not a nice man and doesn't know anything about cinemas, not like you. You know everything there is to know.'

It made him feel decidedly uncomfortable, but in a nice way. He wasn't used to receiving compliments. He'd got nothing but criticism since he was a kid. 'Thank you, Edith,' he said genuinely.

She beamed. 'You deserve so much more, Vince,' she continued. 'You're a nice young man.'

'I don't think so...' he said sheepishly.

'Yes you do, and yes you are. I think you're wonderful.'

Silence slammed in like someone had dropped a heavy weight onto the room. 'Me?' he asked tentatively.

She lowered her gaze. 'Yes, you. I've always thought you were wonderful, ever since I first met you. And I think people have been so, so unkind to you and you don't deserve that one jot. I'm glad Laura Leach found herself another man, because that means your mind won't be on her all the time, and perhaps now you might look at me every once in a while...'

He was stunned, his mouth hanging open. 'Edith, I don't understand...'

'I love you!' she said in a rush. 'There, I've said it!' and she dashed immediately from the room.

Vince sank back into the chair, the wind knocked completely from his sails. Then Edith came back in, sheepishly reaching up to the wall.

'Keys,' she said, avoiding looking at him. She ran out of the office.

* * * *

30

The Price of Sin

The rain came down hard and relentless, the sky a broiling mass of angry cloud smothering the tiniest patch of blue, the wind tearing across the flat land, thrashing and denuding the trees that sat in a dour land brown and shrivelled. Winter seemed to be lurking just beyond the horizon, crawling inevitably towards them. Laura could smell its presence in the air and its cold breath snapped at her exposed cheeks.

The wind buffeted her as she bent down to the headstone and pulled up weeds from her mother's grave. Devereux Towers had its own private graveyard, surrounded by a rusted iron fence, leaning in places as if it too had been tumbled by the wind. It was the last resting place of many a previous occupant. It should have been the last resting place of her father, beside her mother and two sisters, but Laura had refused him his one last wish. The plot he'd reserved next to his wife remained empty.

The graves of her mother and sisters were lined up in the same order as the photographs on her father's desk. He'd been very careful with the placement. There was no room for Laura's grave; she would have been edged out, as she'd been edged out of their life when they were alive. He didn't want her buried here amongst them, next to him.

She rose on hearing the faint sound of a car round the front. Laura wiped her muddy hands down her skirt, brushed back her wind-ruffled hair and painted a dirty smudge on her forehead in the process. She listened nervously, the wind at her back eager to push her towards the sound. She went around the side of the house to check.

Parked out front was a police car. She felt her legs buckle and her stomach screw itself into a tight ball. As she approached, two police officers got out of the car, putting on their caps and screwing their eyes up against the rain.

'Laura Leach?' one of them asked.

'That's correct. Is there anything wrong?'

'Nothing wrong, Miss Leach. We'd like to ask you a few questions, is all.'

For a sickening moment she froze to the spot, unsure what to do.

'Are you feeling alright, Miss Leach?' said the other officer.

'Yes, yes, perfectly well. I suppose you had better come inside, out of the rain.'

She led them into the entrance hall and closed the door on the worsening weather. 'This is some place you have here,' Miss Leach, the officer said, looking about him, genuinely enthralled. 'Reminds me of some kind of movie set.'

'I think it's what father intended,' she said flatly. 'How can I help you?'

'We believe you knew Monica Andrews.'

Laura thought about it for a moment. 'You mean Monica the cleaner?'

'That's right. We understand she used to do work for the family.'

'For my father, yes, when he became too ill to clean for himself. Before he went into a home. He kept her on whilst he was away from Devereux Towers, and she was here after his funeral. I kept her on for a little while but then I fired her.'

'Why was she fired?'

'She wasn't doing the job properly and she wasn't a nice person to have around. I also prefer not to have strangers in the place. Why do you ask all this?'

'Are you aware that Monica has gone missing?'

She shook her head. 'I've had nothing to do with her since she left, nearly two years ago. I wasn't aware she'd gone missing. What has that got to do with me?'

'We're chasing up any leads we can. Did she mention any other places she worked, any friends or contacts? Please think carefully – any shred of information might prove crucial in finding her.'

'We never talked. I knew nothing about her, nothing at all. I can't help you there, officer, I'm sorry.' She stared at him. 'Is that all you've come for?'

The officer glanced at his colleague. Raindrops glistened like little pearls on the dark material of their uniforms. 'You said she wasn't a nice person to have around – what did you mean by that?'

'Just that. She wasn't nice to talk to. She had a way about her that I didn't take to.'

'You live here all alone, Miss?' said the other officer.

'What has that to do with anything?'

'Nothing, Miss. An observation. Have you noticed any strange people hanging around recently?'

'Strange? Define strange.'

'Strangers, should I say. People new to the area, perhaps.'

She hesitated. 'I don't see anyone much. I don't go out that often. Practically everyone in Langbridge is a stranger to me, officer.'

The officer smiled. 'Thanks for your help, Miss Leach. Sorry to bother you; we'll leave you alone now. If you do think of anything else...'

'I'll call,' she said.

She let them out of the door. The wind and the rain saw them hurry to the police car. She closed the door but watched the car through the window, all the way down the track till it was obscured by trees.

Letting out a long-held breath she put a hand to her stomach and doubled-up, wanting to be sick. She choked it back, but not before it burnt her mouth. When she looked at her hands she was horrified at how they shook and she could do nothing to stop them save clasp them together.

She didn't leave the window till night fell; till she was certain the police weren't coming back.

'Is it so wrong, to want to be loved, to want to love?' she said to herself, and recoiled in alarm, because that is exactly what she'd said to Nurse Bradshaw in Bartholomew Place.

'There is nothing wrong in that,' Nurse Bradshaw had replied. 'But it is what you have done in the name of love that is so wrong.'

'I did not plan it,' Laura said tearfully. 'It just happened.'

'Nothing simply happens. You played a wilful part in things, Laura.'

'Please let me out of here, Nurse Bradshaw. I don't like it here and I am not like the others in this place.'

'It is not within my power to grant.'

'Do you think I am a bad person, Nurse Bradshaw?'

She thought hard upon it, and then said, 'My opinions do not matter.'

'They do to me!' She made as if to grab the nurse's arm but she pulled away from Laura. 'I'm sorry. Don't look at me like that. I'm not a bad person.'

'I have to go,' she said. She turned at the door. 'Don't fight things, Laura, that's my advice. And I don't think you are a bad person, but I do pity you.' She lowered her head. 'I can't do anything for you, so please stop pestering me or I will have to avoid seeing you. You don't want that, do you?'

Laura gave a rapid shake to her head. 'Where is Alex?' she asked quietly. 'No one will tell me.'

Nurse Bradshaw's face hardened. 'You mustn't mention that name ever again. You must forget all about Alex. You will have to resign yourself to the fact that you will never see Alex again.'

Laura remembered screaming till she felt as if her throat had been cut by scissors, yet she ignored the pain and did not stop till they restrained her with leather belts and jabbed another needle into her arm; till her brain felt as if it had turned to thick sludge inside her skull and she didn't know why she was trying to scream or who she was screaming for. They tried for years to erase Alex from her mind, and in the end she pretended they had succeeded and stored the name deep inside that far corner of her head where they or their insidious treatments could not reach.

Laura listened to the rain. It intruded on her thoughts, washed away the sad memories. She could not remember the last time she ate. She should feel hungry but she did not. In any case, what was that tiny emptiness compared to the emptiness of her very soul?

Neither did she feel the cold. It was as if her body were turning itself off by degrees and soon all that would be left of it would be the smouldering embers of her tortured mind. One day, even that must burn out, use up its limited store of energy like a star in the cold vastness of space, collapsing in on itself, feeble, exhausted, dying.

She wandered aimlessly though the rooms of Devereux Towers, imagining she heard the voices of her mother and sisters, her father, feeling their presence filling up the place with life again. But now they were only sad echoes only she could hear, reverberating through her mind, fading into the silence of the grave.

Her father's study. Cloaked in darkness. The twisted, angry masks staring at her from the walls. The array of tribal weapons silently mocked her and dared her come closer.

She tore herself away and went to the tower – Laura's Tower – taking the stairs and pausing outside the blue door. She lifted the key that hung around her waist and shed a tear for all that could have been. But she did not enter, for she felt too weak. So she went to her bedroom and lay on the bed without undressing. She could not sleep. The rain hit the glass and made a sound like tearing calico.

Must I be punished forever, she thought? Have I really been so bad that you send me even worse torment to endure?

Yes, she thought; you must take whatever is sent, whatever pain is thrust upon you, because that is the price of sin. Her father had decreed it and so she heard his voice say it still.

Laura did not know how long she had been asleep, but she awoke with a start. She thought she heard a noise coming from downstairs. She strained to hear more through the hiss of silence. The house made all manner of queer noises at night, she told herself. But this was a thump loud enough to penetrate her light sleep and wake her.

She heard it again. Someone was downstairs.

She slid off the bed and padded silently to the light-switch, flicking it on. The bright glare caused her to squint, but instead of making her feel better it only accentuated how exposed she felt, and emphasised the dark void on the other side of the bedroom door. The spiral staircase leading downwards was in almost complete darkness.

Laura crept silently down the stairs, finding the light switch at the bottom. The entrance hall was lit up brightly. There wasn't anything out of the ordinary here. She picked up her father's walking stick – the very same she'd beaten Katherine with – and moved quietly towards the dark archway that led to her father's study. She froze on hearing a faint noise emanating from it.

'Who is that?' she said, her voice uncomfortably loud. 'I'm armed!'

She didn't move for a full minute, but heard nothing more except the rain at the windows. Cautiously she went to the study door, turned the handle and pushed at the solid oak. The room was in complete darkness. Her hand crept around the doorframe and found the light-switch. She flicked it on.

Nothing. There wasn't anyone here.

The curtains billowed a little and she went over to the sash window. It was open by a fraction of an inch and the wind puffing through the tiny gap was cold on her hand. She slammed it shut and drew the curtains against the night, her own reflection in the glass looking like a spirit standing out on the gravel.

A chill embraced her. She looked about her. 'Father, is that you?' she said in a whisper. 'Have you come to haunt me?' She was greeted by silence and she rubbed her shoulder to keep warm. 'Well you can go to hell!' she said.

As she turned to leave she paused by the collection of war clubs, straightening them. She ran her hand over one of them and felt its hardness, imagining the severe pain it had possibly inflicted.

There was nothing to be afraid of, she thought. It was just the wind taunting her. She took a war club from off the wall, carried it up to her bedroom and laid it on the bed beside her, listening to the driving rain outside.

* * * *

31

A Close Secret

It was mid-afternoon and yet the light was as dull as dusk. It had been raining heavily all day, and had not let up once. Today it had reached monsoon proportions, or what Leonard Kimble presumed must resemble a monsoon as he'd never actually seen one, never been further than Somerset. He wanted that ignorance to change. One day he'd see the world, finally escape this dead hole of a place with its small minds and petty, provincial ambitions. Never more so than on a day like today, when the wind whipped off the levels and drove on unchecked through Langbridge, its cramped streets awash, the fields hereabouts sodden.

Dreary, he thought as he paused on the stone bridge that spanned the swollen river. He'd never seen the Lang so high or rushing so fast, its swirling, muddy waters carrying along huge tree limbs and other detritus, thrashing its earthen banks like a petulant child in a tantrum lashing out at its mother, great chunks of earth being dislodged and swept into the churning depths. Some said, fearfully, that if it carried on like this it would break its banks altogether, like it did back in 1947. What did the morons expect, thought Kimble? The damned place was built on a drained floodplain. Anyhow, that was just people getting wound-up, like they always did around here. They see a shooting star and they get all superstitious. There were still those who practised wassailing at Christmas, clanging their pots and shouting like mad around an apple tree, and then pouring a jar of perfectly good cider onto its roots. This was 1976, for God's sake!

The sign was dripping wet. *The Sedgemoor Retirement Home*. It was an uninspiring grey box of a building erected some time in the late-1950s; it was functional, plain, and constructed at a time when building materials were in short supply after the last war. The stopping-off place for pensioners on their way to kicking the bucket. It reminded him of a concrete coffin, now he thought about it, and that was rather fitting.

He rang the bell at the front door and a woman in a pale-blue uniform covered over with a red cardigan answered.

'I'm here to see Mrs Bradshaw,' he said. 'I'm expected.'

'Ah, yes,' said the woman, 'the man from *The News of the World*.' She invited him in. 'Shocking weather we're having,' she said apologetically, as if she were responsible for the rain. 'We get a lot of this in this part of the country. Is it raining where you came from?' She led him to the front desk where he signed a visitors' book. 'You look very familiar, Mr Hemmingway. Have you been to Langbridge before?'

'This is my first time,' Kimble said. 'Can I see Mrs Bradshaw, please?'

She took the lead down a maze of corridors, the air stifling with the radiators being set to high. Bland prints were hung on bland walls, and all the lights had been turned on to fend off the encircling darkness outside the rain-blurred windows. Every now and again a fresh squall threw more water at the panes. The woman paused at a door and knocked.

'Ellen – Mr Hemmingway is here to see you.' She turned to Kimble. 'They've just had their afternoon tea and Mrs Bradshaw normally likes to take a nap at this time, so she could be a little tired.' A faint voice told them to come in and the woman opened the door for Kimble. 'I'll leave you to it. Just call at the desk when you're ready to be let out.' She trotted off brightly down the corridor.

Ellen Bradshaw was sitting in a well-padded armchair facing an electric fire, its twin bars blazing orange. She had a friendly face, thought Kimble, if there really is such a thing; rounded, heavy jowls, watery blue eyes, thinning grey hair moulded into a mass of curls.

Leonard Kimble had been doing some digging. He'd searched the microfiche in the Gazette office, looking for any past article concerning Bartholomew Place, particularly where they mentioned ex-employees. He stumbled across a few leads but most people had either died or left the county and he'd no idea how to begin to trace them. He found one, though, and she had been a nurse at Bartholomew Place – Ellen Bradshaw – who had been living under his nose all this time, here at The Sedgemoor Retirement Home over the bridge and on the outskirts of Langbridge. He contacted her and was surprised at how eager she was to speak to him, and even more so when she heard he was from *The News of the World*. She said she had something she wanted to tell him, something she needed to get off her chest. That suited Kimble just fine. He couldn't believe his luck.

'Good afternoon, Mrs Bradshaw,' he said politely, closing the door behind him. The heat inside the room was almost unbearable, but the woman had a thick blanket spread over her legs, and she wore a hefty, hand-knitted cardigan.

'Mr Hemmingway?' she asked.

'That's right. Call me Ernie,' he said.

'Please, do take a seat,' she said, pointing to a chair by the fire. She looked faintly nervous, her eyes saucer-wide and unblinking. 'Forgive me for saying, but you look rather young.'

He smiled. 'I'm older than I look, Mrs Bradshaw,' he said. 'And *The News of the World* has invested in a raft of young reporters learning their craft; it is a modern, forward-thinking newspaper.'

'A national paper,' she said.

'Yes, famously so.'

'That is good. That is what's needed.'

Kimble sat down and took his wet coat off. He hung it on the back of his chair and removed a pad and pen from the coat pocket. 'I won't keep you,' he assured. 'I just need to ask a few questions about Bartholomew Place.'

'And I need to tell you a few things about it. It's time I let people know about some of the things that went on inside there. Not just there but in other similar places too. It's not right; people's lives have been ruined.'

He was taken aback by the outpouring. 'Ruined? I'm not sure what you mean, Mrs Bradshaw.'

She stared at him and for a moment he feared she had seen through his deception, but she shifted her attention to the fire. 'I am ill, Mr Hemmingway. You get to a certain age and you are beset with all manner of illnesses you never dreamt about as a young person. But such things are inevitable. So many changes happen to you as you grow older. It's like feeling the cold, for instance.' She pulled the blanket further up her legs and appeared to shiver. 'Or seeing things in a different light. Seeing things how they really are – were.' She turned back to him. 'I'm nearly seventy-seven years old,' she admitted, in that way older people sometimes do when fishing for compliments about how they don't look their age. Kimble found that the majority not only looked their age but in fact looked far older, in his opinion.

'You don't look it,' he said, playing the game. 'I've no idea what you're doing in a retirement home – surely you're far too young?'

'And you are a practised flatterer,' she said, smiling. 'All your life still ahead of you, life as yet to be discovered, both good and bad. It's easier for the young to lie, to see things in plain black and white, to accept what others tell you is the truth, is the way of the world, and for you to believe what you think is right and proper. A young person's perspective on the world is not as elastic as it becomes when you get older. When you get to my age you'll see how things become less straightforward. I was like you once. I believed what I believed, believed what I was told. But now I find I question everything. All manner of strange things. I like Beethoven...' she said unexpectedly.

'Beethoven, Mrs Bradshaw?'

'I ask myself, do I love to listen to Beethoven because I like his music, or because to like Beethoven is cultured and his music raised on a pedestal by the musical elite, and to like it is to be like them, cultured? How much of that has influenced me in liking Beethoven in the first place?'

'That's very interesting,' said Kimble, not the slightest bit interested in her ramblings. He wanted to get the silly old duffer back on track. 'So, Bartholomew Place...'

'Now I look back on my life I see where I have been blind, misled, whilst all along so sure in myself that everything I did I did for the benefit of people, for their good. Today I see it clearer than I've ever done before, and I see it for what it is; that I was so very wrong. I'm too old, Mr Hemmingway, to keep these things to myself. Before my time is up I feel I must make some amends for my own part in things, albeit a small part. That is why it was fortuitous you contacted me when you did, almost as if my prayers had been answered. Perhaps you have been sent by God.'

He followed her gaze, which settled on a wooden crucifix fastened to a wall above a cabinet. He smiled uncertainly. 'How long did you work at Bartholomew Place, Mrs Bradshaw?'

'Twenty-five years, give or take a few months.'

'A long time.'

'Time to experience many things. I wanted to help people, you see, for as long as I can remember. My mother, bless her, didn't like me being involved in that kind of work, close to people who were not right in the head, as she used to say – couldn't understand why I was drawn to it. But I saw it as a calling. To support people less fortunate than myself. Ill, but not physically – illnesses of the mind, where the damage cannot be seen, cannot be cut out with a surgeon's knife.'

'That's very worthwhile and commendable of you, Mrs Bradshaw. As I said when we spoke over the phone, I've been tasked with writing an article on the state of our mental institutions, past and present; how they've changed and the levels of care, that kind of thing.'

'Yes, that is something that desperately needs to be written.'

This was going to be far easier than he first thought, Kimble mused. 'I mentioned also that I'd like to talk about a particular patient who resided at Bartholomew Place a number of years ago...'

She shrank back. 'Oh, we can't mention names! Patient confidentiality.'

'Please don't worry about that. Everything will be kept anonymous. We'll call this patient Miss X, shall we?'

She thought about it. 'I suppose that will be acceptable.'

'You were there when a patient called Laura Leach was admitted, correct?'

She struggled within herself. 'No names?'

'No names at all,' he said. 'But a specific patient experience will emphasise the validity of certain treatments.' He thought he was talking bullshit but she nodded in agreement.

'That's true,' she said, as if to give herself reassurance. 'And we will be calling her Miss X, won't we?'

'Yes,' he lied, and found lying was coming far too easily to him.

'And Laura's case was typical of so many young women who passed through Bartholomew Place, if indeed they passed through at all. Some never left. It would be good to use her as an example, as an illustration of the wider malaise.'

What on earth was she going on about, he thought? 'OK,' he said, 'for starters, why was Laura admitted to

Bartholomew Place? I understand from my other source that there was a death involved – is that right?'

'A death. Yes, that's absolutely right. Poor man…'

She fell infuriatingly silent as her mind wandered back over past events. 'Mrs Bradshaw?' he prompted.

'Laura Leach came to Bartholomew Place the same year I retired,' she began, her fingers fumbling beneath the blanket. 'That would be 1959. She was about seventeen years old, as I remember. A snip of a thing. Terribly shaken, afraid, not knowing what was happening to her. I didn't know the full story at first, not till I had access to all her notes.

'She'd been away at boarding school. Bullied relentlessly it appears, which drove her into such lonely depths one can hardly imagine. When she was old enough her father paid for her to take driving lessons. The driving instructor was a young man, married with a child. We never knew his name, of course. It seems she fell for his easy charms, and, perhaps, he genuinely did care for her. But Laura, being so young and impressionable, deprived of companionship and warmth for so long, fell in love with him, or what innocent and impressionable young women like Laura mistake for love. He should have known better, of course – she was only just sixteen. But in a moment of weakness, madness – perhaps even true love – they…' She lapsed into silence again, looking up at Kimble. 'Well, you know. I needn't describe the details. Maybe this was only intended to be a one-off on the man's part. Maybe they both realised the mistake they had made. We shall never know. But as is the way with these things it took only the once and she became pregnant with his child.

'She didn't know what was happening to her at first, being innocent of such things. But it dawned on the deputy headmistress, who noticed the telltale swelling and who insisted on calling out a doctor to examine Laura. When they discovered she was pregnant that's when things blew up. Laura refused to believe the evidence of her own eyes at first, but when the truth could not be ignored, instead of being horrified she was beside herself with joy at the prospect. The sheer magic of a new life, something that she would nurture and give all the love she never had, swamped all other practicalities and misgivings.

The headmaster informed Laura's father at once, and took it on himself to privately inform the young driving instructor. Both parties took it badly. Unable to bear the shame, to face the consequences of what he'd done and the consequences for his marriage, the driving instructor took his own life, apparently dying of carbon monoxide poisoning inside the very car in which they'd conceived the child.

'Laura was grief stricken at the news. But her father came at once to take her from school and bring her back to Devereux Towers. He was immensely angry and disgusted that Laura had not only brought disgrace upon herself and her family but had compounded things by bringing about the death of the young man, tearing apart his family in the process. He heaped full blame for all that had happened on Laura, and Laura alone.

'Abortion being out of the question, she was kept a virtual prisoner in Devereux Towers till the child was born. She named the baby Alex, though it was never christened such, because the child was taken from her as soon as the umbilical cord was cut. She cried out for it as the midwife wrapped the baby in a blanket and carried it from the room. She never saw the baby again.

'Her father could not forgive her. He was already a man with a voice in Langbridge, standing on the town council as well as being from the wealthiest family in the area. He put her behaviour down to a diseased mind and he used his influence to have her sectioned and sent away to Bartholomew Place.'

Leonard Kimble had stopped scribbling on his pad a while ago, engrossed by her story. 'You mean Laura was sent to an asylum primarily because she was a young woman who had a baby out of wedlock?'

She nodded gravely. 'You imagine this to be an isolated incident, young man? Do you know how many women have been put into asylums for this very reason, the country over? How many years some of them stayed in these places? As for Laura, like so many others she was sterilised whilst inside Bartholomew Place, so she could never have children again. They believed people with mental health issues should not have children. So you see that's why I needed to tell my story to you, to the national press. Poor Laura was but one amongst many women who have had to endure this barbarism by our so-called care system.'

'She wasn't mad?'

'It depends who is making the judgement. Pregnancy in one so young was once considered the act of a degenerative mind. The additional suicide of the father was a double blow for Laura. It sealed her fate.'

'But her father – he pushed for this to happen?'

'He actively sought it, yes. Laura was in Bartholomew Place for many, many years.'

'She didn't kill anyone?' he asked.

'Not directly. Her only crime was the opposite – she gave birth. Are you getting all this down, young man?' she said curtly, nodding at his frozen pen.

'Yes, I am,' he said. 'But being held in such a place for all those years – could this have had a negative effect on her mind?'

'It can't have had any other.'

'Could it have made her violent, for instance?'

She frowned at his bluntness. 'Who knows what effect such a lengthy immersion can have on people? Anger, vengeance, an inability to make relationships, suicide – they are all possibilities. The loss of her baby made Laura both inconsolable and angry, till that anger was driven out of her by various treatments. Or they tried. Who knows what kind of legacy that leaves on a sane mind? You must help me, Mr Hemmingway; you must help me bring all this to light by bringing it to the attention of the wider public. For all I know such practices are still going on, even though it is 1976. I need to get my story out for all those women who have suffered and who continue to suffer.'

'And the baby?' he asked. 'What became of Laura's baby?'

'It was given to a childless couple living in Langbridge.'

'And Laura never knew who they were? Never knew where her child lived?'

She shook her head. 'She never knew. It was her father who orchestrated finding the couple and arranged for the baby to be adopted. No one outside Devereux Towers or Bartholomew Place knew of Laura's pregnancy. It was kept a close secret. But even close secrets leak out, especially in a place like Langbridge.'

'Do you know who the child is, and where it is now?'

Ellen Bradshaw's eyes began to water. Kimble didn't know whether it was the heat from the fire or emotion that prompted them. 'No names?' she asked again, firmer. 'You have to promise me that. And it must not go any further than you or I. The child does not know its sad beginnings or who its real mother is. It would be devastating to find out such a thing, as you can imagine.'

'Yes, I promise,' said Kimble, 'it will be our secret. And it is good for your health to get things off your chest.'

'I shall tell you who the child is,' she said, her jaw stiffening. 'But first put away your pad and pen.'

* * * *

32

Caught in a Strong Beam

Martin Caldwell sat behind his desk, his head in his hand. The other hand held a glass, its sides smeared with the remains of the vodka he'd downed. But he couldn't get drunk. There was a time it used to have an effect, not always good but necessary. It dulled things somewhat, took the edge off them. Tonight, though, that edge remained brutally sharp.

The hard bristle of his unshaven chin irritated his hand. He knew he looked a sorry sight; his hair lank and uncared for; dark shadows beneath red and bleary eyes; and he no longer wore a suit and tie. So much for starting afresh, he thought dismally. So much for being able to dump the past, wipe the slate clean, become someone else. Someone new and unsoiled.

God, he wished tonight was over and done with.

He would have poured out another shot but the bottle was empty.

He could call the entire thing off, of course, before it was too late.

But it was already too late and he knew that. Events were rolling on, seemingly uncontrollable and at speed, like a driverless truck hurtling down a steep hill with no brakes. All he could do was close his eyes and wait for the impact. Only then would it be truly over. Maybe, when it was, he could try wiping the slate clean again. Create a completely new life somewhere else.

How ironic, he thought, that in order for him to create his new life, someone else had to die tonight.

For Katherine, life had become painfully intolerable. Life without Felix wasn't a life at all. She could never have foreseen how desperately she loved him. She'd known love before, or something she'd sorely mistaken for love, but all along these types of love had been lies. Only now did she fully understand what the word meant, its joy and its torture, brought into sharp focus only by his disappearance. Something inside her felt sorrow for all those people she'd duped, because now she felt what they must have felt, and it was excruciating. It was eating her up, gnawing at her insides like a ravenous beast and she thought she'd go mad with the agony.

Then there was the envelope, shoved through her letterbox without a stamp. A note from Laura. If she wanted to know where Felix was she had to meet her tonight, on the outskirts of Langbridge. In the car park by a small patch of woodland, a local beauty spot.

Hope rose in her breast. When she got Felix back it would mark the end of this kind of life, she vowed silently. They'd move abroad, settle down and have kids, grow old together.

But if she found out anything had happened to him then Laura fucking Leach was going to pay for it. She was going to suffer anyway. Laura Leach was a dead woman whichever way things turned out, because Martin had arranged it so.

Katherine's expression hardened. When she looked in the mirror she hardly recognised herself. She touched the spot on her cheek where the walking stick had struck her. It was still sore and bruised. The bitch had almost broken her cheek bone. Felix would tell her she'd let herself go. She really ought to fix herself up when she got back, she thought. Get her hair done, buy some new clothes. Christ, it was as if this place and its people had a toxic effect on her. She could feel it attacking her, as if the very air was poisonous. She narrowed her eyes. Stop moping, you sullen old woman, she told herself; you've business to attend to.

She put on a raincoat – it was pissing it down outside. This place was always damp, she thought. She'd be glad to be shut of it. She went into the kitchen and picked up a small knife, which she placed in her coat pocket. She didn't trust that fucked-up bitch one inch.

The rain drenched the car's windscreen and the wiper blades had difficulty in keeping it clear. She peered hard into the darkness ahead; Langbridge was now a mile or so behind her. Beyond the car's headlights there was only the impenetrable blackness of open countryside, the road awash and looking like a turbulent stream. She almost missed the turning to the car park, had to stop, reverse back up the road a little and swing the car round hard. The uneven ground was strewn with deep puddles, the car's wheels dropping into water-filled potholes. She brought it to a halt, turning off the engine but keeping the lights burning, listening to the heavy drumming of the rain on the thin metal roof of the car. The headlights lit up a line of trees, stark and bare and marking the edge of the wood.

She checked her watch but could hardly make out the time in the gloom. Katherine grabbed her umbrella, stepped outside. Cold rain prickled her face, drove into her thin coat. The wind caused the trees to moan in lament, and the sound of the rain pounding the sodden ground was like the hissing of steam from some great engine. The car park was empty. The land all around was empty. It was as if the world had ceased to exist.

'Laura, are you there?' she shouted above the sound of the rain. There was no sign of any car, and when she looked back at the road she saw it was empty. No car lights to indicate anything was coming. If this was some kind of perverse joke, she thought, getting heated up and grasping the knife in her coat pocket…

Then she heard the sound of something moving beyond the line of trees. Thought she saw some kind of movement in the dark undergrowth. She strained her eyes to try to see what it was but it was near impossible. The car's headlights were still blazing, but outside their limited reach it was difficult to make anything out. The sketchy outline of trees against the fractionally lighter band of sky, and that was all.

She wished she'd brought a torch. She forgot how dark the countryside was when night fell. She was more suited to a better-lit urban life and would be glad as hell to get back to it. Katherine narrowed her eyes, her hand lifting the knife out into the open. The sounds stopped. She listened intently.

Nothing. Nothing except the sound of this blasted weather. She was letting her imagination run away with her. Katherine turned back to look at the road. Where the hell was that bitch?

The blow to the back of her head caused her to drop instantly to her hands and knees. The pain crashed into her, her body afire with it. She was vaguely aware of the sounds of splashing footsteps behind her, tried to scramble to her feet, her vision a firework display of sparks. Katherine opened her mouth to scream.

The second blow caved her skull in and she fell flat, dead before her face hit the mud and boiling rain. Her blood gushed in a torrent down the side of her face, into her open eye, washed into a puddle of water that ran into her mouth and filled it.

The third blow from the Fijian war club caused her head to dissolve into a bloody pulp. The end of the club rested there a second or two, in the bowl of her broken skull; and then it was twirled around the mush of bloodied brains and hair like a paintbrush being dipped into a pot of paint, till it was fully coated in a thick, gooey gloss.

Leonard Kimble was horrified. He stood on the bridge overlooking the river, on his way back from the retirement home and his fruitful interview with Ellen Bradshaw. He was initially buoyed up by his scoop. The elation fizzed out when he saw that the river had indeed broken its banks. Where once there had been the familiar silver thread of the Lang there was only a massive lake of water. It looked almost alive, he thought, malevolent nature in the raw.

When he stepped off the bridge he was concerned that the water was already a foot deep, the roads and pathways already submerged. The main street through Langbridge was like a river itself, cars ploughing through the water like tiny beetles. And the rain didn't show any signs of stopping either. In fact it looked like it was getting worse.

Oh, Christ, he thought; I'm going to die! I'm too young to die!

In a blind panic he waded as fast as he could through the rising floodwater, the reflections of the streetlamps splintering and sparking on the water's agitated surface, cursing that he'd never bothered to learn to swim.

Shopkeepers were doing their best to stop the water entering their premises, some of them having produced sandbags and building tiny walls with them, but it was too late – the rapidly rising water brought forth a rising flood of despair and distraught faces. Someone screamed and that made Leonard Kimble panic even more. Get to high ground, he thought. High ground? This fucking place didn't have any high ground. They were all going to die!

The woman from the Empire's kiosk was hammering at Martin Caldwell's office door but there was no answer. 'Mr Caldwell!' she called, 'there's water coming in through the front doors. There's a flood, just like in 1947. Mr Caldwell!' She opened his door and was shocked to see him slumped on the desk, an empty bottle of Vodka beside him. She went over to him, gave him a gentle shake. He stirred, but not by much. 'Mr Caldwell, what are we to do?' He snored loudly and she left him, calling for everyone to get out.

Vince Moody heard muffled screams from the auditorium. He peered through the viewing pane and saw some kind of commotion going on in the dark. A flurry of activity down in the front rows. He checked his projectors were set OK before going down to see what all the fuss was about.

He was almost bowled over by people bursting through the swing doors. He pushed his way through the stream of panicking cinemagoers into the auditorium, and met Edith.

'Vince, there's water coming in, down there.' She pointed to the screen. 'There's tons of it; the building's filling up fast.'

People were vacating their chairs in a hurry, crashing against each other in the mad rush to get upstairs to the exits. Vince could make out the swirling water below, already creeping up to the third row of seats.

'Bugger!' he said. 'Make sure everyone gets out, Edith. Get them to stay calm. I'll switch the lights on.'

He ran up to the projection booth, hit the light-switches and closed the projectors down. When he got back down to the auditorium someone was badgering Edith for a refund on his ticket and the popcorn he'd been made to leave behind; it was a king-size tub, he complained, hardly started at all. Vince persuaded him to leave and he'd make sure he got his refund.

'So has anyone told Caldwell yet?' he asked Edith as they descended the steps to survey the damage. He was surprised at how much water was getting in; the lower half of the auditorium now resembled the local swimming baths.

'He was asleep, apparently. Drunk.'

'Never mind him,' said Vince. 'Is everyone out?' He could see the place was empty except for the two of them.

'I think so,' said Edith. 'Someone's called for the fire brigade and police.'

'We have to make sure all staff are accounted for and safe, too,' he said. 'Double check for customers, check the toilets, things like that; I want to make sure everyone is out.' Then his face paled in horror.

'What's wrong, Vince?' Edith asked as he put a hand to his forehead.

'My stash of old films, down in the basement!' he cried. 'They'll be ruined! I've got to save them!'

'Oh, Vince, don't go down there, you'll be drowned!'

'Just do as I say, and I'll make sure Caldwell is OK, too. I'll be fine.'

'I'd be devastated if anything happened to you, Vince!' she said in alarm, her doe-eyes awash with worry.

Vince leant his head forward and gave her a peck on the lips, surprised at his sudden boldness, and basking in her concern for him. 'I'll be fine, I told you,' he said. 'Really, I will.'

He dashed at once up the stairs to Caldwell's office, and barged in. Caldwell was still asleep at his desk, snoring loudly.

'Mr Caldwell!' he said. But the man was well-under. He grabbed the basement keys off the hook on the wall and hurried down the corridor.

'Where do you think you're going?' said a deep voice behind him.

He turned to see a fireman in his dark uniform and bright-yellow helmet striding purposefully towards him. 'I've got to go to the basement,' said Vince.

'No you haven't,' said the officer. 'That's the one place you aren't going. You know there's a flood, don't you?'

'I've got to get something,' he said, running to a door, swinging it open and bolting down steps. He heard the fireman chasing after him.

'I can't allow that!' he called. 'Get yourself back up here!'

Vince ignored him, something he'd never imagined himself being able to do, ignore authority. He reached the lower floor and plunged up to his ankles in water. It seemed to take an age to get the key into the lock and get the basement door open. Water was gushing down the stone steps like a miniature waterfall into the dark room. He could also see that the entire floor was flooded already and it seemed to be rising up the walls fast. The reason why was because water wasn't only gushing down the steps, it was being pumped up in a torrent from the old well, the underground watercourse that obviously fed it also bloated beyond its capacity.

'Get up here at once!' said the fireman. 'I'll drag you out if you don't!' he warned.

'I can't leave these films,' Vince said, distressed that even while some film cans appeared to be floating others had sunk.

'Nothing is more valuable than your life!' he said. 'Now stop arguing with me, you little prick, and get your arse up here!'

Vince was grabbing an armful of film cans. 'Here, take a few,' he insisted.

'Bollocks!' said the fireman, stomping down the steps towards Vince.

'Don't you care about Laurel and Hardy?' Vince gasped.

'Are you for real?' he said, reaching out and grabbing Vince by the arm in a manacle-like grip that Vince couldn't shake off.

Then, unexpectedly, his hold loosened, the fireman's hand slowly falling away to find his torch. 'Oh fuck!' he said quietly.

Vince followed the man's dumbstruck gaze. Poking above the metal grating of the well, waving around in the bubbling and foaming water, was a human hand. Vince was so shocked he dropped the cans of film into the water, his mouth hanging open.

'There's someone in there!' said the fireman, splashing through the water towards the well. He saw that the hand had been mauled by rats, a finger missing. 'It's a dead body,' he said, shining the torch down into the water, through the metal grating and into the well. 'It's a woman, as far as I can tell,' he said. 'The body is all bloated, that's why it's floated to the surface.'

Vince went over to the fireman's side. He looked tentatively into the churning water, the head of the corpse caught clearly in the torch's strong beam. 'That's Monica,' he said.

'Jesus,' mouthed the fireman. 'Look – look underneath her!' His face paled visibly. 'There's another one. There are two bodies in there!'

* * * *

33

When the Bough Breaks

The older the building the easier it was to get inside, generally, thought Ray Steele, forcing open one of the ground-floor windows. It was little wonder that Devereux Towers managed to escape the attentions of any opportunist thief who happened upon it. Perhaps it evaded attention because it was tucked so far out of the way and looked like it hadn't been lived in for ages, hardly seemed worth the effort. He slid the window up, climbed through into the darkened room beyond. He carried with him a black plastic bag, something bulky and heavy inside, wrapped up to protect it from the rain.

He paused in the blackness, listening for any sounds. Satisfied all was clear he took off his muddy, slip-on shoes and placed them by the skirting board; he didn't want any footprints giving away the fact someone had broken in, wandered through the rooms. He wanted it to appear as if he'd never been here at all.

He tramped silently across the bare boards of the empty room, opened the door. The entrance hall was in complete darkness and deserted. It was late, it was to be expected. Laura Leach was upstairs in bed, unaware what was planned for her. He took out a tiny torch and lit his way to another door across the other side of the entrance hall. Still no sound of movement from upstairs.

He stopped by the door, listened. Clutched the black plastic bag tight and turned the door handle, went inside. This room gave him the creeps – the entire place did – but this room in particular. All these fucking weird African masks and statues and things – who in their right minds would pay good money for that ugly shit and then put it on display? That's the trouble with these people with money, all in-bred eccentrics with no fucking taste.

He went over to the wall of tribal masks, to a chest that stood below them. He carefully opened the lid. It was empty. He slowly unwrapped the object he carried, slipping it from its black plastic cocoon.

The Fijian war club still glistened with Katherine's blood, tiny lumps of something meaty and strands of hair sticking to it. He was glad he'd managed to get it here without the rain washing the blood from it. That had been tricky, given how heavy it had been coming down. He wore black leather gloves so as not to get his prints on the club, but noticed a little blood on them. He'd have to burn them, he thought as he put the club in the chest and closed the lid on it.

It had been all too easy, he thought, breaking in the first time and stealing one of the clubs. Even easier breaking-in the second time round, now he knew his way around the place. All he had to do now to complete his end of the bargain was to get behind the blue door in the tower and then get the hell out of there.

Ray Steele stole quietly out of the study, thinking how this was a piece of piss. He could do this with his eyes closed. It had been a while since he'd had to use his nocturnal skills, and in truth he was quite enjoying the experience. Just like being a kid all over again. It's where he cut his teeth, breaking and entering.

He found the entrance to the tower easily and mounted the spiral staircase, his feet making hardly any sound at all on the old, wooden treads. Finding the so-called blue door was even easier, given that it was the only one that had been painted, with the remainder in the tower being in varnished wood. It was locked, as he'd been told, but he'd come prepared. This type of lock was no problem for Ray Steele. He'd made a career out of opening locked doors.

He took out a small cloth case and unrolled it. It was filled with the tools of his trade, from which he selected the most appropriate pick and set about testing the sturdy,

Victorian lock. It gave after only thirty seconds. You're getting rusty, he thought; used to be far faster than that.

A slight pause to listen for any activity and then Steele pushed open the blue door.

Laura's hand was covered in blood. She stared at it as if the writhing fingers didn't belong to her.

She was sitting on the bathroom floor, the tiles also spattered with blood. She was crying, and when she went to wipe away a tear she smeared blood onto her eyelid, like grotesque eyeshadow. In her right hand she brandished a knife, the blade also smeared with glistening blood. She lifted the knife, pressed it against the flesh of her left arm, denting the skin. With a slow, deliberate movement she drew the blade across her skin, and blood gushed freely from the deep cut, as it gushed from the other cuts on her arm that she'd made that night. The bright-red cut stood in stark contrast to the pale scars of past mutilations.

The pain was tremendous, she thought, biting her lower lip, but it didn't dull the mental pain she endured, not like it used to; it would not go away, the torture continuing unabated. The cutting did not help tonight.

She tossed the knife away, as she'd thrown so many away. Each time the knife had to be fresh otherwise it wouldn't work. It would not release her from her torment.

Oh, Casper! She wept again. Why did you do it? Why? I loved you, I really did!

She remembered the night he came; the night she confronted him with his deception, not wanting to believe he was capable of such a heinous act. She'd almost been willing to forgive him anything. Almost. But it was true – he had deceived her, and though she should have been furious with him she found she only wept for what might have been. She remembered how he cowered in fear before the knife, though she was hardly aware she still had it in her hand. All she wanted was to hear him tell her it he was a fraud. Hear it come from his sweet lips. Only then would she believe it.

When he confessed she calmly unlocked the door and let him out. He paused to turn and look back, angrily calling her a crazy bitch, before getting into his car and taking her new future with him. She never saw him again. Didn't know where he went after leaving Devereux Towers, but guessed it was back to her, to Katherine, to lie in her arms and tell her all the beautiful things he'd whispered so fluently, so practiced, so meaningfully.

When the sound of his car faded into the night she turned the knife she had on herself, cutting and cutting and cutting; slashing her arm, sobbing and cutting some more. Please, she begged, take the pain away. She discovered that he'd left his jacket behind, slumped over the back of a chair and she lifted it up to her nose, smelling his warm presence there, the dashed hopes and her crushed dreams. Copious amounts of blood dripped off her damaged arm and smeared the jacket sleeve. She heard something tinkle and reached inside the pocket. It was a bunch of house keys.

Did she hate him for it? Strangely, no. Her venom was reserved for the woman who possessed him. Not for her callous plans to rob her of money – what was money, after all? No, she loathed her because she had what she believed would be hers. She had Casper.

And Casper – how he looked like the father of her child. So similar, in fact, that she almost wanted to believe he had been sent back from the dead to be her lover once again. Sent back so she could be forgiven his death. God had not abandoned her, the sins of the past forgiven. But He hadn't forgiven her at all; all along God had been mocking her, dreaming up far greater punishments. It was just as her father had predicted; you'll always be a bad person, Laura, he'd told her. You cannot wash away sin. His blood will always be on your hands.

She shook away the hurtful memories and looked at those same hands. Yes, the blood was still there. Blood was everywhere.

Laura heard a noise. The faintest of sounds. Her heart quickened. Someone was in the house. Not far away.

She bent and picked up the bloodied knife from the tiled floor and rose to her feet. The deep slashes on her arm dribbled blood down to soak her hand, down the long blade in thick rivulets; dripped steadily to the floor to splash in a trail of little scarlet rosettes as she padded barefoot to the door.

Ray Steele turned his torch on. He hadn't known what to expect, but it certainly wasn't this.

There was an empty wooden cot pushed against the wall; above it there hung a mobile of chunky, wooden ducks on strings; a tiny chest of drawers decorated with flowers was placed near the cot, sitting on top of this a pile of neatly-folded baby clothes; there was a teddy bear on a stool, its coal-black button eyes watching him; a spinning-top lay beside a carefully arranged set of children's building blocks on a rug; a small bookcase was filled with children's story books; the wallpaper was printed with hot air balloons and birds.

There was nothing odd or special about this room at all. No valuables, no safe. It was a nursery. A nursery without a baby.

He shook his head and smiled to himself, crept quietly over to the cot. It had a name painted on its wooden side: Alex. He squinted against the gloom, played the torch over the cot; there looked to be something inside beneath the soft, woollen blanket. He bent down, peeled the blanket back to reveal a tiny, pink head.

It was a doll. He was getting jumpy over a damned doll!

The scream, shrill and from the depths of the soul, caused him to start violently and he accidentally dropped the torch into the cot. It lit up the blue plastic eyes of the doll.

'What are you doing? What are you doing?' Laura exclaimed, bounding over to the man. 'Get out, get out, get out!' She lunged at him with the knife, narrowly missing his head and spattering his face with droplets of warm blood from her arm. She screamed loudly, yelling unintelligible words at him.

Ray Steel ran for the door, pushing against Laura, his hand catching the knife and he yelled out in pain as the blade scored deep into his fingers. Laura was at his back in an instant, the room filled with her strident yelling. In the dark, Ray reached out to steady himself on the banister. He felt the searing pain from his bloodied hand, which slid down the banister on the blood as easily as if the thing had been greased. It caused him to lose his footing on the stairs.

He tumbled momentarily into a black void, and then his head crashed against the hard, wooden treads, his body cartwheeling uncontrollably down the stairs, his ears filled with the sound of a devilish, screaming banshee.

And then he came to rest and all was silent. He was on his back, his head facing down the stairs and he could just make out the strange, unnatural angle of his broken arm. But he could feel no pain. He should be feeling pain!

'Help me,' he said plaintively. 'Help me.'

He was aware of a shadow looming over him. He couldn't make out the features of her face, but her hair was like a ragged halo, her breathing deep and heavy. He saw the knife in her hand. 'I can't feel my legs,' he said, sobbing. 'And my arms - I can't feel those either. I can't feel anything!' He could feel tears though, as they ran hot down his temples to his ears. "I think I've broken my back... You've got to help me!'

'Who are you?' she said, her voice hoarse.

'Please help me – I could die!'

She looked at the knife. 'Yes, you could, if you didn't get help soon. It was you who broke into my house before, wasn't it?' He was blubbering. 'I knew someone had been in. Tell me it was you and I'll call for help. You might have all manner of internal injuries. You might be bleeding to death.'

'Don't let me die,' he pleaded. 'I beg you – I don't want to die!'

'It was you, wasn't it?'

'Yes,' he panted, 'it was me.'

'So why did you do that? Nothing was stolen.' She bent down, closer to his face. Her breath warm on his cheek. 'I'm sticking the point of my knife deep into your arm. Can you feel it? I'll bet you can't.'

He shook his head. 'I can't! I can't! Please…'

'But something was stolen, wasn't it?'

He nodded quickly. 'Yes, I stole one of your old clubs from the study.'

Laura sat down on the step beside him. 'One of my father's war clubs? Whatever for?'

'He paid me to do it.'

'Who paid you to do what?'

Help me, please…'

'Who paid you to do what?'

Martin Caldwell – he paid me.'

'I don't know anyone called Martin Caldwell,' she said.

'He's the manager at the Empire cinema. He paid me to kill Katherine, the woman who tried to con you. He told me to make it look like you'd done it, because he said he knew you'd been harassing her.'

'Go on,' she said evenly.

'Get me some help! I'm not saying anymore!'

'Then you'll die here on the stairs.'

He tried to make his arms and legs move, but failed, gasping. 'He wanted people would blame you,' he said. 'So I stole one of your clubs…'

'What of Katherine? Have you killed her?' She said it matter-of-factly, which terrified him. 'I'm not saying any more!'

She plunged the knife into his arm at a point where he could see it. 'Look how deep it's going in, and yet still you can't feel any pain.'

'OK, OK, I used the club to kill her tonight. She's dead. The plan was to plant the club with her blood on it here then alert the police in some way. They'd find the club and put two and two together. It's downstairs, in the study inside a chest. Martin wanted to get rid of Katherine once and for all – she was blackmailing him, and he wanted you to take the rap. Now please phone for an ambulance. You have to help me!'

'You soiled my baby's room,' she said hollowly. 'You defiled it. You might have woken the baby up.'

'There is no fucking baby!' he said, coughing on blood. 'It's a doll!'

'Keep your voice down. Little ones are such light sleepers.' She began to sing a lullaby, rose to her feet and ascended the stairs, dropping the knife. It bounced down the stairs and landed near Ray Steele's anguished face.

'Where are you going?' he said, his voice choked. 'Don't leave me here. I need an ambulance! I've told you everything – you've got to help me!'

'*When the bough breaks the cradle will fall...*' sang Laura, going to the blue-painted door. She went inside, slowly closing the door behind her. '*...and down will come baby, cradle and all...*'

* * * *

34

Rulers of an Empire

The clod of earth thumped against the coffin lid, the hollow sound like that of someone kicking against a door, he thought. The next handful of dirt tossed into the grave sounded like rice being dropped onto an open umbrella. It fascinated him. He had been like this all morning – no real emotion, no sadness, just a series of vacuous observations, almost as if he weren't part of the events taking place around him. Some kind of heavenly spirit sent down to observe the comings and goings of earthly mortals.

For Vince Moody this was his first funeral. A rite of passage he could tick off his list. He'd been to weddings and christenings and this was the final piece of the trilogy. Poor Laura. He didn't have to attend, of course. He wasn't family. He never really knew her and she never knew him. Their lives had only brushed by each other for brief moments in the Empire cinema. Ships in the night, and all that. But he was over Laura Leach now, thankfully. It had been a passing phase, a temporary madness from which he'd recovered, and Edith had been crucial in helping him down the recovery road.

Edith was standing beside him, looking down at Laura's coffin. He thought she looked even more beautiful dressed in black, with her hair tied up into an elegant knot, not unlike Audrey Hepburn from certain angles. She moved her hand closer to his and he felt her cold fingers enmesh with his. Their breath came out in clouds to mingle, become one, breath that drifted gossamer-like over the open grave. She'd been eager to attend the funeral, and he'd no idea why. Perhaps she wanted to make sure she was gone from their lives, see it with her own eyes; eyes which were curiously moist, he thought.

Laura had been found dead in the stream near Devereux Towers. She'd taken her own life a few weeks after she'd told the police everything. No foul play suspected, they said. She was depressed, on medication, had been for years. She'd been in Bartholomew Place for a long time. Inevitable, was a word someone used. Maybe it was, maybe it wasn't. In her will she'd left all her money to a children's home somewhere, which Vince thought was very thoughtful of her. Devereux Towers was up for sale and already a prospective buyer was interested in turning it into a hotel. But he couldn't dredge up a single ounce of the feelings he once had for Laura. Why was that? Surely there should be something he could let her have, a last tear, a final tiny morsel from his heart? But no, not a single thing could he release for her, and maybe it was because Edith had become the centre of his attentions now; she soaked up everything he had like a black hole swallows up light.

Before the funeral service in church, Edith had told him how handsome he looked. She openly admired his new haircut, his new shirt, his new suit. How different he looked, she said. A real change had come over him, and it was a change for the good. He was manager now and looked the part, too.

His promotion had come as a surprise to him. It was, in part, recognition of his long service with the cinema, his positive actions on the night of the flood when his manager was asleep and drunk in his office – actions Edith had been all too eager to embellish when interviewed by the bigwigs from HQ. But of course they also needed someone to replace the thoroughly disgraced Martin Caldwell, a safe pair of hands. They wanted to lay the memory of Martin Caldwell to rest as quickly as they tumbled earth into Laura's grave.

The police arrested Caldwell within a day or two of the flood and the discovery of the two bodies in the well. They charged him with their murder. The evidence was clear –

pregnant Monica had been blackmailing him – Vince had told the police as much, told them all he knew. And they found his missing Oscar statuette in the well, its base dented from where it had caved Monica's skull in before he disposed of her body. And the other body, the man's, this belonged to the guy whom Caldwell was living in fear of. Caldwell's sordid past came flooding out as quickly as the water did from the well; how he'd used the fire-axe by the door to finish off Felix before dumping him in the well too. They say he wasn't dead when he was pushed in, but that he drowned. The fire-axe was also found in the well. The thing was, Caldwell might have evaded detection hadn't a botched attempt to frame Laura for the murder of Felix's girlfriend sealed his fate. The man who broke into Devereux Towers with the intention of planting the murder weapon, confessed everything to the police.

Caldwell denied everything, very convincingly, but the evidence against him was overwhelming. They had motivations, they had murder weapons, they had bags of evidence from interviews with Empire employees, and now Martin Caldwell was about to serve a life sentence for committing three murders. Who'd have thought it?

Poor Laura; she'd suffered so much at their scheming hands, had no idea what she was involved in, what part she was to play. And now she was dead, just like Ophelia, said Edith. Vince had no idea who Ophelia was, but didn't say anything so as not to betray his ignorance. But he ought to forget Laura now, because Edith and he were together now, a couple, a unit; they were soulmates. They even whispered tentatively of marriage in a year or two. In the meantime Vince was taking driving lessons, and by the end of the New Year he hoped to have passed his driving test. There was a lovely MGB-GT he had set his sights on. A beauty, only a year old. As manager of the Empire he could afford to take out a bank loan now. By Christmas he'd be driving around Somerset in his very own sports car. Who'd have thought that, too? Even his mum and dad started to smile at him when they spoke, and finally began to say encouraging things about him to other people.

HQ had suggested that once Monica's body had been released for burial Vince should attend the funeral. He didn't have to, they said, not really, but now he was manager he had obligations. She had been an employee. He should show his face, for outward appearances if nothing else. After all, it had been a tragic affair, and no one deserved to get murdered, not even Monica. Buy a wreath, on behalf of the company. Not too expensive though, because budgets were tight, what with the planned refurbishment and all. So he'd get to go to his second funeral soon.

Vince looked up. There was no one else stood around the grave but the vicar, Edith and himself. Not one relation to mourn Laura's passing. Standing some distance away he saw Leonard Kimble. He had his hands in his pockets, shoulders hunched against the bitter cold. And he was smiling, which Vince thought a little odd. Smiling at Edith and him. Kimble gave a quick wave and then walked away. What was he doing here? Was that business or personal, thought Vince.

Edith and Vince walked back to the Empire. It was currently closed because of the refurbishment. Builders were coming in the next day to cap off the old well with concrete and re-concrete the entire basement floor as part of the planned changes. Vince also had a couple of interviews to carry out with prospective new projectionists. HQ thought it best if fresh faces were brought in. a clean slate. Vince had argued the case that he should have a deputy manager and had managed to shoehorn Edith into the new role, making the most of her brave actions and utter commitment to the Empire on the night of the flood. HQ agreed with scarce a bat of an eyelid. He guessed they were simply glad to get things moving along and get back to normal.

That afternoon, Edith and Vince informed a young man that he was to become the new projectionist when the cinema reopened for business.

'The future's going to be big for the Empire,' Vince said to him. 'We've got great plans for the place – more screens, more X-rated films in an evening, more bums on seats, securing your future and mine...'

Edith smiled openly at Vince's newfound confidence.

'You and I, we're going to make this place special,' she said when the new projectionist had left.

'We are,' he agreed, kissing her and never failing to marvel at how cushion-soft her full lips were. 'It belongs to us now. We're rulers of an Empire!'

* * * *

35

Truly, Madly, Forever

Edith left Vince making a phone call regarding the building work going ahead the next morning. She was so happy, and decided to wander the empty corridors to take in all that they had achieved. She could hardly believe the swift turn of events. There was so much to be done, she thought. The Empire would be transformed under their joint managership. Once more it would become a place of dreams.

'Ah, mine, all mine,' said a voice behind her as she stood before the massive cinema screen imagining all the movies as yet to be projected upon it.

She turned. 'Leonard,' she said. 'You surprised me.'

'Lenny,' he said. 'Why so formal all of a sudden?' Leonard Kimble strolled down the centre aisle towards her, his footsteps muffled by the thick carpet. 'The flood did a lot of damage,' he observed, nodding at the muddy-grey gunge on the ruined carpets in front of the stage. 'Going to cost something to get it all fixed.'

'It was being refurbished anyway,' she said. 'I saw you today, at Laura Leach's funeral. Did you know her?'

'I knew her better than most, I guess. The entire story was good for the Gazette, though; good for me too, if I'm honest. That level of scandal in Langbridge will not come around again in a hurry.'

'I'm pleased for you,' said Edith.

'You don't like me, do you, Edith?'

The comment wasn't expected. 'What on earth makes you say that?'

He shrugged. 'The way you look at me. The way you talk to me. Little things.'

'What is it you want, Leonard? If you need to speak to Vince he's up in his office.'

'Yes, good old Vince. Done well for himself out of this, hasn't he?'

'He deserves to do well,' she said.

'Why him, Edith, eh? I mean, he's a born loser, a nobody. He looks like a baboon wearing a suit. Why would you choose someone like him over someone like me?'

'Vince is a nice, gentle-hearted man. I don't think you ought to be saying such things. You shouldn't even be in here. You're trespassing, so I think you should leave.'

'You really think you're someone, don't you? I know your mum and dad; they think they're better than anyone else with their fancy Volvo, avocado-coloured bathroom suite and lawn sprinklers.'

Edith made as if to walk past him. 'It's time you left now, Leonard, before you say something you shouldn't. If you don't leave, I'll – '

'You'll what?' he said, grabbing her by the arm, jamming his face close to hers.

'I'll tell Vince.'

'I'm *so* scared!' he mocked. 'You're all the same, you women – you girls. Tarts, every last one of you, only good for one thing.'

'Let me go, you're starting to hurt me! What's gotten into you?'

'What would your precious Vince say if he knew the truth about you?'

She frowned deeply. 'I've no idea what you're talking about. Let me go!'

'I know who you are.'

She yanked her arm free. 'You're crazy, Leonard!' she said, storming away up the aisle. 'I'm going to get Vince.'

'Your mum and dad – they aren't your real parents, Edith.'

Edith stopped in her tracks and turned round. 'What are you babbling on about? Of course they're my real parents. Are you ill or something?'

'Ever wondered how your mother managed to conceive, given that she'd had a hysterectomy a few years before you were born?'

'That's not true! I'm going to get the police.'

'But it is true, Edith. I've seen hospital records and spoken to the woman who knew your real mother. You were adopted, Edith. They're not your real parents. Mad Laura Leach was your real mother.'

Edith was speechless, the words she wanted to say drying up on her tongue. A swarm of strange, disturbing thoughts stung her mind. 'Why are you creating all these absurd lies, Leonard? What do you hope to gain from it?'

He came towards her. 'They're not lies, Edith. You were the result of an affair between Laura and a married driving instructor. He killed himself because of it; she was put into Bartholomew Place because of it. Want to know what your real name was going to be? Alex – Alexandra, that's what Laura called you, but that was never the name they were going to christen you. You were taken from her at birth and given like so much unwanted and troublesome baggage to a nice, discreet couple who couldn't have children. You've been living a lie all this time. Just think if word got out you were actually loony Laura's bastard child, your mother the suicidal Witch of Devereux Towers. Why, Vince wouldn't want you, would he? Not now he's a manager and on the up. You'd become the laughingstock of the town, someone people would point out when you walked down the street. There's that bastard, Edith – or is it Alex? They love that sort of thing around here. And think about it; proper legal channels weren't followed when you were adopted, either. All done on the quiet. On the sly. Your dad was a crafty old geezer. Pulled the right strings to make it happen, keep it hush-hush. Your mum and dad might even go to court for it. At the very least they'd have to leave Langbridge. You all would. So you see, everyone's been living a lie. You're a nobody, Edith; the result of a sordid affair with so-called parents that were willing to take a child to satisfy their own shortcomings and help cover the whole thing up. Technically, you don't belong anywhere.'

She sat on one of the cinema seats. She often wondered why there was no resemblance to her mother and father. Why they avoided talking about her birth, or why they couldn't provide a birth certificate – destroyed, they said, or lost; or why they talked so cruelly about Laura Leach when she came back to Devereux Towers. And of course it made sense why her Aunty Liz always referred to her as the Miracle Baby. Her mother had been barren, she said; she couldn't have children and God had smiled upon them...

'You have proof of all this?' she said quietly.

'Oh yes, lots of it. It's all true.'

'Does anyone else know about this?'

'Not yet. And they needn't,' he said, reaching out and putting a hand on her thigh.

'What is it you're after, Leonard?'

'Isn't it obvious? I want you. I always have.' His hand squeezed her leg, then travelled down to the hem of her skirt.'

'You want me?'

'For starters, yes. We can talk how your parents can help financially a little later. Don't come over all innocent, Edith; you know what it is I want from you.' His fingers ran up inside her skirt, traced a line along the inside of her thigh.

'I've never done that kind of thing before, Leonard...' she said, her eyes filling.

'A virgin? Don't worry, I'll teach you everything there is to know. I've even bought us a pack of condoms from the machine in the toilet.'

She placed her hand on his, stopping him. 'Not here.'

He licked his lower lip. 'Where, then?'

She rose from the seat. 'Follow me,' she said sullenly. They went through a set of doors behind the stage.

'Where are you taking me? Why not do it here, behind the screen? No one will see us.'

Edith stopped. 'You don't have to be like this, Leonard. Why can't you just keep quiet about it all? Why be so nasty?' Her eyes were glistening with tears.

'Because absolute power corrupts absolutely,' he said. 'And I like the idea of being able to get exactly what I want.' He pointed. 'Hurry up and get us to where we're headed.'

They wound their way through dingy corridors, down a flight of steps. Edith eventually paused at a door. 'Please, Leonard. Reconsider...' she said.

'Through there?' he asked. 'What's through there?'

'The basement,' she explained.

His eyes lit up. 'Where they found the bodies?'

She nodded. 'It's quiet; no one comes down here at all. We won't be disturbed.'

He rather liked the idea. The thought of having sex in the very place they'd fished out the two stiffs caused him to get all heated up and he suddenly grabbed Edith by the throat. His hand groped roughly at her breast. He tried to kiss her but she averted her head. There was the sound of ripping cloth as he tore her blouse, revealing her lacy, white bra. Kimble's eyes widened in animal anticipation. 'Fuck it,' he said. 'I want to do it right here, against the door!' He let his hand fall to the hem of her skirt, hoisted it and placed his fingers firmly between her legs, moaning as he felt the soft, resisting mound beneath.

'Leave her alone!'

Vince couldn't believe what he was seeing. He'd been on his way to the basement to check out something following the phone call with the builders, needed to get back to them with more information. His surprise morphed into anger when he saw what Kimble was doing, the pale band of flesh beneath the torn material of Edith's blouse, and her terrified face.

'Fuck off, Moody!' Kimble snarled, continuing to hold Edith by the throat. 'Can't you see that we're busy?'

Vince rushed forward. 'I said let her go!' He grabbed hold of Kimble and tore him away from Edith. Kimble released her, lashed out with his fists and sent Vince reeling backwards with a couple of well-placed blows.

'And I said fuck off, you moron!' said Kimble.

Shaking his dazed head, Vince cried out in rage and launched himself at Kimble again, who tried to fend off a rain of blows, covered his head with his arms. But he wasn't so easily beaten and he threw his entire weight at Vince, bowling him over to the floor. He kicked him in the ribs and Vince wailed in pain.

'Stop it! You'll kill him!' cried Edith.

'Shut up, bitch! I told you he was a fucking loser. You'll get what's coming to you in a bit.' He bent over Vince who was doubled-up in agony. 'Hear that, Moody, you little weed. I'm going to fuck your precious little bitch and I'm going to let you watch. And guess what? She'll let me do it, too, without a tiny fucking squeak of protest, because I know what I know.' He sent another boot into Vince's side, then another, his teeth gritted, his face a devilish mask.

The next instant, Kimble's head lurched sideways, his skull split open at the back, his blood fanning out to splash the walls and the door. He sank immediately to the ground beside Vince, not a single word or breath coming from him and he lay there, a lifeless mound of clothes. Blood oozed into a large puddle on the floor.

Vince looked up. Edith was holding the new fire-axe she'd removed from the hooks on the wall. As soon as he realised what had happened he scrambled painfully to his feet, clutching his bruised ribs. 'Christ, Edith – what have you done?'

'He was hurting you,' she gasped. She dropped the axe to the floor. It clattered noisily. 'I was afraid he was going to kill you.'

'Oh shit!' Vince said, looking down at the still form of Leonard Kimble, the back of his skull missing, a bloody pulp sitting inside the rest of it. 'Do you suppose he's dead?' It was a silly question. 'We have to call the police,' he said, and looked up at her. 'Are you alright? Was he trying to rape you?'

'I had to do it, Vince, I had to! I didn't have a choice. He was raping me and he was hurting you. I had to make him stop, like I had to make all of them stop. They were hurting us, can't you see?'

Vince's eyes narrowed. 'Edith, you're not making any sense.'

'I did it for you, Vince. It was all for you, because I love you!'

Vince sank to his knees, reaching out and touching Kimble on the shoulder. 'Jesus, Edith, you've killed him. What are we going to do?' Then his face screwed up in thought. 'What are you saying, you had to make all of them stop?'

She licked her lips, tried to regain control of her breathing. 'I killed Monica,' she said.

'Don't be ridiculous, Edith. You're in shock, is all.'

'I'm telling you the truth, Vince. I killed Monica. I did it for you, and me, for both of us.'

'Why are you talking this way? Stop it, Edith, you're getting hysterical and you're starting to frighten me. Martin killed Monica. The police arrested him, they had all the evidence.'

'I made it look like it was Caldwell who did it.'

Vince clutched his head, dazed. His vision began to swim. 'Do you know what you're saying? Stop it. Help me think about what we're going to do about Leonard.'

She took hold of his arm, shook it. 'Vince, I killed Monica!'

He stared into her watery eyes, observed how her lower lip shivered like it was cold. 'Why? Why would you even admit to that?'

'Because it's true, Vince.

She shook her head slowly. 'Monica told me she was going to get rid of you, get you kicked out of the Empire. You didn't deserve that. Or her constant, poisonous nastiness. One day I heard her arguing with Mr Caldwell in his office, saw her storm out, telling him she'd show him just how much trouble she could be if he didn't do right by her. She was really riled up. She stomped off and Caldwell saw me outside in the corridor. He told me she was having a bad day and to go keep an eye on her, so I did. I followed her down to the basement. When I looked inside I saw her taking some of your old films out of their cans and piling them on the floor. She had a box of matches and was about to set light to them.

'I told her to stop it. She was steaming-mad at Caldwell, and said she'd burn the fucking Empire down if she had to. I guess she knew the films were already a fire hazard. She was in a state and maybe she didn't know what she was doing, being so angry. I told her that the films belonged to you, but she laughed at me, told me to get the fuck out of there and mind my own business; and the fire would be enough to get you the sack if nothing else.

'It all happened in an instant. I went down into the basement, told her to leave the films alone, and when she wouldn't I picked up one of the cans and hit her over the head with it. She began to scream, loudly, so to stop her I hit her again, and again, on the side of the head.' She pointed to her temple. 'To keep her quiet.'

'You killed her?'

'No, she wasn't dead at that point.' Edith had stopped crying. Her face was now all but expressionless, her eyes blank. 'She was barely conscious, but not dead. So I thought about things for a bit and then I went upstairs to the cleaners' cupboard. I'd saved Mr Caldwell's Oscar statuette from the trash can when I cleaned his office – I thought it such a shame to get rid of it, especially as Mr Caldwell's wife had bought it – and stashed it away in one of the cupboards under a pile of junk. I took the Oscar, came back downstairs...' She sucked in a deep breath. 'And then I hit Monica over the head with it. That's when she died, there and then. I told Caldwell she'd gone home. But I didn't feel anything for her, not a single thing. She was a horrible, horrible woman.'

'It was you that dumped her body in the well?' said Vince. She nodded quickly. 'And you used Caldwell's statue so that if she were ever found people would suspect it was him that killed her, not you.'

'That's right. I did it for you, Vince.'

'For me? You murdered someone for me?' He shook his head. 'That can't be true, Edith. You couldn't do something like that, not you! It's not in you!'

'I did it to protect you, Vince, because I love you. And because I wanted the best for you, for both of us. That's why I had to kill Felix, too.'

'What? Christ Almighty, Edith, tell me this isn't true! Tell me you're making all this up!'

'I think he'd been to see Laura, and something obviously didn't go right because he was furious. He came round to the Empire to find you. It was very late, I was on my own at the kiosk and Felix was stone-drunk. He grabbed me, told me to take him to you and that he was going to kill you for what you'd told Laura, for spoiling his plans to con her. He remembered me, you see, from the night he came and beat you up. I was afraid for you, Vince; I didn't want him to harm you, not again. I think he would have killed you, he was so mad.

'And that's when it all came together in my head. How I could make things better for you and me, Vince. How I could make the Empire ours. I told him you were in the basement, brought him down here, just like I did with Leonard. I unlocked the basement door, told him you were down there, and as he went down the steps I took the fire-axe from the wall and hit him in the back with it. He fell down the steps to the bottom. He lay there. He wasn't dead. I undid the bolts on the metal grating again and dragged him over to the well. He was heavy, but I did it eventually. I let him fall in and put the grating back on. He wouldn't hurt you, Vince, I made sure of that.'

'Oh my God!' said Vince, getting to his feet and looking down at Kimble. Realisation crashed in. 'You brought Leonard down here so you could do exactly the same to him!'

'He was trying to come between us, Vince. He wanted to harm us. He was saying things…'

'You planned it, didn't you?' said Vince incredulously. 'You planned it so that Caldwell would take the blame for all this. Why, so that I could become manager? Is that it? And if the storm hadn't happened and the bodies hadn't been accidentally discovered…'

'I'd have found some way of notifying the police,' she said evenly. She went up to him, put her arm around his waist and drew him close. 'They all got what they deserved, Vince. Nothing can come between us now. No one can hurt us anymore. It doesn't matter if Caldwell takes the blame, does it? Who cares about him? He's a nasty man, Vince. I mean, you're manager now, aren't you? He's out of the way and paying for doing all the horrid things he's ever done in his life. They're all out of the way now. Just like in the films, the bad cowboys in the black hats get what's coming to them…'

Vince put a shaking hand to his dry mouth. 'Cowboys? Are you mad? Think about this seriously; we have to go to the police, Edith, because what you did, that was premeditated murder. And you've gone and killed Leonard, too! If I go along with that I'm an accessory, or something; I've aided and abetted and tons of other stuff they'll lock me away for and then throw away the fucking key! Jesus, what kind of a woman *are* you?'

'I'm a woman in love.'

'That's no excuse! We've got to go to the police…'

'I'd go to prison,' she said flatly. 'But I don't have to.'

The thought of Edith being taken away from him ate at his brain. But he didn't know what he should do. 'We haven't got a choice; we have to tell them,' he said. 'We should tell them what you've done, tell them about Leonard. Oh Christ – what are we going to do about Leonard?' he exclaimed, stepping smartly away from the bloodied corpse.

'We don't have to admit anything and we don't have to say anything about Leonard either.'

'He's dead, Edith! He's dead and he's here, if you hadn't noticed! He's not going to go away, is he? None of this mess is!'

She opened the door to the basement. 'It can all go away,' she said. 'We put his body in the well, like I did with the others. Tomorrow the builders are coming in to cap the well and lay the entire floor with concrete.' She squeezed him tight. 'Look at what we've got now, Vince. We've got each other and we have the Empire all to ourselves. Do you really want to give all that up?'

He couldn't bear looking at Kimble's leaking skull. 'No, of course I don't, but…'

'We put him in the well,' she said calmly, 'weigh him down so that he sinks. No one will ever know he is there. You saw what he was doing to me, Vince; he was going to rape me. He was a bad man. Did you want that to happen to me? Did you want him to rape me?'

'No, you know I didn't.' He stared at her quietly-composed face. She smiled at him. It was no longer the smile of the young woman he'd first met. There was more depth to it now, like it was a smile that came from a life long-lived. It spoke volumes. 'You planned it…' was all he could say.

'For you. For us. They've had their turn as pretty little butterflies, and now it's our time, Vince. You and me together. No one can stand in our way. Our love is far too strong.'

He thought about it. He didn't want to give up his managership before it had even started. In a few years he could be area manager, then who knew? Maybe national director one day. Nor did he want to give Edith up. He'd only just discovered love – real, physical, all-encompassing, soft-lipped, soft-bosomed, emotionally invigorating love. His life had changed almost overnight and it could all be taken away from him just as quickly. 'Yes,' he said, his voice hushed, his breathing more relaxed, 'you're right; they deserved it, all of them.' Edith kissed him deeply, meaningfully. He felt her probing warm tongue wet on his lips. 'You do love me, don't you?' he said, holding her by the shoulders and staring into her eyes. 'You're not just saying it?'

'Truly, madly, forever,' she said. 'Why do you think I did this? I did it for us. That's love. That's *true* love, like in *Annie's Song*. I want to drown in your laughter, and die in your arms, Vince!'

'I would hate anything bad to happen to you, Edith,' he said. 'You mean more to me than anything in the world.' He looked about him. 'And this place really is ours now, like you say. This is our chance to change things. Together we're stronger, aren't we? We're a team. And, damn it, you're right; nothing should stand in our way. We'd lose everything we've only just found, and that's not right, is it?'

'You know it makes sense, Vince,' she said.

'I love you, Edith,' he said. 'And I don't aim to let you go.' He bent down to Kimble's dead body. 'Give me a hand down the stairs with him. Then I'll fetch my spanners and take off the grating over the well.' He looked at the lake of dark, sticky blood spreading across the stone slabs and running in rivulets down the walls. 'And maybe you ought to fetch a mop and bucket,' he said.

* * * *

Dear Reader,

Thank you for purchasing 'MOUSE'.

If you enjoyed this novel, I would be grateful if you could take the time to let other people know and put a review on Amazon. I personally read them all and take every review very seriously. As readers your thoughts and insights are extremely valuable.

Yours,

Daniel M. Mitchell

Other novels by D. M. Mitchell available on Kindle:

SILENT

THE KING OF TERRORS

MAX

THE HOUSE OF THE WICKED

PRESSURE COOKER

THE FIRST D.M. MITCHELL THRILLER OMNIBUS

The Dormann
Book Nook

Made in the USA
Lexington, KY
10 May 2014